# RECRUIT

IRON LEGION | BOOK 1

DAVID RYKER
DANIEL MORGAN

RYKER'S ROGUES

# 1

*Planet: Genesis-526*
*Earth Date: 2734AD*

All the glasses rattled on the table top as a freighter swung around the dustball that was Genesis-526, and slingshotted into deep space.

I sighed and watched the surface of my drink settle.

"All's I'm saying is that," Zed belched, "Ninety-Three could definitely benefit from a Sim-Stack." He shrugged and drained the last dregs of beer before slamming the cup down on the steel table top. He was a skinny guy, a tuber like me, grown for purpose, with a shaved head.

Sybil squinted at him, one eye half closed. He was older, Ex-Federation Ground Corps. Dishonorable Discharge. I watched him choose his words, fishing drunkenly for them. It was crazy that, for anyone from off-world, getting shipped to Genesis-526 and being put on terraforming duty was the worst punishment conceivable. For us tubers, it was a *career.* And a life-long one at that.. Not like we had a choice, though. I stared at the flat surface of my beer, watching it bubble slowly. I wasn't much in the mood for drinking. I wasn't much in the mood for anything.

"Sim-Stack, eh? You just want to," Sybil hiccoughed, "get your digital di—"

"Hey!" Zed cut back in. "I appreciate the fine form of a woman as much as any guy — probably more so considering how fucking few of them the almighty goddamn Federation saw fit to grace this barren rock with — but that's not what I'm talking about."

"For once," snorted Crash, the ex-Federation cargo pilot who'd ploughed into one of the moons off Zebox while he was flying shit-faced. They called him Crash for obvious reasons.

"I've never been off this fucking planet, alright?" Zed snapped, sucking on his empty cup. "I've never seen anything other than goddamn dirt and algae. I don't want to fucking die here, not without seeing somewhere else, *something* else."

I grimaced but stayed quiet. I knew that ache.

"Listen, kid," Sybil kicked back in, sighing, "the universe ain't all it's cracked up to be, alright? Terraforming for a colony planet's not a bad gig. It's safe, secure, and you're making a decent—"

"You developed Stockholm syndrome, or are you just a fucking idiot, Syb?" Crash drained his beer and cocked an eyebrow.

I looked at the three of them, an utter bunch of misfits, and wondered how the hell, firstly, that it was our responsibility to turn a planet into something habitable, and secondly, that I'd somehow managed to throw in with three guys I could barely stand. I shook my head. I could already see how the conversation was going to go — Syb and Crash would start arguing about the Federation, both ragging on it and defending it at the same time, angry at themselves for fucking up their lives and getting stuck down here. And Zed would just get shitfaced, and then cross them both, and then they'd brawl, get kicked out, and we'd get stuck with the bill for the damages. And I'd have to foot my part, despite not getting in the middle of any of it. I was sick to my back teeth of it — of them. And then, after all was said and done, they'd stagger home and fall into bed, wake up hungover and bruised, go to work, pretend like everything was peachy, and then go do it all over again.

I left my drink untouched and stood up, pulling on my jacket.

"And where d'you think you're going, Jim?" Zed piped up.

I tried to smile but found it hard. I knew this was my lot in life, but I didn't want to get reminded of it every single night. "I'm not feeling drinking tonight, guys. I'm gonna see if I can't squeeze in some overtime."

I saw their looks of disapproval at my intention to do any more than the bare minimum required by the Federation. In truth, my options were either stay and listen to their bullshit, head back to my cramped little hab and lie in bed staring at the ceiling until sleep swallowed me up, or get back to work and earn a few extra credits. At least the last option might afford me a little bit of luxury to make my existence just slightly less unbearable. The wage we got was hardwired into the system from the Federation protocols that governed the universal currency — Federation creds. It was practically impossible to earn enough money to do anything other than sleep and eat. And if you wanted to drink, you had to forgo one of the others. Syb and Crash, for all their bickering, shared a hab like a pair of kids, freeing up enough cash to get drunk enough every night to forget they were consigned to this life until they both died of old age — or cirrhosis, whichever came first. Any way you spun it, things were spread thin. But the Federation liked that. It kept us in line — kept us controlled.

"Overtime?" Crash laughed. "Fucking scab." There was venom in his voice, like it was an affront to him. If he didn't have so much bile in him, or a habit that needed quenching, he'd probably be out there too. But he did, so it was easier to try to make me feel bad about it than face his own demons. I just let it roll off my back. I was used to that now.

The others mumbled in agreement. I shrugged and turned away, waving over my shoulder. Before I even reached the door, they were back to talking about the Federation, and how it was fucking them three ways from Sunday. Underpaid. Overworked. Taken for granted and not appreciated. Because, of course, who wouldn't want three discontented and mutinous drunks in their ranks?

The Federation didn't care though. They were just one group in a thousand just like them in every settlement from here to the poles and back. The Federation fucked everyone, though. It's what they did. They ran half the universe.

I WALKED the length of the steel catwalk outside Marcy's, one of two bars in Ninety-Three, one of the terraforming settlements on Genesis-526. The settlement itself was a mess of stacked habs, loaded on top of each other, tied together by catwalks and walkways, covered by a huge dome. In a couple hundred years, the dome would come off — but for now, the air outside was lethal, so the dome stayed, keeping us safe, keeping the air in. Keeping the stink in. I hacked and spat the stale air over the railing, watching it sail into the murky depths below. It splatted on the ground with a dull slap, hidden by the darkness, and a grunt of indifference rang up. People lived on the ground — but no one bothered with them. They were fade-outs. We called them that because that's what they did. They just *faded out.* Either they stopped working, or retired, or just pissed away their money until they couldn't cover hab-rental. Either way, they lived under tarps, sleeping on anything that kept them off the ground — the sludgy, algae-covered ground. No one went down there if they could help it. The fade-outs didn't take kindly to workers. They'd shiv you for a couple of credits. They had nothing and the Federation wouldn't do shit about them — nothing except scrape them up and toss them out when they finally did *fade.*

I pushed the thought out of my mind and kicked down off the catwalk onto another one, clearing the miniature ladder that connected them. The fade-outs didn't need thinking about, or pitying. Everyone was fighting for what they had out here. They were the ones who'd given up. My Blower was calling. It was the only place I felt comfortable. Most people hated the claustrophobia of it, but for me it was the opposite. I liked that isolation, that feeling of protection, that feeling of power, of moving something big like that, of having so much strength at my fingertips.

I went on autopilot, and before I knew it I was scanning myself into the airlocked hangar of one of the surface ports. The Blowers, terraforming machines like snowcats, with treads and autonomous arms, were lined up in a row — mine, Zed's, Crash's, Syb's. I headed across the catwalk suspended over them and dropped onto the roof of mine with practiced ease.

I popped the hatch and climbed into the cockpit, a windowed bubble equipped with a chem shower for decontamination following a walkabout, and not much else. I pulled the hatch shut after me and basked in the silence as it sealed.

The hangar was dark and still, and the only light in the cockpit was coming from the clock on the center console that told me it was about two hours to sundown.

I settled into my chair, sponge bulging from the cuts and gouges in the fabric, and pulled on my headset. I pushed the ignition switch and the system buzzed to life, the console lighting up. Telemetry and readouts filled the screen in front of me, and then settled into the corners, and a big smiling face popped up in the middle of the screen.

"Sal," I sighed, glad to be feeling comfortable again.

"Good evening, James," she said in her dulcet tones. "A little late for work, isn't it?"

Sal was about as close to a woman as I'd ever been. The settlement wasn't exactly a hotspot for women. Without them there, it was one less thing for the drunken, dishonorable terraformers and traders to fight over. As such, they were few and far between. But it didn't really bother me. You couldn't miss what you'd never had. Sal was the closest I'd ever come, and she did alright for me. I shrugged. "Never too late to earn some money."

"If you say so. What would you like to do?"

I took a breath and reached for the joysticks, pushing into the throttles with my heels. One for each track. "Pull up all available overtime jobs."

"Of course." The screen filled with a list of titles, none of which seemed appetizing.

"Prioritize those with the highest pay."

"What's the magic word?"

"Please," I laughed. Sally was full of sass for an AI. Her old driver must have been more polite. Or maybe she just liked to remind me who was in charge.

"Sorting."

The jobs rearranged and I expanded a few, casting them aside with a swipe of my fingers. I wasn't looking for anything hard, or dirty. "Any suggestions?"

"I can see that a radio relay is in need of repair."

"How far out?"

"Thirty-one kilometers."

"That's a trip." I rubbed my eyes. The other option was just going back to the bar, and the thought of that was even worse than trekking thirty kilometers into the desert at seven at night. "Screw it." I tapped on the job and marked it 'in progress.' Sally pulled up the coordinates and plotted a course. The telemetry showed up in a dotted line on the windscreen. A tiny green blip flashed in the distance, somewhere beyond the hangar doors.

"Whenever you're ready, James. Systems are all functioning correctly."

"Thanks, Sal. How about some music?"

"What would you like?"

I smirked. "How about some rock?"

"Martian?"

"Earth, for a change."

"Would you like me to choose?"

I hit the button for the airlock doors and they began to part. The cab rocked gently as the air washed out and normalized the pressure. "Sure. Make it a classic. Pre-Expansion."

I planted my feet and we rumbled into the desert beyond Settlement Ninety-Three just as Born to be Wild kicked up.

It took almost an hour to reach the coordinates. It turned out that it was a simple enough thing — a cable exchange that needed rerouting. Usually, this was droid's work, but just like everything on Genesis-526, the droids seemed to be too broken down to do their jobs. The Federation was supposed to take care of all that — delivering supplies, providing new equipment, but they didn't. It was a big job, looking after a thousand planets, and some little dust ball in the middle of an undeveloped system wasn't at the top of their priorities list. So here I was, doing droid work. And yet, the peace and quiet was almost nice. And of course the extra credits were a welcome bonus.

I pulled my feet off the throttles and let the engine settle to idle. "Sal, would you be a dear and route the audio to the external speakers?"

"Sure thing, James," she said softly as I got out of my chair and stretched my neck.

I stared at it for a second, the cracked veneer, the sponge sticking out of the tears, the word 'FUCK' unceremoniously carved into the headrest by one of the previous owners. Guess even his manners ran out at some point. Or maybe it was because of behavior like that that Sal developed her authoritative air. I couldn't say. It was against policy to discuss former employees. I'd asked what had happened to him when I'd first climbed into Sal, but she'd told me straight. And we'd just sort of gone on from there. I'd be lying if I said she hadn't softened some since then. I curled my lips down. But fuck *what*, exactly? Was it an exclamation of anger? *FUCK!* Or maybe a statement of hopelessness. *Fuck.* Or was it more an act of rebellion? *Fuck this. Fuck that. Fuck everything.* I couldn't say, but whatever they were trying to say, I got it.

I pulled on my walker suit and slammed the helmet down, listening to it seal with a hiss. The hatch that led outside was accessed through a chute — a glass screen that slid out of the wall to seal off the cabin, and then opened into the air above. I hit the release button and felt the dust and sand swirl around me. I wasn't an engineer, but this was easy money. I took the ladder in hand and climbed out, looking around at the endless sea of pale orange dust streaked with green and brown veins of algae. The beginnings of oxygenation. But there was still a long way to go — another half a dozen centuries before anyone would take their first rancid, stinking, sulfur heavy breath of surface air.

One of the restaurants back in Ninety-Three, the bubble-domed excuse for a town I called home, had a landscape like this painted on one their walls. I asked the owner about it once. He told me it was called a *prairie*. It had come in a pre-painted pack from the Federation. He'd never been to Earth himself — no one ever had. It was a thousand light years away.

He'd said that 'Earthscapes' were reproduced from datafiles and shipped all over the universe — wherever humans were. For some reason there seemed to be a focus on that. On remembering 'home' like it was some fairytale land to travel back to one day. From what I'd heard it was a wasteland. There was nothing much left to visit except ash and sludge. But then there were people who said it was everything but. They were all rumors, millennia old, drifting across the universe. So which was right? Maybe both were true in different times. Either way, I'd never know unless I saw for myself, but I didn't think that would ever happen, so what was the fucking point in giving a shit? It was a pretty picture, so what did it matter?

I clenched my fists in my rubbery gloves and let myself down the external ladder into the shadow of Sally's square body. The Blower cast a long dark square in the sinking sun, red and tired on the horizon. I went to a storage hatch on the dark side and got out my tool bag.

I circled her, knocking on the chest-high treads with a wrench, drumming to the beat of the song blasting in the thick air. I wondered what sort of fun and games they had in the jungle, and what exactly a jungle looked like.

The dust hammered my walking suit as I approached the exchange, a half-buried metal box that regulated cable currents across the surface. The steel had already started corroding and the door was hanging half open. I stared at it, wondering how in the hell they thought it'd last for another seven hundred years. I grimaced, realizing that they knew it would last because they had chumps like me to come and fix it every time it broke down. I repaired the door first, the route of the problem. Without it, the wires inside were exposed. The wind and dust had already eaten through the rubber and into the metal. I did what I could. It really needed replacing, and I put that in as a note, but I knew it'd just stay like it was until it needed repairing again. I shut the door and got up.

It was dark by then and the stars were glittering overhead. I looked up at them and paused. One was big. Really big. And growing, fast. I narrowed my eyes, watching it. A freighter coming in for a slingshot? No, wrong angle. Satellite falling out of orbit? No, too small.

As I was trying to figure what the fuck it was, it burst into flames, hitting the atmosphere. The shockwave staggered me and I stumbled backward, dropping my tools with a clang. "What the fuck?" I mouthed in my suit. I reached for my comms link and opened it. "Sally, sitrep — what the hell's going on?" I dragged my eyes away from the swirl of fire around it and made for the Blower. Whatever it was, it was big, and it was coming in fast. My heart was hammering in my chest, my breathing suddenly tight. The figures blinked furiously at me in the corner of my visor. "I detect a large incoming craft. It appears to be a Federation vessel." Her voice was calm and sweet, as usual, but it didn't do anything to dispel the adrenaline surging in me.

I made it halfway back to the Blower, kicking dust up behind me in a thick cloud, before the noise hit me like a wave, nearly throwing me over. The ground started to rumble, and my insides coiled up like a snake. I staggered sideways and plunged onto my knees, skidding in the red earth, my breath fogging in my visor. I twisted around just in time to see it, white hot and smoking, sailing over the desert like a huge torpedo. The air split around me and all the hairs on the back of my neck stood up. I swallowed hard to pop my ears, but they wouldn't listen. My eyes tingled and my teeth felt furry. My brain stammered and the air whined in my ears. Electromagnetic repulsors. It had to be. That was the only thing that had effects like that. My comm faded to static and crackled in my ear.

Electromagnetic repulsors were used on the biggest Federation sub-orbital vessels to stop them destroying half the planet on entry. And they only used them when they were coming in for a landing. But we weren't expecting a delivery, and especially not from something that size — so what the hell was it doing here? I scrambled forward. I had to. If I couldn't make it back to Sally before it passed overhead, they'd rip me in two.

I got no more than ten feet before they crushed down on me, and then sucked me backward into the air. My feet left the ground and there was nothing I could do. Ahead, the Blower reared onto its hindquarters and somersaulted backward like a toy truck. I tumbled forward and over, catching sight of the huge black underbelly of the ship above, broken by blue ports firing out thrust and repulsor jets. The heat sent the sensors on my suit wild and my screen lit up in red and white, flashing madly as I swirled through the air, screaming in my own ears. All I could feel was heat. My skin felt like it was peeling off, sizzling like seared meat.

My skin burned inside the suit, threatening to blister and bubble, and everything else went numb in the haze of pain. My teeth clattered together and my eyes stung. My brain fizzled and stuttered and the ground and sky flashed in turn as I was dragged through the jet wash, a leaf on the wind. The engines howled above me and every bone in my body shook and jostled against the others.

I dragged red hot air into my lungs and felt my eyes glue shut. My stomach lurched in the force and I spewed sickly bile into my helmet. It washed up the glass and gummed in my hair. I retched hard, choking on the smell and liquid. I kept my eyes closed and the inside of my face exploded in a plume of pain as the acid rose into my sinuses.

My ears rang like bells, and then there was silence, darkness, weightlessness. Impact. Screaming. Pain. Crying. My heart beating in the darkness, hard and fast like drums.

And then, nothing.

# 2

When my eyes opened, all I could see was darkness. I pulled my face back from the visor and felt my face peel from the acrid bile dried on it. The HUD readouts glowed in the darkness, bright against the sand, speckled and cold beyond the glass. I moved my hands and felt the sand around me shift. The slow pulsing of blood in my ears died away and I became aware of the pain in my joints and back. I thought about my chair in my cockpit, wherever the hell it was, and the word carved into the headrest. I sighed and made a mewling noise, understanding it now more than ever.

Fuck.

I pushed myself out of the sand on shaking arms and onto my knees, feeling it drain off my back and pool around my heels. My throat was razor blades and my head felt like it'd been hacked in two. I swallowed painfully and sat back, breathing hard, the gravity of the situation sinking in. My heart was hammering again and my HUD told me that my oxygen was below fifteen percent. It flashed in red and yellow, burning against the endless ocean of sand around me. I tried not to look at it. A huge gorge had formed in the sand and a canyon ran into the distance toward Ninety-Three. The glow of the two moons that hung over Genesis-526 played softly on the ridges of churned earth. It was the trail left by the Federation dropship that had tossed me like a ragdoll. I stared into the abyss, wondering how the hell I was going to get out of it. I reached up and pressed the comm link on the side of my helmet. It clicked uselessly in my ear. The electromagnetic field must have fried the circuits. My breath sounded shaky and my eyes stung. There was no sign of my Blower, no sign of anything. My fists curled at my sides so hard the rubber of my gloves groaned and twisted.

It was a goddamn miracle I was alive, and the fact that my back wasn't snapped was pretty fucking astounding. Though it wouldn't be worth shit if I suffocated to death in the middle of nowhere. No. I couldn't think like that. I gritted my teeth and tried to shake off the feeling of hopelessness. It wouldn't budge. I sucked in a hard lungful of vomit-stricken air and watched the number in front of me plunge to fourteen percent. The Blower. Where was the Blower? I had to find it. If I did, I wouldn't suffocate. Then I could go from there. It was just one step at a time. Shit. I had to think. It couldn't be too far — walking distance, at least — I hoped. I was near to it when we were tossed. It must have been close by, and close to the surface. If it wasn't... I didn't really want to think about that just then.

The flicker of courage waned as quickly as it'd risen and I collapsed forward and swore, sucking in the putrid stench of vomit, trying not to think about it being splattered and smeared all up my face. I gritted my teeth and willed myself not to give up — not to accept death, no matter how heavy I could feel it on my back. I had to get up. I had to think.

My comm was fried. Shit. That wasn't good. But my HUD was still functional, sort of — and that meant that the EM field hadn't fried my electronics. If it had, my respirator would have failed and I'd have asphyxiated before I even woke up.

There was that, I supposed. Comms weren't working because the antenna in my helmet only did short range, relaying off the Blower. It must have been the Blower's antenna that was shot then — snapped off in the carnage, no doubt.

I pulled up my hand and opened my wrist readout, a holographic display suspended over a projector on my glove. I moved through the screens, cursing the ancient equipment that the Federation gave us. Any halfway decent suit would have been built with long range transmission. Getting out of here would be as simple as sending out a distress call and getting picked up. This suit was a relic, though, and was about as advanced as a Gollaxian sea slug. I swiped until I came to the map and zoomed out. Seemed like the geolocator was still working on my suit. I was a tiny white blip in an undulating sea of gray. I breathed a sigh. It was something. The Federation Standard Issue Colony Surface Suit, or a Walker as most people called them, was the workhorse of the settling world. From mining colonies to settlements all across the known universe, these suits were in action. One of their base functions was a sonar pulse — usually used while on scouting missions to check for subterranean water sources, mineral deposits, or in my situation, a buried Federation Blower 400 named Sally.

I selected the option and held my breath between my teeth. "Well, here goes nothing," I muttered to myself. I pushed the button tentatively and watched a white ring ripple outward from the blip on my map. Nothing came up at first, but just as it started to fade, a faint white shape glowed to the east. I stared at it, watching it disappear back into nothingness. It was thin, but it was all I had. It was almost two hundred meters away, following the line of the canyon.

I stared at my feet, buried in the soft sand, and swore. My oxygen had dropped to twelve percent. I didn't know if it was enough. If I set off, it would dwindle faster. I'd be breathing harder, consuming more. If I stayed put, I could conserve it, but the chances of anyone finding me were slim to goddamn none. I turned my head, hoping to see some light on the horizon — a search party or passing ship. But there was nothing. Just an endless black canvas.

I decided, and with a grunt, I rose out of the sand and set off, ignoring that the effort of doing that alone had reduced my O2 level to ten percent. I hit the sonar pulse every few seconds to make sure I was on track, trying desperately to keep my breathing steady. The soft sand torn up by the ship was making it harder. Every step had me sunk up to my knees, and every heavy gaited stride was burning precious airtime. My heartrate hadn't dipped below a hundred and ten the entire time, and I could feel the beads of sweat trickling through the vomit clinging to my skin. I minimized the display and pushed on. I didn't need to be reminded how close to suffocation I was. The thin air and the rattling of a near empty tank in my ears was enough.

When a pulse told me I was right on top of it, I stopped. To my left was a drop-off of about twenty meters. It was sheer at first, and then flattened, leading to the canyon floor. I stood on the mount of churned earth, staring into it. I had no tools, nothing to dig with, and the sonar was telling me that the Blower was about ten meters down. And even as small as it was, the tiny display in my peripheral was clear as day. Single digits. I was out of time, and there was only one thing to do.

I turned left and edged towards the precipice. "Fuck it."

I stepped off and plunged through the cool night air. My feet hit sand and I crumpled into the ground, somersaulting forward down the slope. I threw my arms and legs out and skidded to a halt in a cloud of dust, breathing hard. My oxygen was failing. I had to get up.

I turned and scrambled up the slope on all fours, jabbing at the sonar continuously. Dirt ran in streams around my knees as I clawed my way upward. I hit the vertical wall and started digging. It was all I could do. My hands pulled at the earth and it came away in soft chunks. An overhang formed and then fell on me. It clattered on my helmet and back, but it didn't matter. I had one option now, and that was dig. Dig. Digging was all I could do. The Blower was in there somewhere. I'd either find it, or die trying. My teeth ground together and my visor fogged with each ragged breath. The bead in my oxygen tank rattled on empty with each inhale, squeezing the last of the remaining gas into my tubes.

The words 'Critical Warning' flashed on my visor and I watched through them as my fingers scraped and pulled at the bottomless wall of dirt. A thought crossed my mind and almost stopped me dead.

What if it wasn't the blower? What if it was a rock? Or something else? A chunk of clay or some crashed ship or machine from centuries back? What if I unearthed something completely useless? I thought about it, and wondered if I'd burst out laughing, or just burst into tears in my final moments before collapsing backwards, choking on my own vomit and hot, putrid breath. It was almost poetic, or maybe just the way that life goes.

The Federation would have birthed me, and it only seemed fitting that they would kill me, too. James Alfred Maddox, age nineteen, presumed dead. Body never recovered. Another casualty in the crusade for universal domination. All people, one Federation. I scoffed and then sputtered, my lungs struggling to open. My fingers reached out meekly now and tore at the sand. My O2 hit zero and the words changed to 'Oxygen Depleted.' I gasped and sucked on the vacuum and my lungs started to crackle. My ears popped and squeezed like I was underwater and my eyes ached. My vision blurred in the negative pressure and I retched hard, the vacuum trying to fill itself with my insides. My fingers left the sand instinctively and I clawed at the seal on my helmet. I sank back into the dirt and scrambled, kicking and swimming away from the impending suffocation. I flailed, searching frantically for the release. Blackness pulsed in time with my heart. It closed in like a tightening aperture. My head was pounding, diaphragm crumpled into a heap against the bottom of my empty lungs. My heels kicked dirt and it rained down on me, submerging me, drowning me. No. I couldn't stop yet. The air. The air outside. It was toxic, but it was better than nothing. What was it at the last reading? Thirteen percent oxygen saturation? I couldn't remember. It was almost half the safe threshold and even lower than the planetary target. It would hurt. Hell, it would kill me, but it might have been a few seconds more. I just had to get my fucking helmet off. Where was the latch? Left side. Right. I had to find the next seal. There. Good. My fingers moved along it frantically. *No! Slow. Slow down, goddamnit.* I had to keep my breath tight, not panic. My lungs clamped shut. I couldn't breathe. The pain rushed up behind my nose like pins. Ignore it. Push through it.

My eyes stung. I shut them, tight. I didn't need to see. It was my fingers I needed, not my eyes. Where was the fucking latch? My eyes throbbed. I had to find it. There. Wait. No. Yes. There. My fingers closed around it and lifted. They were fat, heavy, useless. Lift it up. There, now push.

It clicked and hissed and gas rushed in. I sucked a lungful of half oxygen half *whatever else* was flying around out there, but it didn't matter. It was something. I clamped my mouth shut and threw off my helmet. It bounced and rolled down the slope. I blinked and my eyes burned in the atmosphere, scrabbling desperately to unearth myself and sit up. The stars glowed above, hazy in the methane thick air. My head was swimming, my blood filling with all the wrong gases. I tried to unbury myself, kicking at the earth. My feet churned uselessly. Come on. I wasn't going to die in the sand like a worm. *Come on!*

Kick. Kick. Kick. Clang.

My boot heel hit something solid and my neck snapped my head down so hard it clicked. I stared in the twilight at the exposed metal hull of the Blower in front of me, covered with sand on all sides, but there it was. My eyes widened in shock and it was everything I could do not to scream with joy.

I ignored my aching lungs and heaved myself forward, cheeks puffed. I breathed into them and then back into my lungs, raking every measly second of consciousness I could out of whatever air was knocking around inside my mouth.

I kicked it again and more sand peeled away. The porthole of steel widened. I kicked it as hard as I could and sand started to cascade around the edges. I threw my feet into the corners of what was exposed and the sand ran like water, streaming down around me. It was on its side, top toward me, which meant the hatch was somewhere. I reckoned I had now more than about twenty seconds of air before I passed out, and that was being generous.

Adrenaline surged in me and through a pinprick of vision I watched my hands hit the steel and spider sideways. I couldn't think — only do.

I brushed and heaved at the chunks of dirt until my fingers sang.

The darkness had all but closed in when the hatch hinge burst from the sand and glinted in the moonlight.

I exhaled, unable to hold it any longer, and choked on the oxygen-deprived air. I ran my fingers around the edge and found the handle, up to my elbows in sand. I yanked it up. It took two goes before it gave, and then a torrent of sand unfastened itself and poured down on me. I fought to stay up, clinging to the handle with everything I had, and dragged myself through it, into the tube, pulling the door behind me. It sealed and the cabin lit up, blinding me. I collapsed onto the wall, the whole machine upended, and I watched distantly as my hand weakly stretched out for the big red button. My fingers touched it and my mouth opened. More air rushed in, hot and dusty. The button clicked, and I closed my eyes.

In the darkness, the hiss of oxygenation pierced the air and my lungs collapsed, squeezing out whatever was in them. My lips were parched, cracked, my head covered in sand, my suit filled with it down the collar. It itched and rubbed and grated on my skin, but I was alive, and that was all that mattered. I swallowed hard and coughed, then retched again, vomiting earthy bile onto the ground under my chin. The glass screen showed me the cockpit ahead. All my shit was everywhere, tossed around inside a giant tumble dryer drum. The cabin was bathed in red warning lights and the windshield was cracked and covered, totally buried. The surge of hope ebbed quickly, and the realization that I was still very far from home, and very far from being out of the woods, sank in.

I dipped in and out of consciousness for a few hours while my body filled with oxygen and expelled all the poison in my veins. When I finally had enough in me to lift my head, it wasn't far to dawn. I chewed on my oversized tongue and grumbled, forcing myself upright. Hunger gnawed at my belly and thirst clawed at my throat. I'd vomited out everything that was in me and now I was running on empty. Every part of me was aching and it wasn't hard to figure out why. But there was no time for rest. Not yet. The oxygen tanks were bigger in here than my suit, but they wouldn't last forever.

I had to get back, somehow. I had to raise a signal, get a distress call out, or something.

I clambered out of the chute and shed my walker suit, tossing it, sand and vomit clad, back inside. I shut the door and stood on the wall, steadying myself on the floor with my hand. I went for the decontamination shower first, and after unhitching the nozzle, managed to turn it into a hosepipe. It wasn't warm, or pleasant, and the stench of chlorine was unavoidable, but the dried sick flaked off my face and out of my hair and pooled between my feet, which was a much better place for it. I used my dirty shirt to soak up what I could, and then tossed it into the chute along with my suit. I found a spare one lying around and pulled it on before going to the controls. I pressed the ignition button, but nothing happened. "Sally?" I called to silence. The internals must have been damaged. I wasn't surprised. The engine was probably trashed too, filled with sand or torn apart in the melee. The cockpit ran off a separate power source, but functionality was severely diminished. Not even enough to power Sal. Shit. I knew she was okay, just *sleeping,* or as good as, but still - hearing a friendly voice would have been a welcome reprieve from the darkness of the cabin. I wasn't liking the claustrophobia so much anymore.

I flicked the comms switch and opened all channels. "Mayday, mayday, this is a distress call. Come in." The line crackled gently. "I repeat, this is a distress call. Does anyone read me?"

Nothing. Shit. A cold sense of dread crept up my spine as I stared at the windows, totally black. It was the sand, and it was blocking the signal, which wasn't surprising — but it still sucked. But I couldn't dwell on that now. Panic would be the worst thing. I had to stay focused, concentrate on getting out, not on being trapped in. I twisted the console until it was sort of facing upright, and held the manual reboot buttons. After a second it flickered dimly to life. An emergency power banner appeared and then rose to reveal a schematic of the Blower. Almost every portion of it was flashing red. I tapped on the engine and a message appeared: 'Intakes Blocked — Clear debris before ignition.' I kicked it hard and growled. The image strobed before settling down. No engine, no comms, limited air supply and exactly zero fucking chance of someone stumbling upon me. It'd be morning before anyone even thought to look, and from what I could work out, the wash of the jets had tossed me who knows how far from the relay I was fixing. Being found and rescued wasn't a very likely prospect. I needed to figure something else out. If it wasn't for the walker suit, I would have been dead. I couldn't believe I wasn't already. But, even now that I was in my Blower, time was still limited. The oxygen levels were falling fast, and the filtration system wouldn't be pulling any fresh air in from outside either, not with all this fucking sand. It looked like most of the critical systems were damaged, the engine wouldn't fire, and the power cell was running at twenty percent. The Blower had taken a harder landing than me, that's for sure.

My fists curled and I pushed back from the console, looking around. Alright. I had to figure this out. How was I going to get out of there? I sure as hell didn't want to expire on that dirt-ball of a damn planet. Born, live, and die, right there on Genesis? No thanks. I sighed. I had to think of something.

It took me thirty minutes of leafing through the technical manual of the Blower 400 before I found something useful. By that time, the air was getting soupy, sticking in my throat and squeezing my lungs like sodden sponges. I tried to ignore it, focusing on the task at hand. It was a lot easier without my vital signs flashing in my face.

The Blower 400 was equipped with a set of autonomous arms, which were attached to a motor that was attached to the subframe that connected the cockpit to the hull. The cockpit itself was a plexiglass dome and a space behind. The back end of the Blower contained all the motors, gearing, engine, and everything else that a motivated individual could need for reshaping a landscape. I traced my fingers in the dim emergency lighting over the dotted lines of the exploded diagrams, looking at the couplings and linkage.

A minute later I was prying up an access hatch I'd never accessed before. I pulled the emergency toolkit from under my seat and then went to work. About eighty screws and bolts later, the couplings were un-attached, and then I was following what was called the 'Emergency Submersion Cockpit Ejection Sequence,' which in layman's terms basically blew the cockpit free of the carcass, leaving it free with only the arms attached. Apparently, if a pilot was stupid enough to drive their rig into a body of water, it would sink — go figure. But the cockpit was filled with air, and pressurized, and as such would float if detached. So, in-built was the ability to do that. Doing so would engage a miniature power cell capable of running life support systems and the arms for a couple of hours. Maybe enough to dig myself free and make it some of the way home, dragging the dismembered carcass of the Blower. Maybe.

I took a rotten breath and pulled the lever. An explosion blew the cockpit free of the body and the sand shifted around it, rumbling deeply. Wisps of smoke drifted up out of the hatch, and then the cockpit settled again. The emergency lighting died and was replaced with the glare of the standard white halogens. The console's screen lit up, filled with a series of bars brimming with green. The label said 'Energy Levels.' A smiling face flickered to life on the windscreen, too. "Good morning, James."

I sank back onto my haunches and grinned, relief flooding through me. She might just have been wires and pixels, but seeing her face was a huge comfort. Tears formed in the corners of my eyes. "You don't know how good it is to hear your voice, Sal," I sobbed.

"It's good to hear you too, James. I detect major structural damage to most systems, including our communications. Would you like to conserve remaining energy resources to await assistance?"

I smirked and levered myself into the seat, strapping myself sideways so I could resume control. "If we did, I don't think anyone would come for us." My hair flopped off the side of my head as I reached for the arm controls, grabbing hold of two gyroscopic handles. I flexed them and gears whined against the sand, like a strained grunt as it gave everything it could to shift the tons of earth crushing them.

"So, what would you like to do?"

"Let's go home."

# 3

Settlement Ninety-Three was a bit of a shit heap.

From the outside, it looked like a giant soap bubble filled with coal. The clear dome arched over the town, lined and stained by algae growth both inside and out. While it was essential for oxygenation, it got everywhere, and covered everything in a thin layer of greasy green filth. I could see it looming on the horizon, a dark growth on the pale sand.

The buildings were a collection of shanty-shacks assembled from old ship and rover parts, bolted onto Federation habs — square-shaped blocks that could be stacked modularly. They were smooth and rounded off on the corners to create a sense of 'cleanness,' but every single one was streaked with algae, scraped up, battered, bruised, and decorated by the inhabitants in some way, so the whole thing looked closer to a shanty town than anything else.

The main gate into Ninety-Three was a huge round airlock that fed inside, measuring around thirty meters across. A circular plate with a segment missing rotated into the ground to allow entry, and then closed off behind the ships or Droids that came in and out, before letting them through the other side. Above it was the entry tower — a double height hab unit with a miniature airlock on its viewing deck which led outside — manned by a couple of Federation sentries armed with plasma rifles. They sat around playing cards mostly, waiting for their shift to end. There was no wildlife to fend off, and there was nothing to get raided for. It was just standard protocol, and it was boring as hell to man.

The guy on duty that morning was named Jackson, I found out years later when I ran into him on Tracelon-3. He was six feet tall, and had yellowed teeth.

It was almost seven in the morning, and he was coming off the tail end of a night shift. He was leaning back in his chair, feet propped up on a table, hat pulled down over his eyes. When the droid he was on shift with started squawking, he fell backward and sprawled to the floor.

"Unknown entity approaching," the droid yelled without warning, stepping back through the open door to the viewing deck. He was an 8C — humanoid with built-in binocular eyes and speakerbox for a face. A standard Federation sentry droid — a hundred years ago. Not exactly the most *refined model.*

Jackson scrambled to a stance, throwing the tail of his Federation duster back off his head. He grabbed up the scope on the table and ran to the window.

The droid stood next to him. "Subject is at seventeen degr-"

"English, dammit!" Jackson growled, ramming the scope against his eyes.

"Straight ahead, a little to the right," the droid as good as sighed.

Jackson dialed in his scope and honed in on the approaching entity. "What the fuck?" he mouthed, dropping the scope and staring into the planes beyond the glass, still drowned in the murky gloom of the dawn.

I WATCHED as a fleet of Treaders raced out to meet me — half tank, half troop transport, rolling fast and leaving a cloud of dust in their wake. I let off the handles and the cockpit teetered. It'd taken some doing, but I'd managed to dig myself out eventually, rolling the entire thing sideways into the canyon. After that, the filters had kicked in and the air had started circulating, which was something, at least. Then there was a lot of dragging, swearing, and falling, until I figured out that with some gentle persuasion, the arms could be positioned to lift the cockpit into the air. After the first hour, I managed a couple steps, and after that, I was walking, sort of. More like tottering. Still, it was a lot faster than crawling. I mean, it was a feat by any stretch of the imagination, whether I looked like some demented crab or not.

The Treaders circled me and ground to a halt. The dust blew over like a wave. I heard boots, then rifles cocking, and then nothing. I waited for the cloud to pass and found myself staring down the barrels of half a dozen rifles pulled tight against the shoulders of Federation sentries.

"Identify yourself!" one yelled.

I grunted and ran my forearm across my head, flicking sweat all over the floor and windows. "James Alfred Maddox," I called through the speakers.

They stared in at me, sitting in the cockpit of Sally's battered and dismembered corpse, likely seeing nothing but a filthy, grubby kid through the cracked glass. I couldn't blame them for not welcoming me with streamers and a parade. I lifted my arm to show them the barcode tattoo emblazoned there. Standard issue for any colony tuber. "Don't believe me? Come in here and fucking scan me."

"I would advise politeness in this situation," Sally said gently.

"Oh, I'm way past polite," I said through gritted teeth.

One of them did, and recoiled at the stench in the entry chute. I swiveled on my chair and smirked as he dropped in. "Sorry." I stood up and offered my arm. "Been kind of a rough night."

They stuck an emergency breathing mask on my face and dragged me out of there, throwing me into the back of one of the Treaders without telling me what the hell was going on. In the distance, the Federation dropship that had tried to kill me lay dormant behind the settlement. I glared at it, willing it to burst into flames, but it didn't. It just sat there, not giving two shits about the kid it'd nearly torn in two. And what was worse was that no one answered when I asked what it was doing there. Everyone leapt in and the Treader took off at pace, leaving the cockpit, and Sally, beaten and bruised in the dust. I watched her shrink into the distance, broken down in the dirt, and wondered if they'd bring her in for repairs or just scrap her, and whether my lobbying would make the slightest bit of difference. Either way, I figured I could pull her AI core and put it into the next Blower — if they gave me one at all. It all came down to whether or not I could convince them that it wasn't my fault. It wasn't, of course, but I wasn't sure they'd like the story too much. Little did I know that was the last time I was going to see her again.

I was basically frogmarched back through the airlock, despite my protests. The Federation sentries didn't seem concerned about my health at all, and just more than a little pissed off that I'd managed to total one of their Blowers. They were giving me the silent treatment.

The door hissed closed behind us and we were back inside Ninety-Three. I never would have thought I would have been glad to breathe that recycled air again, but just then I was. One of them pulled the mask off and I sucked it down gleefully. The Federation dropship loomed behind the glass beyond the habs like a humongous beached whale, half obscured by the slime.

I waited, but the sentries didn't seem to want to let go of my arms. "Hey guys, you want to let me go? I can walk on my own." I struggled against them but they wouldn't budge. They just marched me into the gap between the two nearest buildings where sand became street, and then stopped, holding fast.

"Come on, guys!" I pleaded. "It wasn't my fault."

They didn't reply.

I jerked my shoulders, but they held tight. "Seriously, what are you gonna do to me? I can't afford to pay for that damn Blower..." I ground my teeth. "I didn't do anything. It was that dropship, it..." I tried to smile but they wouldn't meet my eyes. "Look, guys, can't we just—"

They leapt straight and both saluted with their free hands. I snapped my head around and froze, watching three figures clad in

Federation gray marching toward me. There was an officer at the front, visor pulled low, hands behind his back, rod straight, striding hard, flanked by two guards, plasma rifles hanging at rest.

They approached quickly and stopped. The officer, a Porosian on the older side of fifty, looked me up and down, recoiled at the smell of me, sighed, sneered, and then nodded. They were an odd race, almost like humans, but with pinker skin and slits for noses that flared when they breathed. "Show me," he demanded through thin lips, voice strained to speak one of the human tongues.

One of the sentries lifted my arm roughly and turned it over. The officer pulled up his hands and ran a scanner over my barcode. It beeped and he looked at the screen on it. "James Alfred Maddox. Nineteen." He looked me in the eye and then turned the corners of his lips down. "He'll do. Take him away," he said harshly.

The two sentries handed me over to the two soldiers and then disappeared. The officer looked at me indifferently.

"What the hell's going on?" I squeezed out.

The officer stared at me for a second, and then cast his eyes at the huge black shape visible through the glass dome between the buildings. He smirked. "Conscription."

I WAS strong-armed all the way across the settlement. They weren't letting go. The streets were empty, except for the Federation Soldiers. They were swarming, like groups of wasps, knocking on doors, chasing down settlers and colonists, subduing the ones who fought back, tasering and cuffing the ones that fought back hard. Anyone between the ages of eighteen and forty, by the look of it. Conscription, though? What the hell were the Federation into that they needed to roll through Genesis-526 looking for recruits? I asked, but got no answer. I guess we were just resources like everything else that could be mercilessly dredged out of a planet flying the Federation flag. I grimaced at the thought, feeling the squeeze of the Federation boot against the back of my head. *Eat it. Eat this shit!*

When we got to the Spaceport, a run-down square of a building that blockaded the airlock that suction-cupped to the side of whatever ship was docked, I was thrown into a line and the soldiers and officer turned and walked away. Someone jabbed me in the ribs with the muzzle of a rifle from the other side, and I shuffled forward toward the gangramp. Behind me and in front were dozens and dozens of people — big, tall, human and not. Most tubers were human — we were easy to grow, apparently, so most of the recruits were human. The other races, though, were all humanoid, carbon-based, oxygen-subsisting. We got a lot of different species through. Outcasts, dregs, nomads, fugitives, runaways. Anyone looking for a fresh start that didn't care where they landed. And you'd have to not care to be okay with landing on Genesis, and then settling down in Ninety-Three. The only work to be had was terraforming or maintenance. Neither were exciting prospects, so they didn't attract the best crop of people. All shit flows downhill, I guess, and Ninety-Three was right at the bottom of one.

I swallowed and caught the eye of one of the soldiers guarding the line. He was gripping his rifle tightly, and his finger looked twitchy. I kept my head down instead, and tried to focus on the fact that I'd at least be able to check something off my bucket list.

I'd always wanted to get off Genesis; I just never envisioned it happening like this.

Twenty minutes later, I'd been scanned, tagged, and strapped into a seat headed for orbit. The countdown rang through the cargo bay and I stared at all of the scared faces around me. None were from my crew, but I didn't think about that for long. We worked together, but we were never close. It was a rotating cast, ever changing. Getting close to people just wasn't something you did. I knew some of the guys in the line from around. Others not so much, but none of them were soldiers. You could tell by the look in their eyes. I wondered how many would be dead by this time next year. We'd heard the stories of Federation incursions. I hoped they weren't true. I licked my dry lips, dying of thirst, and tasted the dried bile on them, sour and sickly sweet. My heart throbbed in my throat and I realized that I was gripping the harness with white knuckles. I'd never flown before and my breathing was shallow. I'd had enough excitement for one night. I just wanted to go home and fall face down in bed. Maybe cry a little. Maybe a lot. I felt the tears come again, and my mind whirled with what was to come. I swallowed hard and felt an iron lump in my throat, hot and sharp.

For a second I thought about what would happen to my hab, to all my stuff after I was gone. Then I realized that I had nothing to leave behind except dirty laundry and a couple of shiny rocks I'd found on the surface. Almost seemed stupid to collect them now.

And then the countdown hit zero and the thrusters kicked me in the ass.

## 4

"This is bullshit," a kid in front of me scoffed. He must have been no more than eighteen. The sides of his head were shaven, and I could see a Parthacion tattoo running up his neck out of his collar — weird symbols and tribal lines. They were war-paint for the Pathacions, supposed to bring good luck in battle. They were the rage among the kids, if you were into that sort of thing — getting tattooed in some back-alley somewhere just to show off to your friends. Then again, he looked exactly like the sort. I didn't know him — probably from another settlement — but I knew his type. He had a bit of cockiness about him — obviously didn't have much experience working for the Federation. Maybe he was from off-world, sent to Genesis as a punishment to serve community service. Maybe he was a runaway. Either way, I didn't care, and I didn't want to ask in case he decided to tell me. My head was pounding and I needed to sleep. All I knew was that the Federation weren't big on shit-talkers.

I kept quiet, but he continued. "I don't fucking get it," he announced, his volume rising.

We were in line, queueing through the hangar of the Regent Falmouth, a Class I Federation Carrier — basically a flying space station. Our dropship had been swallowed up by the hold and then we'd been ushered out through the pools of sick left by those who'd never gone orbital before. I hadn't either, but I'd also not eaten or drunk anything for sixteen hours. But it was the fact that I'd barely slept other than being knocked unconscious and almost suffocating that was making my fuse short. "Shut up," I grunted at the kid. He was two people ahead.

"I mean," he continued, ignoring me, "why the fuck have I got to be up here? Who the hell do the Federation think they are serving up a conscription notice, huh? When I—" He cut off suddenly and faced front. The thudding steps of a Federation mech cut through the din. It sidled slowly by, huge machine gun in its arms. It was at least twenty feet tall, more than three times the height of any of us in line. Across the armored body, the word 'F-Series' was emblazoned in white.

Along with everyone else, I stared at the huge lumbering beast as it stomped past, square shouldered and armor plated, a little camera ball rotating two thirds of the way up the bulbous body like a swiveling eye. But I wasn't enamored like them. People had an obsession with them — and sure, they were *cool.* We'd all heard the stories. Heroes. Epic adventures. Saving lives and destroying the forces of evil. But I figured they couldn't all be true, if any of them were. Inside that angled, steel-shod body was just a regular person. There was nothing amazing about them.

Someone whispered "House Cat" behind me. I turned half on.

"What?" asked someone else.

"They call them House Cats," the first voice said again.

"Why?"

"'Cause you need nine fucking lives to pilot one!"

Some people laughed. I didn't. I watched it go indifferently. The Mechanized Corps were the Federation's elite arm, sure, but when your entire force is made up of colony workers — farmers, miners, terraformers — how good do you have to be to be 'elite'? Most soldiers transitioned into Exo. I'd read up on it when I'd turned eighteen — thought about enlisting. It was the only way to get off-world and out of my job, and for a while, I thought it seemed better than being a 'former until the day I kicked it, but with ninety-six percent of troops landing in Exo after assessment, and with the current three-year survival rate at seven percent, I didn't really fancy my chances. 'Forming didn't seem so bad in comparison.

The House Cat trundled out of range and the kid with the tattoos piped up again. "I could just slip out of line now, jump a guard, take his rifle, jack a cruiser, and then *boom,* out of the hangar and straight to freedom. No way you're going to catch me in the Exo Corps, dying like some fucking idiot — like the rest of you fucking idiots." He snorted like he was hot shit.

I rolled my eyes.

"Yeah." He nodded. "Got it all planned out — next time one of those dumb-shit sentries comes waltzing by—"

"Will you just shut the hell up?" I snapped. I couldn't control it.

He turned to face me, one eye half closed in some mild attempt at menace. "The fuck you say?"

The two people between us moved out of the way, all wanting to just keep their heads down, and he stepped up. I sighed. That lack of sleep was killing me and I was in no condition to fight, but the headache was begging me to knock this guy's teeth into the back of his throat, on the verge of collapse or not. "I said shut your fucking mouth."

"You wanna go?"

"To dinner?" I raised an eyebrow, the anger bubbling up in me. I'd had the night from hell and I felt like kicking his ass might let me exorcise just a little of my frustration.

His fists curled. "I'm gonna kick your ass, you—"

"Piss off, kid."

"Right, that's it." He smiled in a way I'm sure he thought was menacing.

He wasn't gonna hit me. If he had any intention to, he would have done so already. He was waiting for someone to step in, or for a guard to intervene. But it seemed that no one really gave a shit. All of the people in this portion of the line were from Genesis, and as such, all of them had looked into enlisting — pretty much the only way to get off planet without stowing away on a ship and hoping you didn't get found — and knew that the seven percent survival rate was what lay ahead. As such, no one really had much reason to give a crap about anything. I wasn't feeling especially fresh, and I just wanted the guy out of my face. I didn't feel like catching a hook, so I defused. "Look, shit-head, you're pissed off, I get it." I dropped my tone a little lower. "But swinging for me right now isn't gonna do anything for your chances of getting out of this. Smart money says to bide your time, you know?"

He glowered at me. "Oh yeah, got it all figured out, huh?"

"No," I admitted. "But if I was gonna make a break for it" — which I was pretty sure I was at some point, considering the odds — "I'd pass through Transit and wait to be dispatched. Pulling some stupid shit's going to be far easier on a troop transport than it would be on a Federation Carrier. Hell, staring down the barrel of a death sentence, maybe you could even get a few recruits onboard to help you, yunno, *even the odds.*" I was talking out of my ass. I didn't plan to start a mutiny, but I would have definitely been looking for an out after transitioning. I figured, though, the idea of leading his own little band of merry men would appeal to the kid. I watched the gears turn in his head and then after a few seconds he nodded like we'd come to some sort of unspoken agreement. I tried to sigh quietly enough that he wouldn't hear as he turned around.

We all shuffled quietly forward toward what now looked to be SimPods in the distance. There were hundreds of people ahead of us in the line, and the hangar was abuzz with activity. Ships being loaded up, mechs being moved, soldiers patrolling, and every now and then some unlucky soul making a break from their line, running to who knows where. They usually got about ten steps before one of the patrolling drones hit them with a taser disk. After that, they crumpled, seized, and were dragged away. There was no escaping the Federation. Not ever. I guess I was more used to it, being a tuber, than everyone else was. I stared at the barcode on my arm. I'd always belonged to them.

Two hundred and twelve minutes later, I ambled up to a yellow and black line and had a rifle shoved in my face. "Wait there," I got told by a soldier. I watched the kid with the tattoos sidle up to the SimPod and climb inside. The door closed and hissed shut, and a red light flickered to life overhead, accompanied by a timer that reset itself to zero. The pod was a big oval, like an egg.

I sighed and looked at the floor, at my dusty boots, and caught a whiff of vomit. I'd still not had a decent shower or been allowed to sit down, or been offered anything to eat or drink. I was dreading the Sim — there's no way I'd be sharp enough to do well at it. The whole thing was designed to weed out the bad from the terrible — the worst then went to be cannon fodder in whatever war was being fought close by that required bullet sponges, and the less horrible recruits would be shipped off to some distant planet to fight for something they didn't give a shit about. It was all covered in the 'After Your Enlistment' pamphlet, except not exactly in those words. Looking around, I couldn't imagine that anyone would be here voluntarily. I wondered how many were.

The light went off and the door opened. Tattoos strolled out, grinning. He cracked his knuckles. "Piece of cake." The timer read twenty-three seconds.

"Get moving," the soldier with the rifle growled. "Down there, keep left."

The kid went around the pod and disappeared. There were dozens lined up, all with their own lines of recruits being ushered in.

"You, inside," the guard ordered.

I took a breath and stepped up onto the steel rungs and into the egg. The door hissed shut and a screen came to life. *STAND ON THE X.* I looked at the floor and moved over the white X in the center of what looked like an omni-directional treadmill. A rod descended from the ceiling with a set of goggles on one side, and a fake plasma rifle on the other. *PUT ON YOUR HEADSET,* the screen ordered. I obliged.

The goggles sucked on my face until the world outside disappeared and then a jolt of pain lanced through my skull. A quiet buzzing lingered in my ears for a second, and then it started.

THE DROPSHIP RUMBLED NUMBLY. I looked around at all the new Exo recruits, held against the wall between the arms that would soon enough let them go and plunge them into some alien hell.

I stared around at the nondescript helmets, all facing forward, and almost lost myself to the idea that it wasn't real. I let myself smile and flexed my fingers around the butt of the rifle and looked down, turning it over. Humph, it felt like the real thing. Just a second ago it was plastic and light. This felt like steel. It was heavy and I could feel the surface slick with the chamber grease. The goggles were doing more than just showing me a virtual world. I couldn't figure out how, but I knew this was deeper than the simple VR goggles I'd saved up a year for back on Genesis to kick back with some video games when I was off the clock.

A buzzer sounded in the cargo bay and a red light started strobing. On the catwalk between the two rows of troops, an officer, grizzled and gray, stepped down from the next compartment. He was wearing a pilot's suit, and his face was covered with scars. He had his helmet under one arm, and the other was gesticulating. "Troops," he yelled over the sound of explosions outside the ship. "It's almost time. Your objective is simple. Survive. We need boots on the ground. Overwhelm the enemy forces. If they're shooting at you, you're shooting back, got it? These fuckers are big, they're mean, and they won't think twice about putting a bullet in you."

He turned, his eyes roving across the helmets of the troops strapped up ready to drop. I looked at my arms and legs, at the exo suit. Hydraulic and sprung, my joints felt light, my arms strong. Struts protected my chest and shoulders, rose around my neck — armored me from whatever was coming next. I swallowed hard and then the floor dropped from under me.

The belly of the ship opened and I plunged out along with everyone else. Smoke and fire swirled below and the dropship peeled away into the clouds. We all hit the ground in unison, bounced, and then sprang forward toward cover instinctually. The air was a mess of bullets and plasma rounds.

The ground was carved up with shell holes and craters. In the distance, dark shapes seethed in the smoke, and the cries of some alien species, pissed off at the Federation, rang in the air, punctuated with the whistle of mortar fire and the fizz of plasma rounds.

My shoulder hit the broad side of a foxhole and I pinned myself against the ground. The HUD in my helmet lit up like fireworks, displaying vitals, callsigns of the friendly troops around me, as well as measuring distances to alternate cover, and the chances of reaching it without incident. I shook my head but it wouldn't budge. How the hell was anyone supposed to see anything in these things?

A troop sank down next to me and gave me a thumbs up. I returned it, trying to convince myself that none of this was real, but the ache in my shoulder was arguing against that hypothesis. The soldier showed me three fingers, then curled one down, and then the next. When his fist closed, he leapt to a stance and scrambled over the top of the fox hole. He didn't even stand up straight before he got blown backwards by a plasma round. He landed a couple meters away, half his chest missing. I swore inside my helmet and stared around, watching soldiers in every direction get blown apart.

"Get moving!" A voice rang in my helmet. "Sitting on your ass ain't going to win this war, soldier! Go, go, go!"

I rolled onto my hands and knees and looked for cover. The HUD told me that I had a 72 percent chance of making it to what looked like the remains of a building about ten meters away. My adrenaline was surging, and it was keeping everything else at bay. I couldn't feel the hunger or thirst or fatigue I knew was gripping me, and despite *knowing* this wasn't real, it felt like it was. The goggles had to be interfacing with my brain somehow. Basic electric signals to simulate feeling. Simulate muscle movement. Simulate the sounds and the chemical reactions. But it felt off, somehow. The ground felt smoother than it should and, despite the explosions and projectiles flying overhead, I couldn't feel any wind or disturbances of the air on my skin. It was good — better than I'd ever experienced, but there was just enough to cling onto to keep reality and this world separate.

I climbed out of the hole and my feet hit asphalt. I stole a glance sideways and realized I was running down a road. Stacks of bricks and what remained of walls littered the battlefield. This used to be a town.

I dived under a missile that peeled off a mech in the distance and rolled through a broken doorway.

The ground rumbled behind me as a dropship swooped in. Its hold doors opened and it popped out a dozen F-Series Federation mechs decked out in white and blue liveries. They landed hard and then pounded forward, loosing machine gun fire into the distance from their rifles. The muzzles chattered and spat flame.

The last out was a different sort of mech, taller and sleeker than the House Cats. It fell halfway to the ground before its thrusters kicked in and kept it aloft. It drew two huge pistols and started punching rounds into the smoke ahead of us. A rifle popped up from its shoulder and glowed blue before spitting a plasma round into the distance. Something exploded.

It hovered forward, directing the House Cats and barking orders at the troops over comms. "Move up, soldiers. Collect some scalps!"

I swore inside my helmet and breathed hard. Peeking up over the wall, I laid my rifle across it and starting putting shots into the air. I didn't know what I was shooting at — there was nothing to shoot at. It was like firing into water and hoping to hit a fish. The House Cats drew level with my position and pushed up the rise toward the enemy front line. It must have been easier to wade into fire knowing you had twelve inches of steel protecting you. I looked down at my flak jacket and thought about how the guy in the foxhole had been blown apart. It was more for show than anything — a placebo. Around me other exo troops rose from their holes and fell into line behind them, taking cover behind the thick steel hulls of the House Cats. I watched them creep on ahead and the voice came back. "Deserting your unit is an offence punishable by death, soldier. Show us what you're made of. Move up!"

I didn't feel like getting killed. I was guessing it was going to hurt like a bitch, judging by the way that pain was triggering all over my body. However the headset was sending impulses, I could feel things. Not little things, like dust or wind, but the stony shrapnel punched at me as it rained down on my head, tossed by a stray shell shot from whatever the fuck we were fighting.

I grunted and scrambled back onto the road, taking cover behind one of the F Series there. It fired incessantly. Two other troops fell in next to me and we all strode forward. My helmet crackled with static. "Hey, exos!" The voice was hard, female, no-nonsense. "You're my goddamn eyes, alright! You cover my flanks. Let's get these fuckers."

I stared up at the back of the F-Series in front of me. It was the pilot talking from inside the suit, cocooned inside her steel shell. I nodded, but I didn't know to who. We surged forward, me covering left, the other two covering right. The House Cat picked up the pace and we followed. I kept my eyes left, shooting at everything that moved, ducking under fire when it came in, crouching close to the F-Series and firing through its legs when it came under attack. My heart hammered in my chest, but I wasn't dead yet, which I was pretty happy about. I had no idea how long I'd been in — it felt like a long time. My mind flitted back to the kid with the tattoos — twenty something seconds. He must have been putting on a show. He'd been cooked by the time he got to the first foxhole. Must have been, but I didn't have the time to consider it just then. I knelt down and pumped a dozen rounds into one of the things that was swimming in the smoke. The air was thick with it. Everything was burning. Wreckage of buildings, downed craft and mech, shell holes — everything. The smoke was thick and acrid. The alien stumbled under my fire, writhed in the air, and then collapsed. It was on all fours, at least three or four times the size of a human, with a tail and a long face — reptilian maybe? Couldn't say. I kept firing.

One of the troops behind me clapped me on the shoulder and I turned, the sensation dull and vague. A muscle twitch more than anything, but real enough in the moment. He nodded his head to the right and motioned for me to follow him. He pointed toward a set of only half-destroyed buildings. Cover. *Real* cover. He motioned for me again to follow. I wondered if they were real recruits, like me, in a SimPod, or if they were just digital apparitions.

"No," I said, shaking my head. "We have to cover her." I looked up at the House Cat towering over us, pummeling the reptilian enemy with the Samson rifle she was wielding.

They looked at each other and then grabbed for my arm. I shrugged them off. They tried again, pointing to cover. I pushed one of them back and the other lunged for me. "Come on, man! We're going to get killed out here!"

I hit him with the butt of my rifle and then shoved it in the face of the other one. "Hey, we were told to cover her! I'm not just going to bail."

"Shit, man! She's a fucking Federation pilot and she's protected by twelve inches of Zephod Steel! We're going to die and it'll be for nothing," the one on the ground growled. "This ain't our war, man. I'm not dying for the Federation. It's not my choice to be here."

We stayed silent for a second, but I didn't lower the rifle.

The pilot shouted "Contact!" through the comms and I wheeled around, pinning the trigger. We both fired on the same reptilian thing rushing us, firing its own rifle into the House Cat, and it seemed almost pointless for me to be there at all. My rifle was like a peashooter compared to the F Series above me.

I glanced over my shoulder. The two exos were gone. The House Cat went to a knee as the reptile fell and ground to a halt in front of us. Its mouth opened, and its tongue lolled out, blue and forked between the hooked teeth. I swallowed hard and fought the bile back into my guts.

"Cover me," the pilot yelled. "I'm reloading!"

"You're fucking kidding, right?" I called into the ether.

"Eleven o'clock!"

I swore and dashed between the legs of the House Cat, slamming my shoulder against the inside of the knee for cover. I span out and pinned the trigger, filling the air with muzzle flash. A reptile rushed up toward us between the destroyed buildings and absorbed my rounds without slowing down. It was nearly on us when it faltered, stumbled and clattered to the ground. I dove to the side to get out of its way and it slid straight into the House Cat, bunching against its leg.

"Shit!" the pilot yelled.

"Shit? Shit what?" I dashed back to the fallen corpse and laid my rifle across the hulking jawbone, using it as a rest while I chased down one flanking us with a stream of bullets.

"Bullet jam!" she grunted.

"Bullet jam? You're not fucking serious!"

"It's no good. Punching out!"

"Punching what now?"

Before I even finished asking, the hatch on top of the House Cat blew open with a burst of flame and the pilot soared into the air on her seat. She sailed into the clouds above and was gone. The F Series sagged a little but remained upright. I stared around in disbelief. There were no exos nearby, I couldn't see any other mech, and there was no sign of any sort of support.

Dark shapes swam around me, circling like sharks. I hunched down behind the monster's head and looked up at the mech above me. I couldn't believe she'd just left me. I gritted my teeth, regretting not going with those two exos now. The Federation didn't give a shit.

I growled and threw down my gun. Fuck it, I wasn't going to go out like this, feeling sorry for myself. If they wanted to play like that, then fuck their simulation.

I planted my boot on the jaw of the reptile and launched myself upward, hooking my fingers over the rungs that ran up the front of the House Cat. I swung my legs up, caught purchase and hauled myself inside. The pilot's seat was gone, but there were caged footplates below me and haptic gloves in front. I slammed my feet into them and pushed my hands in, flexing. I felt the arms and legs judder to life on the F Series and it stood upright. The hatch closed automatically and the entire front of the cockpit filled with screens displaying everything outside. I couldn't help but grin as I pulled up the rifle. I clicked the trigger but nothing happened. Guess it really was jammed.

I sighed and cracked my neck. "Alright, Jim, you can do this. Just like the Blower, huh? Arms, joysticks — same thing."

I figured that being behind the twelve inches of Zephod Steel the exo troop had mentioned would be a better option than risking my ass outside. As I took my first step forward, and fell flat on my face, though, I started to wonder if that was the case.

## 5

My hands found the haptic gloves, not unlike the controls of my Blower, and my feet settled into the cages, suspended and hinged. The pilot had ejected with a seat strapped to her ass, and the distinct lack of one in the cockpit was noticeable. The controls moved the arms and the legs and without anything to get fixed to, it was like trying to stand on liquid. The F-Series lurched sideways as I tried to find level and then flopped forward, beyond my control.

The hull hit the ground and rang like a gong. Without a harness or seat, I sprawled into the screen in front of me, crushing the gloves and my hands underneath me. The arms of the mech followed and pinned themselves under the F Series. I couldn't move. The weight of my own body on my own arms, combined with the weight of the mech on its arms, meant that I was stuck.

A voice rang out inside the cabin — stiff and robotic. "Proximity alert. Enemies approaching."

"Who's that?" I called back, trying desperately to roll the House Cat over.

"I am this F-Series' integrated AI assistant. Who are you?"

"I'm the person trying not to get fucking killed!"

"Affirmative. DNA scans reveal you are a Federation Enlisted Troop. Self-destruct sequence deactivated."

I twisted my arms and managed to shift onto my side, dropping the jammed rifle in the process. "Self-destruct?"

"It is standard protocol when a Mechanized Unit is commandeered by a non-Federation entity. Caution: enemies are approaching."

"Shit," I panted, trying to wheel the F Series around. It was almost impossible without being strapped into a seat. My body was flopping around and I had nothing to pull against. "Is there anything you can do about it?"

"I am able to deploy grenades, though line of sight is required. A smokescreen is possible, though."

"So I can be blind *and* lame? No thank you," I grunted, flattening my hands on the ground in front of me. I pushed back as much as I could, suspended in the cockpit from the gloves and foot cages, and scrambled to a stance.

"I detect an imbalance in the equilibrium sensors. Are you fully harnessed?"

"Fully harnessed? There's not even a fucking seat in here!" I turned as quickly as I could to face the red outline running at me on screen. The words 'Automated Defense Protocols Activated' popped up on screen and a barrage of miniature grenades exploded out of the shoulders of the F Series, obliterating the incoming reptile.

"It is not advised to operate a Mechanized Unit without being harnessed in. It is recommended that the pilot ejects. Ejection sequence started," the voice announced.

"What!? No! Abort!" I yelled, turning and throwing my fist into another reptile that was trying to flank us. I met bone with steel and felt the skull crack under the force. It reeled backward and scrambled in circles. It was long, with muscular fore and hind legs, with armor plates secured right into the scaled skin. It had huge claws, and a strange-looking weapon slung across its back — half firearm, half melee club.

"Negative. Pilot does not have authorization to abort."

"What do you mean I don't have authorization?"

"I outrank you," he said flatly.

My proximity sensors went wild and I turned to face another one. It came at me hard, slashing with its claws. I threw my arm out but it connected with nothing but air. The reptile weaved under me and sank its talons into the gaps between the armor plating, driving me backward. I swore loudly inside the cabin and felt the back of my helmet crack against the inside of the hull.

"Ejecting in three, two—"

"No!"

"—one. Ejecting."

A loud click rang out below but there was no seat to eject. At the same time, the hatch above me blew open and out of reach. I leapt up instinctually to grab it but it was too high. I met the eye of the giant reptilian alien clambering over the hull for just a second before its jaws closed around my head. Its teeth sank into the flesh on my neck and I screamed, pain ripping through every fiber of my body. The world went black, and then I died.

I TORE the goggles off and threw them down in front of me, panting hard. My neck was tingling and my eyes were stinging. I breathed raggedly and looked up at the screen in front of me. The words 'Neural Link Terminated — Simulation Over' were burned on it in white.

"Son of a bitch," I grunted, standing straight. The door to my left hissed and light bled in around the edges. My head was pounding when I stepped out. The guy with the rifle told me to go left and I did. Before I rounded the corner, I stole a glance up at the timer above the door. It read twenty-eight seconds. What the fuck? It'd felt like forever. Time dilation. I'd never experienced it, but I'd heard about it. Not that it felt like that, though. Like being kicked by a horse. I didn't think my headache could get any worse. I was wrong.

I made my way down the walkway, and stopped. Ahead, I could see Tattoos talking to a couple of soldiers. They nodded to him, and then he looked at me. They followed his gaze, and then turned toward me. Tattoos smirked, and then walked off.

The soldier at the front was humanoid, but not human, tall with dark green skin. I didn't recognize the species. He looked comfortable carrying his weapon, like he knew how to use it. "James Alfred Maddox?" he asked loudly.

"Yeah?" I said back, conscious that I was leaning into the balls of my feet.

"Stop there. You need to come with us," he said, striding toward me.

I tilted to the left and looked at Tattoos — his sly grin, his cocky gait. Motherfucker. He'd sold me down the river. That shit about jacking a transport. He'd told them. Told them that was what I planned to do. My fists curled and anger flared in my belly like a twisted fire. I looked left, and then right, at the rows of SimPods standing next to each other, each with a gap between. My eyes moved upward, looking for the Federation drones I knew were buzzing overhead.

"Hey," the soldier yelled, going for his rifle. "Don't you dare —"

I didn't let him finish. I broke right and ran hard. My muscles groaned and ached. No food. No sleep. No water. I was running on fumes and adrenaline, and I didn't think they'd last long. I dragged as much air into my lungs as I could and sprinted between the pods, darting between two lines before the soldiers administering them could turn to grab me. I stuck close to one of the queues and ran hard. I had no idea where I was going, but it didn't matter. I'd fucked it. I was running from Federation soldiers in a Federation ship, with an impending charge of trying to incite mutiny. If they caught me, that was it — prison, or more likely, I'd just catch a bullet for *resisting.* In my peripherals, I caught sight of flashes of gray Federation uniforms between the recruits standing in line. Shit. One moved in. I halted for a second and skipped a step. He lurched through the line and made a grab for me, but swooped in front of me, sprawling to the ground. I leapt over him and went through the gap he'd made in the line. Another came at me and I sidestepped him. His fingers closed around my jacket and I ducked, spinning out of it. The sleeves slipped over my hands and I heard the soldier swear. I felt his hand graze my shoulder but I kept running.

The third one was quicker, sitting low on his heels, hands spread. The lines were dense either side and I was boxed in. He watched me come and I went right, pulling back my elbow for a swing. He knew how to fight — he was trained, and big. I wound up the punch and he went to block it with all the time in the world. I turned into my toes and lashed out backwards with my left heel instead of following through with the punch. It connected with his thigh and he staggered backwards, crying out in shock. Now I followed through with the hook, landing it as hard as I could on his cheek. It was like hitting iron. My knuckles rebounded off and he screwed up his face in anger, but didn't go down. Shit.

His hand flew up and I felt the sharp prongs of a taser pierce the flesh under my ribs, and then the fuzzy tongue of ten thousand volts. My body convulsed for a second or two and I stumbled backward, my muscles not my own. I watched through the thickening haze as he stood straight and massaged his face, scowling. "You're a dumb fuck," he said, spitting blood.

As I fell, I couldn't have agreed more.

I GOT DRAGGED by the arms out of the hangar and into a brightly lit corridor lined with halogen lights. The din of the hangar disappeared, and doors flashed past, each even more blandly metal and nondescript than the last. We passed into another corridor and then into an elevator. I was still barely conscious and my feet wouldn't even go under me. Whether we went up or down, I don't know, but when we stopped moving, the pace continued. One of the soldiers dragging me put his palm on a scanner and a thick set of doors opened to reveal a wide space. In the center was a hole that led down to the lower level, and all along the sides of both floors were narrow doors. In space or not, I knew what cells looked like. I tried to swallow, but the muscles in my neck just floundered a little. They took me up to a cell and threw me in. The door slammed shut and I was left with a steel cot and a seatless toilet.

I lifted my head off the smooth floor and climbed onto what was more akin to a shelf than a bed. My head was still pounding, and despite the bright lights, I fell asleep pretty quickly, though it was more like passing out from sheer exhaustion.

How long it was before I woke up, I couldn't have said. The doors shot open and a woman walked in. She was almost six feet tall, and had her hands clasped behind her back. Her blond hair was pulled back into a tight bun, and she had a gray naval cap on with some silver stars pinned to the side. Must be an officer. She stared down at me, limp on the cot, and rolled her eyes. "Sit up."

She had the sort of look that told me she wouldn't ask twice, so I did. Her hand moved from behind her back and she held up a communicator slab, staring indifferently at it.

"James Alfred Maddox," she said, looking at me over the top of it. "Do you know why I'm here?"

"Look — it was just a joke, alright? I was trying to shut him up. I'd had a really bad —" I started talking, but she silenced me with a flick of her wrist.

"I don't know what you're blathering about, but a simple *no* would have sufficed." She sighed, obviously discontented with her current job. "I'm here because of your simulation score."

"Like I said, I've had a really bad —"

"Did I ask you to speak?" Her voice was hard. "Interrupting an officer is an actionable offense in the Federation Corps — but, considering your current predicament, and the circumstances that brought you here, it doesn't surprise me that you didn't consider the implications before you opened your mouth."

I stayed quiet.

"Your score, as I was saying, is the reason I'm here. What do you have to say for yourself?"

"I, uh," I started tentatively, "Had a really bad... Night? I haven't slept, and... There was a dropship that took me in its wake... I was doing some overtime and... The thrusters, they... My Blower was... I mean..." My head was spinning. I couldn't form sentences. "I nearly died, and... I'm having a bit of an *off day*." I rubbed my temples. The headache was coming back.

She huffed. "An *off day?*"

I nodded.

She raised her eyebrows and shook her head lightly. "Then I'd be curious to see what a good day looks like. You scored in the top twelve percent of all recruits. You were in the top five percent across most of our scoring metrics. You did exceedingly well, by all accounts."

I was speechless. "I did... well?"

"Yes, quite." She put the communicator away. "The simulation is designed to weed out the worst recruits, and gets progressively more intense and difficult the longer it goes on. Those who last the longest score the best. The initial landing and scramble for cover — seventy-eight percent survival rate. The first move from cover, over the foxhole — forty-three percent survival rate. Reaching further cover — twenty-nine percent. Surviving until the Mechanized Corps arrived — sixteen percent survival rate. Moving to cover position behind the F-Series — eleven percent survival rate. Reaching the integrity test — eight percent. Passing it — two percent."

"Integrity test?"

"The two simulated soldiers telling you that they're moving to find better cover. More than eighty-five percent of all soldiers left the covering position and moved to cover."

"Oh." The words weren't really sinking in. They felt vague and distant. All I could think about was drinking something. Eating something. Curling up in a little ball and sleeping.

"Less than one percent of all simulations following your path lasted until the F-Series pilot ejected. After that, there are no rates. Very few survive more than a minute or two of simulated-time. It's not designed to be continued after that. We have all the information we require by that point."

I swallowed but said nothing.

"We use these simulations to determine the suitability of ground troops for deployment. You are very capable, and very ready, by all accounts — *off day* or not."

I stayed quiet, sensing there was more coming.

"However — it was not the time that you lasted, or the fact that you passed the integrity test, that's the reason for my being here." She put her hands behind her back again and stood at attention. "It's that you went for the F-Series following the pilot's ejection."

"Was I not supposed to?" I asked quietly, my stomach churning.

She stuck out her bottom lip. "There's nothing built into the simulation to prevent it — it's just not something we've ever witnessed a new recruit attempt." She arched an eyebrow. "Tell me, why did you assume the controls?"

I felt like she was looking for a specific answer, and I didn't think the actual reason would be it. "Instinct?"

Her eyebrow went higher. "Is that a question?"

"Instinct," I said more firmly, convincing myself it was the answer, and that it wasn't because I thought that was where I'd be safest from whatever the fuck those aliens were.

She nodded slowly. "Very good. We would have let you carry on, but we wanted to stop you before you developed any... *bad habits.*"

"Stop me?" I cocked my head. "Wait — you did that? You opened the hatch?"

"Not me personally, but —"

"You killed me!"

"You look very much alive to me, Mr. Maddox," she said coldly.

I cut myself off and reined myself in, remembering that I was in a cell for assaulting a Federation soldier. She hadn't mentioned it yet, but I had a feeling it was coming. I waited for her to speak again.

"Most Federation pilots are hand selected out of our elite academies. Potential pilots are trained from a young age in combat and reflex training, spacial awareness, advanced tactics and strategy. They're in peak physical condition, and mentally much sharper than the average soldier. The best of the best." She took a breath. "Recruits are never transitioned into the Mechanized Corps, Mr. Maddox. But then, it would be idiotic to ignore what we saw today. To have the instinct to try to assume control of an F-Series in the heat of battle, a machine that pilots spend years trying to gain control of — let alone using it to kill two Vangosokons, and all without training, a neural interface chip, or even a seat? Well, what's that old Earth saying — *actions speak louder than words?"*

I tried not to smile. It was a goddamn fluke, and a blur too, but I wasn't about to say that. While exo troops had less than a one in ten chance of surviving their first deployment, pilots had a much better statistical likelihood of not kicking the bucket.

She sighed again. "It's the reason we sent those two soldiers to apprehend you — to bring you directly to me immediately following the simulation."

"Ah," I said, feeling like I should acknowledge it. They could have said that instead of just running at me with rifles.

"And, had you waited to be addressed, you might have found that out. Instead, you fled, disobeying a direct order from a superior — also an actionable offense. You then proceeded to evade two Federation soldiers — one of whom was a private first class — the second was a corporal."

I thought I caught her smirk for a second, but I dared not look at her for more than a moment. She cleared her throat.

"And the third, who you *assaulted,* was one of our on-duty master sergeants. He tells me that you feinted a punch, staggered him with a kick, and then struck him in the face. Is that correct?"

I clenched my jaw. "Yes," I squeezed out. Tubers were treated like shit growing up. Like animals — bullied and kicked around. I used to fight a lot as a kid. Older kids. Bigger kids. Groups of kids. I was used to it, to throwing punches and receiving them, too. Though I felt like those skills I'd developed to save my ass were about to bite me on it.

"Are you aware of the punishment for a recruit striking a senior officer?"

"No." I guessed it wasn't good.

"Expulsion."

"From the Federation?"

"Into space."

I gulped.

She waited for a few seconds before she went on, letting me shit myself a little more. "Have you ever had any hand-to-hand combat training?"

"Training? No. Not exactly." Unless she counted getting beaten to a pulp by bigger kids than me.

"And you've never partaken in any pilot training of Mechanized Units in the past, simulated or otherwise?"

"No."

"And yet you managed to hit a Federation master sergeant — twice, and pilot an F-Series to reasonable effect — considering the circumstances, at least." She did smirk this time. "I'd say you have the makings of a pilot. So let me be very clear here, Mr. Maddox. In very rare cases, the neural link established in combat simulation can leave echoes in the mind of recruits — images and feelings that persist even after the simulation has ended, that can sometimes cause erratic, even violent behavior. Do you see what I'm saying?"

I was afraid to answer, that my hope to survive just a little longer was clouding my judgment.

She looked down and stepped further in. "Let me be candid here, Mr. Maddox. It's my job to find the best pilots and transition them from the academy into active duty. I didn't expect to find a potential pilot today — especially not fresh off a dropship from a colony planet in the middle of dead space. But that seems to be what's happened. So I'll say this once, and believe me, once I leave this room, the offer will have expired, and you'll be left to the hands of the Exo Corps' Disciplinary Committee." She drew breath and held up the communicator again. "I have in my hand a signed medical assessment from a Mechanized Corps medical officer stating that, after his assessment, it is clear that you were experiencing simulation echoes, and that was the reason for your behavior following the simulation. As such, your actions are inadmissible and no further disciplinary action will be taken. However, Mechanized Corps medical officers are only permitted to provide medical reports for those in the Mechanized Corps. James Alfred Maddox, if you accept this proposal, you'll be immediately transitioned into the Mechanized Corps Combat Training Program, along with a crop of recruits from the Regent Falmouth's Mechanized Corps Pilots Academy."

"And, just hypothetically," I began tentatively, "what would happen if I declined? Hypothetically..."

"The likely answer? You'd be sedated and then fired into the cold depths of space on course for the nearest star," she said flatly.

"Then I accept," I answered quickly.

"Good." She turned on her heel and moved for the door, pausing only when she was across the threshold. "James Alfred Maddox — welcome to the Mechanized Corps. A transport will be waiting for you outside. Please don't take long."

I stood up.

"But before you go" — she sighed, turning her head away and screwing up her face — "take a shower. You smell like vomit."

# 6

I was shown into the detainment facility's shower block, and instructed to wash — thoroughly. I did so, along with hanging my head back and drinking as much shower-water as I could stomach without a thought about whether it was safe to or not. When I got out, my clothes had been disposed of. The guard took pride in using the word *incinerated.* He smirked as he tossed me my new ones — a gray recruit's uniform. It was tight in all the wrong places and folded up across the chest, velcroing in at the shoulder like some ancient doctor's smock. They also tossed me a pair of boots and a pair of clean socks, both of which were about as comfortable as I'd ever put on, and I doubted they were designed to be. Colony planets didn't get top-class supplies. That was apparent.

I was ushered out and down a set of hallways until I was in what looked to be a miniature train terminal. The ceiling was vaulted and curved, and along the platform were different painted sections, denoting who could stand and enter the train at which points. The train itself was three cars long, silver and bullet-shaped, clad in glass. It was empty, save for the officer that had addressed me in the cell.

I stepped onto the polished floor and stopped. She turned half on and squeezed her lips into a tight ring. "Well, it's not *much* better." She turned back to the train. "But it'll do."

I stepped up next to her and she shook her hair.

"No. Privates stand behind officers. Your position is denoted by rank." She motioned me backward and rolled her eyes. "Down here they may be lax with their rules, but when we get up top, it won't fly. The officers will look for any reason they can to hook your ass —" She paused and cleared her throat. "To demote you back to Ground Corps."

I measured her carefully, the way she stood, held herself — the slip. I smirked. "Can I ask your name, Officer...?"

"Everett. Second Lieutenant." She returned the curious gaze. Her face was angular, her expression flattened by practice. She held herself stiffly, shoulders back, chin up. Her skin was like poured porcelain, her eyes a dark shade of teal. I tried not to stare too long.

"Have you been an officer long, Second Lieutenant Everett?"

Her face hardened. I could tell she hadn't, but she wasn't about to admit it outright. Still — the look was enough. "It's time to go."

She stepped toward the train and the door opened. She turned to face me once inside and watched me enter. "Look, Airman Maddox, this is highly unorthodox. Usually, you'd be transferred back to the Academy, but... You've already *aged out* of the education sector. You're just too skilled to be put into Basic in the Ground Corps. However, this puts you in a very difficult position. Basic training is much more rigorous in the Mechanized Corps. The airmen you'll be training alongside will be much further ahead than you. They'll be faster, stronger, and more experienced. They'll be the best that the Federation has, groomed and educated from youth with a single purpose — to pilot Federation Mechanized Units. The academies do not accept walk-ups, and they don't give free rides. Every person where we're going," she said, jabbing the button and closing the doors, "will have earned their place." The train took off, deeper into the Carrier. "They're strict, and they won't go easy on you, do you understand? Each and every one of them will have a chip on their shoulder. It's a highly competitive environment."

"A pissing contest, you mean," I snorted.

She cleared her throat, and tried not to laugh. There was no way she was one of these jumped-up Mech Corps pilots. There was no way you'd talk about your own like that. She must have come up through Ground Corps. She ignored the remark. "I'd advise that you don't let them know that you're not transitioning from a pilot's academy. Work hard. Keep your head down. Study, and get yourself up to speed. There's not going to be any special treatment for you, and you'll face the same tests that they will, and should you fail even a single one —"

"I'll be *hooked back down to Ground Corps with the other animals?*" I grinned.

"Ahem." She stood straight as the train decelerated, paused, and then began rising vertically up another rail. "Quite."

We stood in silence for a few seconds until the train pulled up to a platform and the doors opened. "This is it." She proffered the door and I stepped off.

I paused on the platform and turned. "Aren't you coming?"

She smiled briefly. "No. They don't like GCs up here."

"I —"

She held her hand up. "Save it. If you manage to screw it up, you'll be tossed back down with us animals, don't worry about that." I saw a flicker of something in her eyes and I struggled to put my finger on it. "Good luck, Airman. You're going to need it." The flicker came back, and I saw what it was. Sadness. Regret.

I opened my mouth to say something else, but she closed the door and the train peeled away and disappeared, her steely eyes glittering through the glass.

I had no way to check, but if I could have, I would have put money on her having been enrolled in one of those fancy pilot academies. Maybe she'd even graduated to Basic. Who knows. But, at some point, along the way, she'd stumbled. Maybe failed a test. Maybe looked at one of the tightly wound officers with a bit too much zeal. She'd gotten the hook, and been tossed down to Ground Corps.

I hung my head and sighed. She was working her way up, but

still, my stomach twisted up a little and I felt a flash of guilt. This wasn't my choice, but I felt bad that it'd been her mandate to deliver me here. I made a mental note to apologize for my derisiveness if I ever saw her again. Everett. I committed the name to memory and let myself smile at the fact that she'd managed to beat that seven percent rate.

I turned back to the platform and stared up at the words over the doorway ahead. Level 16 — Mechanized Corps. I clenched my teeth, held a breath, and went toward it.

I PASSED through a set of sliding doors and into a corridor. It was all white, with appropriately patriotic slogans painted on the walls and ceilings. A desk sat in the corner, with a bored looking airman attending it. I cleared my throat as I approached.

He looked up at me and raised an eyebrow. "Yes?"

"I'm, uh, here for Basic?" I said, not quite sure where I was going, or what I was supposed to be doing.

His eyebrow arched higher. "Where've you been?"

I jerked a thumb over my shoulder and almost let slip about the Sim. "Er, I just got transferred."

"From where?"

"The Academy."

"I never saw you there. I got transitioned three weeks ago. What wing were you in?"

"No — it wasn't this academy."

"Which academy?" he asked accusatively.

I sighed and put my hands on the desk. "Look, buddy," I said, trying to take on an authoritative tone, trying to remember what Everett had said. Competitive. Chips on their shoulder. I'd grown up with kids looking down on me for being *less* than them. I knew what they were like, how if you gave them an inch they'd take a mile. I had to sell it, or just like when I was a kid, I'd be shit on their shoe forever. "I'm under orders. Just like you. I was told to drag my ass out here, and get myself into Basic." I met his eye. "I haven't just hauled myself across six damn systems and a billion miles of space to have some jumped-up rookie airmen get in my face, alright?" I tried to keep my voice even, but I was bullshitting. "I was told not to tell anyone my business, and if they asked, I was told to tell them to go fuck themselves. So, come on — ask me."

He stared at me, not really knowing what I meant.

"Come on, ask me. Ask me again where I just came from and what I'm doing here. Come on."

"I, uh," he stammered. "Where di —"

"Go fuck yourself."

He clenched his jaw. If he was stuck on desk duty out here, I made a guess that he wasn't a model pilot. I didn't say anything else before I turned and walked off. If it was going to be like Everett said, then I needed to walk in there with my dick swinging. They didn't know me, but if they were all as tightly wound as the guy on the front desk, it'd only be a matter of time before they got on my back and gave me the third degree.

I headed for the double doors at the end of the hallway and didn't look back. I got through them and came to a fork. There was an arrow pointing left toward 'Administration.' I followed that. I needed to figure out where the hell I was going, and what the fuck was going on.

A maze of white, shining corridors led me to another nondescript door with the same word painted above in ubiquitous gray. I approached and it opened. There was a curved desk in the middle of the room, and a row of doors behind it, all adorned with the names of various officers. I approached it, and a droid sat up in the chair. It was standard house-droid, but had been dressed up like a Federation airman for show. Its skin shone brightly in the light, its round, camera lens eyes focusing on me as I approached. Its voice box lit up as it spoke and LEDs danced behind its mesh teeth.

"Good afternoon, Airman..." It trailed off. "My apologies, I don't seem to recognize your data signature." It stiffened suddenly, a red light coming to life on its forehead. "Identify yourself," it demanded.

I stopped in my tracks. House droids weren't usually the confrontational sort. Must be a militarized version — and I wasn't keen to find out what that meant. "My name is James Alfred Maddox. I'm a recruit. Here for Basic?"

It narrowed its apertures on me. "Do not move." Its brain whirred in its skull for a few seconds, and then the red light disappeared. "Welcome, Probationary Airman Maddox. You're late."

"Late?" I stepped forward. "How can I be late?"

"Your induction began twenty two minutes ago."

"I didn't know anything about an induction."

"Being late is an infractionable offense. This will go on your record."

"My record?"

"Speaking freely to a ranking officer without express permission is an infractionable offense. This will go on your record."

I ground my teeth and took a breath. "Permission to speak, sir?" I didn't know how the hell a house-droid could be a ranking officer, but I didn't like the look of that seven percent.

"Granted."

"Can you direct me to the induction room?"

"Your induction is being conducted by Major Meyers. His office is on my left. Thank you." He gestured to a door behind him and I nodded as politely as I could before I breezed toward it, knuckles ready to knock. I watched them shake as I raised them. Nerves. Hunger. Fatigue. Trepidation. They all swirled like some horrid cocktail, gnawing at my guts, coming out on my skin in a thin sheen of cool sweat.

I stopped at the threshold and listened. I could hear voices inside.

"—all due respect, sir, this is bullshit!" It was a woman's voice.

"Airman Kepler!" a guy boomed back. "This is not up for discussion. I don't like it any more than you do, but these are orders, this is what is happening, and this is your mandate. Do you understand?"

I heard her grumble.

"You're to babysit this *whoever* the hell he is until he bombs out of Mech Corps, is that clear? There's no way that some colony tuber is going to—"

I knocked, hard, and both voices halted immediately.

"Enter," the guy said.

I did and found myself in an office, modest and square, paneled white like every other square inch of the level sixteen. The guy, who I assumed was Major Meyers, was a big brute with round shoulders and a receding hairline. His chest was pinned up with medals and I could see scars snaking up from his collar over the side of his face. Reconstructive surgery had been kind to him, but it must have been a bad tangle. I could see the same scars on the back of his left hand as it clasped the right on the wooden top in front of him. His jaw was set and he looked pissed off.

The girl must have been my age, maybe a year older. She was tall, athletic, with muscular legs hugged by her pilot's trousers, and a crop of short brown hair that was swept up and back, and shaved on the sides. She was sucking her cheek and glaring at me. "Nice of you to finally join us," she snorted.

Meyers scowled for a second. "Kepler, wait outside."

"But —"

"Now, Kepler."

She huffed and then stormed past me, closing the door harder than was necessary. When we were alone, Meyers gestured to the seat in front of his chair. "Mr. Maddox, sit."

I did. The chair squeaked.

"You're late, Maddox."

"I—"

"That wasn't a question." He sighed. "Look, I'm going to be straight with you here. This isn't exactly—"

"Protocol?"

He narrowed his eyes at me.

"Sorry."

He ignored it, but I had a feeling I'd only get the one. "All of our pilots here have transitioned from Federation academies. Do you understand that? They've been trained their whole lives for this, taught tactics, history, strategy. They've been taught hand-to-hand combat, weapons training. They've been conditioned for what's in store. Simply speaking, they're the best of the best. And you think you can just waltz in here and take control of a mech, and what, be a hero or something?" He shook his head in disbelief and I already knew this entire thing was going to suck.

I waited to see if he'd talk more or if he genuinely wanted an explanation. "I didn't think anything — sir." I added the last part quickly. I took a breath and looked him dead in the eye. "To be perfectly honest, less than twelve hours ago, I thought I was going to die. When that dropship came in over Genesis, it scooped me and my Blower —"

"Blower?"

"The Blower 400, a mid-sized terraforming unit equipped with —"

He silenced me with a raised hand and I cleared my throat.

"Sorry. It picked us up in its wake and tossed us like ragdolls. When I came to, my oxygen was spent, and I couldn't see my unit anywhere. I almost died. Had to dig my way back into it. After that, well, it wasn't any easier. I had to decouple —"

The hand again. "Get to the point."

"It took me hours to get back to the settlement, at which point I was detained, frogmarched to the dropship and strapped in. They shot us into orbit, and then put us in line. By the time I got to the SimPod, I didn't know which way was up. I was just trying to survive. I didn't know what I was doing, and I wasn't trying to be clever or brave." I hung my head, a little ashamed of that. I was supposed to be putting on a show. "When I saw those soldiers coming for me, I assumed the worst. Next thing I know, I'm being dragged out of the brig and sent here. I got kicked off a train out there and then found my way here. So, like I said, sir, and with all due respect — I don't think anything, because I don't know anything."

He drummed on the desk.

"But if you're asking me if I'd like a chance to be here — well, you know better than me whether those Ground Corps survival rates for new recruits are accurate. And if you were me, sitting where I am, and someone said to you — you can either stay down there with those guys, or you can try your luck upstairs... Well, what would you do?"

"I'd be inclined to say that if you think what we do here hinges in any way, shape or form on *luck,* as you put it," he huffed, "then you're in for a very rude awakening."

I blinked hard, pissed that I'd used that word. In fact, I probably should have kept my mouth shut altogether and just nodded and apologized. Maybe I thought there'd be some humanity in him, like with Everett, or that this might actually not be so bad. I'm not quite sure how I managed to delude myself into thinking mandatory military conscription would be anything other than prison, but I'd done it.

"Kepler," he called, beckoning her from the door.

She stepped in and closed it behind her, putting her hands behind her back and standing to attention.

"This is Airman Maddox. He is in your charge."

"Yessir," she replied.

"I don't really think I need a babysitter," I started, though the remark wasn't even acknowledged.

"Make sure he knows where he's sleeping, what our schedule is, and where he can find the things he needs. Uniform. Books."

"Books?" I cut in.

"Your first Mechanized Corps Basic Training Written Test is in three days. If you fail, you'll—"

"Be kicked out. Yeah, I get it."

Kepler snorted. "Keep cutting off an officer and you'll be kicked out," she mumbled.

Either Meyers didn't catch it, or he ignored it. He shifted in his chair. "If you're here, then you're a pilot in training. I don't give two shits what your Sim scores were — if you're here, you're living under MC rules. Kepler will make sure you find your quarters and get settled, and I've asked her to keep an eye on you, too — show you how things work."

She grunted with indignation at the thought.

"Thank you."

"Oh, it's not for your benefit. You've got no idea how anything works, and I don't want anything here disrupted because you don't know where to put your boots. Incidentally, at the foot of your bed."

I chuckled in as friendly a way as I could. He scowled. It wasn't a joke.

"Now, get out."

I nodded slowly and then stood up. Kepler was already in the hallway, staring at me with as hard a look at Meyers was from behind. Seven percent was starting to sound pretty good.

# 7

"So, it's Kepler right?"

She stopped and turned into the balls of her right foot before I had chance to react. Her hand shot out and the heel of it slammed into my chest just below my collarbones. She drove me backwards with strength I hadn't really considered she might have had, and my head cracked against the paneled wall. She kept me pinned there, side on, leaning into my throat with her fist. "Let's get one thing straight." Her eyes narrowed. "We're not friends. We're not going to be friends. And I don't give two shits about your goddamn Sim score, alright? This isn't some fucking game — not some simulation you can pass and impress everyone in. We all earned our places here, and there's no way some jumped-up fucking tuber from some spit of dirt in the middle of fucking nowhere is going to make himself into a pilot. You got that?"

I nodded, wanting to rebut, but I figured that making enemies of *everyone* I came across might be a bad idea.

"Good. Meyers stuck me with this detail for one reason, and one reason only — because he trusts me. He trusts me to make sure you don't fuck up too badly in the first five minutes. He trusts me because

I'm the best. I was the top of my class, and I'm going to graduate Basic in the same place. Got it?"

I nodded. I really didn't like this big and bad act, but I didn't have the energy to challenge it, or the inclination to make another enemy before I even got started.

"So shut up, listen, watch, and stay the fuck out of my way. I've got too much riding on this to get caught up in whatever pity-party fucking sideshow the Federation brass have cooked up." She snorted and shook her head, releasing me. "Fucking Sim scores. I'd like to see you pull that sort of shit in a Full-Immi," she muttered through gritted teeth, turning away.

"Full-Immi?" I asked, rubbing my throat.

She scowled at me but said nothing. I struggled to keep up as she walked, her long powerful legs keeping a steady pace. When we finally reached a splay of hallways labelled with their destinations, she stopped and turned. She was breathing hard and trying not to show it. Beads of sweat were glistening along her neck and I could see her pulse hammering there. She'd tried to make a show of the walk, leave me behind, make it tough for me. Guess she didn't know that growing up on a colony like Genesis-526 breathing oxygen-poor air and sucking through a breather half the time would do wonders for your lung capacity and muscle oxygenation. I felt fitter all of a sudden. The air quality aboard the carrier was much better than I was used to. For Kepler, though, having come up through the *academy,* breathing liquid fucking gold, she was accustomed to it, so her fitness level and my sudden oxygenation seemed to be cancelling each other out, much to her dismay. She squeezed her lips into a grimace that didn't suit her and tried to look like she didn't give a shit about anything.

"I've gotta study. I've already lost an hour to your shitty time-keeping skills, and I've gotta keep my spot—"

"At the top of the class. Yeah." I sighed. If she was going to go, I was wishing she'd just leave already and give me some peace instead of just deriding me.

Her fists curled. "You've got a habit of interrupting people. It's kind of fucking annoying."

"I've heard."

"You consciously trying to be an asshole?"

"Just got a knack for it."

She narrowed her eyes at me. "Mess hall is down there." She pointed down a corridor. "Breakfast at seven. Lunch at one. Dinner at seven. Think you can remember that?"

I nodded.

"Quarters are down there." She pointed down another corridor. "You're in room 8B — the only free bed in there. Seems you picked your day to arrive. We just lost a recruit. Couldn't handle the pressure." She said it like it was a premonition. I tried to ignore the tone.

"What room are you in?"

She smirked. "Yeah, right." She shook her head at me and I watched her fists uncurl. "Down there, you'll find laundry, supply rooms, and the Upper Training Deck. The main hangar is reserved for most of the GC's stuff. We get our own one. We try to keep the riff raff out when we can. Doesn't always work." She looked me up and down and then turned on her heel. "In your dorm by nine. Lights out by ten," she called, striding toward the Training Deck.

"It was 8C, right?" I yelled as she approached a corner.

She flipped me her middle finger over her shoulder, and then disappeared.

MOVING through the hallways was disorienting. It took me fifteen minutes to find room 8B. I'd looped back on myself twice trying to get to it. It turned out the hallways were arranged in grids, which was confusing. When I got to it, I let myself in, found the entire room to be empty, and then left. The room was pristine, and there was nothing out of place. I had no idea how I'd be able to find mine, especially not without anyone in there to say *hey, it's this bed.* And I hardly wanted to go opening trunks and drawers to check for underpants before slumping down on my cot.

Each room had eight bunks in it, and with a one in sixteen chance, I didn't like my odds. I had no idea where anyone would be and no idea where to even start looking. I sighed and leaned my head against the outside of the door. My headache was coming back.

Softly shuffling steps snapped my attention around and I looked up to see another Federation House-Droid moving toward me, carrying an armful of folded uniforms. He saw me and stopped.

"Airmen are supposed to be in afternoon training." He sounded surprised, or at least as surprised as he could with limited voice fluctuation capabilities.

"And that would be… where?"

"Upper Training Deck. I must report —"

I dashed toward him, hands up. "Hey, hey, hey — there's no need to report anything."

He looked at me. "But it is protocol to report infractions committed by airmen and other Federation personnel to a ranking officer."

I could tell there was no arguing with him. Androids didn't buy into semantics or context. It was all black and white with them. I smiled instead. The droid in the administration area hadn't been able to read my identity. I guessed that all Federation personnel would be biometrically scanned for ID purposes, but I hadn't been brought in for that just yet. "Don't suppose you can scan my ID, right?"

"Negative. Identify yourself immediately, or I will be forced to restrain you."

"In that case my name is Airman Kepler.," I grinned. "And being such a big advocate of the rules around here, I suggest you do report me. Now, which way to the Upper Deck?"

When I got to the Upper Deck, I was immediately pulled aside, reprimanded, and then sent straight to medical, where they gave me more of a thorough going over than I'd ever had before. They were pissed off that I was late. Apparently, Kepler was supposed to take me to Medical, but she'd cut me loose early — to try and screw with me.

It was hardly the sort of hazing I was used to. It was almost cute. While the doctor had me bent over the table, he told me that I'd put him behind schedule by near enough an hour, and for that, he was going to have to be *quick,* which apparently meant *rough.* I gritted my teeth and tried to think of a happier time. I couldn't come up with one.

After that, I'd been directed to Psych Eval, where my sense of humor had gone down just *wonderfully* with a shrink wound up tighter than the droid had been. After that, I was given a crash course on Mechanized Corps etiquette by a Federation droid that usually oversaw the Federation history self-study sessions. He was dry and fast, and almost as rough as the doctor had been. He went on explaining saluting, addressing, and everything I could need to know to be a mindless robot in training to pilot a mindless robot. He'd given me my schedule, as well as my bunk assignment, and informed me that my clean changes of clothes would be already in my trunk — the droid I'd passed in the hallway had been carrying them, go figure.

IT WAS seven in the evening and I was shoveling down the first decent meal I'd had in over a day in the mess hall, sitting at a table all of my own, when the shit hit the fan. Or, more accurately, when Kepler hit me.

I was pushing meat-flavored paste into a pile with a plastic spork when she slammed my head forward. It bounced off the back of my hand and rebounded. Pain shot through my forehead and into my skull.

"You think that's funny, huh?" she snarled, planting her foot next to my knee on the bench.

I blinked the stars from my eyes and pushed my tray away. "Fuck," I grunted in pain, pressing my hand to my forehead.

She open-handed me on the side of the head. "Huh?" I was aware of two other bodies behind me. Cronies? Muscle? An audience?

"Not especially," I mumbled.

"You know they pulled me in? Meyers pulled me back in, got me up on misconduct toward a Federation droid and absence from duties without clearance." She slapped me again. "It took me forty minutes to convince him I wasn't trying to pull some shit, and get him to look at the security footage to prove it wasn't me." She went to slap me again, but I caught her wrist and held fast.

"You fucked with me, I fucked with you," I said flatly. It wasn't smart, sure, but it was the only language these kids would understand. I wasn't about to let myself get pushed around again, not when the Federation already had a chain around my neck.

There was fire in her eyes and her cheeks were flushed. She was angry — but more so, upset. "You almost cost me *everything,*" she hissed.

I felt guilty all of a sudden. I tried to swallow it. "Then stay the fuck out of my way."

She ripped her hand back and curled it into a fist. "You need to learn your place, tuber." She curled the other into a fist and stood straight, splaying her stance. "Get the fuck up, so I can knock your ass back down."

I spread my hands on the table. "You think that's a good idea? Want to be pulled in *three* times in one day? There's a lot of people in here."

She smirked and cracked her neck. "Don't worry, it's been taken care of. There's an understanding here. We take care of our own shit. Pilots don't need anyone else to sort it out. So long as it's... sanctioned. We're a family, all of us, and we don't like anyone messing that up. You get it?"

I looked up, towards the officers' tables, and found them distinctly empty. I swallowed, my guts heavy, heart thumping slowly, squeezing at the back of my eyes. The feeling was dread. "Look—"

"Get up."

She had pull. With the officers? She and Meyers were close — that much was apparent — or at least close enough to talk as freely as she had earlier. Everett had said that they were tight-knit up here. So what, Meyers had pulled her in, they'd gone over the footage. He'd seen that Kepler had ditched me, and that I'd tried to screw her over, and then... What, she'd told him she wanted to beat my ass, and he'd just said *okay?* I was finding it hard to buy, but maybe they just wanted me out. It sounded like everyone here had been through the wringer and I'd just dropped in from nowhere, skipped the years of training and studying. Were they just trying to make it so bad for me that I begged them to kick me out?

I pushed back from the table and stood. Growing up on a colony was no picnic, especially as a tuber. People didn't like them. In adulthood, it was more like being a social pariah. Terraformers were outcasts as it was, but no one else was wont to bother with us. We stuck out too — *Tube Defects*, they called them. Some had it much worse than me — skin discoloration, lack of hair growth, vocal malformation. I got off lightly. All I had to contend with was one side of my head being white, apparently where I'd leaned against the side of the tube. Growth in the early stages was stimulated with electricity, but it also affected pigment in the cells if a portion of the body was touching the contact point. Made it easy to pick me out. Made it easy for kids to pick me out. As an adult, it was being shunned. As a kid, it was being cornered, bullied, beaten on. It wasn't fancy Federation training, but it was learning not to get your ass kicked from a young age. I'd been schooled by a House droid built in with Federation Curriculum in the Education and Development Facility in Settlement One on Genesis before being sent to Ninety-Three. Though that was a fancy way of saying *orphanage*. Still, I was no stranger to having some purist want to take my lunch, or just throw me a beating for no real reason at all. We were all there together, all in the same boat. Most of the purist kids were orphans from other planets, brought to new colonies to get an education and a jump start on life. The only thing they got was a jump start on was serving the Federation. I got that. They were bitter. Full of anger. Hell, who wasn't? But they thought that gave them the right to beat on tubers. We were easy to pick out of a crowd, and I think that's all it was. And now, it was like being back there all over again. I was different. Different enough to unsettle them, to make them question their fragile little pedestals. And it'd painted a target on my back.

I sighed and stepped out of the bench into the gap between it and the next one over. I got a look at the two cronies. Guys, our age, reasonably big. Not too big to take one at a time — probably too big for both at once. But first, I had to contend with the pissed-off twenty-year-old-girl standing her ground, ready to throw a punch. I could tell there was no getting out of it, so I put my hands up and beckoned her toward me. "Come on, let's get this over with," I muttered.

Then she hit me, and I went down, and stayed there, and I hoped that it would be the end of our relationship. But it wasn't — not by a long shot.

# 8

Basic training was far from basic, and on top of that, it kind of sucked.

The first hurdle to clear was the written test, which I was told would come once every two weeks, and would cover everything from mechanical operation of the Federation mechs to the history of the Federation, the history of war, tactics and warfare, sciences and mathematics, and philosophy — which was actually just politics mostly. It was a stroke of luck that the first examination was on Federation history. Being a colony kid, we'd grown up having their history rammed down our throats. I didn't breeze through it by any means, but I passed, which was everyone's first problem.

The first day, when I'd had my wings clipped by Kepler, I'd sort of thought that she'd just shape up to be the bully, and everyone else would be much nicer. I was wrong. Word spread pretty fast that I was some colony-jumping tuber who'd somehow cheated his way into the Mech Corps. No one took lightly to me being there, and the result of that was a solid four months of hazing, where they'd do everything they could to bounce me out of there. Everything from jostling me to get me to drop my lunch to dumping buckets of water, and worse, over me while I was sleeping. And that was just the kid stuff —

during combat training, they definitely weren't exercising the 'reasonable constraint' that they were instructed to. I was sick of getting elbowed and kicked, but it wasn't enough to get me out of there. I didn't think anything would be. Whatever they did to me, I'd had worse. Their idea of 'hardcore' was far from it. They were rich kids, private schooled, born with silver spoons in their mouths. Growing up in a colony orphanage was a fight for your goddamn life.

The thing was that with every passing minute, the carrier we were on drifted farther and farther from the only place I'd ever called home, and closer and closer to a place where most of the ground troops would likely die. As such, I had no intention of finding myself in the melee, not when there were rumors swirling that the Federation was on the brink of war on a planet called Zelebos over resource appropriation, where the indigenous population was the Zelebosions, a race of humanoid jungle dwellers that outsized humans by three to one, and could rip one clean in two with a flick of the wrist. The idea of jumping into battle with them didn't sound very appealing.

I was trying to stay cool and collected. And from the outside looking in, I think I might have been pulling it off. In truth, I was hanging on by my fingernails. I'd dip out of quarters to the bathroom after lights out and spend a couple of hours studying on the toilet, locked in a cubicle in the most remote bathroom I could find. Or I'd wake up an hour or two early, snag some extra sim-time on the ground and in the F-Series. I was almost getting the hang of it, which was great, considering that we had an examination coming up. Full immersion simulation, with the time dilation turned right up. We'd be under for a few hours in real time, but inside, it'd feel like weeks. I didn't know how to feel about it. Everyone else had done it a few times in the academy — or so they kept saying. Telling me what a mind-fuck it was. How it'd break me. I tried to ignore them and keep my head down. And yet, as it loomed, I couldn't help but feel a little sick. I didn't know what to make of the whole thing. I got the bare bones of the concept, that it was about accelerating the way your mind processed information. Inside, everything was in ultra fast forward, but from the outside it was normal. Of course there were the horror stories — the psychotic breaks, the seizures, the hallucinations. But I figured if I'd come through the orphanage on Genesis and made it out without any lingering psychological issues, then this wouldn't be what broke me. I figured that it was just the academy kids, swaddled from birth and raised weak.

THE UPPER TRAINING Deck was warm, and the air smelled like stale sweat and heavy breathing.

The ground flashed under me, disappeared and then reappeared. I slammed into it and the wind jumped out of my lungs. A guy called Jonas was standing over me, tall and thick like a tree. He rolled his eyes, cracking his knuckles.

I stared into the ceiling high above and listened to my heart thundering against my chest. The rafters swam with dust and shimmered in the haze of the halogen lighting. The room was about five football fields across, and was used for everything from hand-to-hand combat training, which was what I was currently engaged in, to target practice, to maneuvers and tac training, to simulation. Three hours in the morning, two in the afternoon.

I'd been getting my ass kicked for four months. Kepler was the golden girl, and my stunt had bought me no favors. Apparently she came from a long line of Federation officers. All pilots. All top of their classes. She had a lot to live up to, and she was doing it. There wasn't an officer in the ranks that hadn't come up with her brothers or her father, or uncle, or someone. And there wasn't an airman in the ship who didn't know her family's name — except me, of course. And that seemed to give her some sort of authority. People listened to her, gravitated to her.

She was pegged to be the youngest female pilot in history, and held most of the training records already. That much was common knowledge. There wasn't a recruit in the ship who didn't want to cozy up to her, ride on her coat-tails. She had a chip on her shoulder about it. Something to prove. Apparently, me snagging the top sim-score, and without even meaning to at that, really pissed her off. I was hoping that letting her deck me would have been the end of it, but it wasn't. She made it her mission to get me out of the Corps, and she was using all her pull to do it. She was picking my sparring partners and choosing the biggest, meanest fuckers there. She was choosing my sim environments, my target practice routines, the scenarios for my tac training. All she had to do was offer to organize it and the instructors were happy enough to let someone else do the paperwork. She was making it as difficult as it could be in the hopes I'd fail — incidentally, she was just making my training a lot more thorough than anyone else's, which wasn't a bad thing. I was trying not to show it but I was busting ass to stay in the Corps.

"Get the fuck up," Jonas grunted. He wasn't human, but he wasn't far off. The Polgarians were a humanoid race with dark, ridged skin, ridges on their skulls and arms, and a far higher muscle and bone density than humans. As such, hitting him was like hitting an anvil, and getting hit was like running into traffic. They paired Polgarians with Polgarians for sparring, humans with humans, but today there was an odd number of both, and I drew the short straw.

I lolled my head sideways and cast a glance over to the sim-pods. Kepler was standing there, hips locked, arms folded, short hair hanging loose over her ear, smirking. She watched me, and her cronies sniggered. They always seemed to be a rotating bunch — hungry airmen all trying to suckle at the popularity teat. When she'd hit me, I'd gone down, and she'd blown off some steam, but she was holding a grudge. I think I made the right call, though. She was lighter than me, but she still hit like a fighter. I watched as she'd ground her heel in, twisted into her knee, and thrown from the hip, giving it everything she had. I could have stopped it and clocked her, and I'd stayed up nights, sponging the blood from my nose or cheek after a tangle at afternoon sparring, thinking about it. All it would have achieved, though, was getting me kicked out. The only reason I wasn't gone already was because I wasn't fucking up. I wasn't biting back and I wasn't picking fights. Boots filled with petroleum jelly, socks with the toes cut off, towels being stolen while I was in the shower. They thought it was treatment enough to get me to go, but they were private school kids who'd all grown up with a silver spoon in their mouths. They thought this was hard? They'd obviously never taken a look inside a Colony Education Facility. That was hard. That was getting a pillowcase put over your head while you sleep and having six kids punch you until your ribs cracked.

I dragged in a breath and rolled over, spitting blood onto the mat. I got to my feet and shook off the stars, curling my fists. It was taking a while to get to know how a Polgarian fought. Lots of up-close-and-personal stuff. Grapples. Throws. Shoulder barges. Elbows and knees armed with jutting spines. They hurt the most. Only got caught with them once. That was enough. I thought I had it figured out now, and it'd only taken two weeks of being tossed around by Jonas to do it.

Despite being bigger and stronger, Polgarians were a little slower, and weren't really much for blocking. Their hard exterior made landing painful blows more difficult, but they weren't impervious, and like all humanoid species, had soft spots. Things that dangled on humans dangled on Polgarians. Thumbs still hurt when they were bent back. They needed their eyes to see and their throats to breathe.

I cracked my neck and raised my hands, circling. Jonas grinned and raised his. "Want more, huh?"

I could taste copper. "If you've got it to give."

He lunged forward before I had chance to finish and I leapt back, stepping left and right. The last time I'd tried this, it hadn't gone so well. Now, I hoped I knew better.

He came at me with a grab and I fended it off, shunting his outstretched fingers with the flat of my hand. They bent back and he curled them in and sucked his hand to his chest, eye twitching. He lunged with his right instead now, in a wide swipe. I got inside it and threw my arm up, feeling it connect with my forearm. I ignored the pain and lashed out with a kick instead, low and hard into his inner thigh. The thickly knotted muscle absorbed the blow, but with no hardened and ridged skin, it struck home. He sagged backward to a knee, his leg moving outward, and I took the chance. I wound up my arm and lashed out with the bottom of my knuckles, connecting hard with his ear — the softest part of his head, left undefended by the arm clutched to his chest. He yowled and keeled backwards, protecting his face, shocked more than anything. I didn't let up. He never had, and that anger was bubbling up.

I threw my foot into the soft patch between his abs and chest and shunted him backward, leaping after him and throwing my other foot over his shoulder. He scrabbled for me, but it was too late, and I twisted hard toward the ground and pulled him over, locking one leg around his throat and the other over my foot to keep it there. His hands were beating on my legs like drums. I caught one by the fingers and found the thumb. It took both of my arms to wrestle one of his into submission, but I had him by the neck; the question was whether he'd pass out before I had to let him go from the blows. His fist beat on my thigh and knee and I gritted my teeth through the pain, squeezing as hard as I could on his throat until I felt it close.

He wheezed and flopped, but I wasn't going to let him go. If I did, he'd beat the hell out of me. No, I was too far gone now. I had to keep going, whether it was right or not.

My legs ached and my blood gushed in my ears, deafening me to the cries of the other recruits around the mat who were all chanting and yelling for Jonas to get up. Boos and screams of indignation rang through my head as I starved his brain of oxygen. They faded away with every hard beat of my heart as my muscles filled with lactic acid and throbbed.

I didn't know how long I was like that, but out of the darkness I felt hands on my chest and shoulders. My legs loosened and I was dragged off Jonas, who gasped and rolled onto his side.

Two airmen had hold of me, one on each arm. They looked grave.

"Jesus Christ!" the instructor, a human by the name of Shaw, yelled. "You're not trying to kill him, Maddox!" He let the pad he was holding slump at his side and put his hand on his head, which was speckled with thinning gray hair, shaking it.

Jonas gasped for air on the ground and the two guys dropped me. I hit the mat and rolled to my knees. Everyone around me was staring blankly, like they were pissed off at me. Figures. No one said shit when Jonas was laying into me — tossing me around, hitting me in the back of the head, ignoring tap-outs. I raised my head and locked eyes with the nearest guy, staring him out until he looked away. No one would say shit. No one really gave a shit. They were all too concerned about what anyone else thought to really have an opinion of their own. I was the bad guy, and that was it. The villain to hate. I shook my head and spat blood onto the ground. Fucking vultures, all of them, staring down their noses at me, the only tuber in the Mech Corps, waiting to see if I'd get hurt, or worse, so they could be there, just to *see* it.

Shaw made a turning motion with his hand. "Alright, that'll do. We'll break for today."

Everyone dispersed slowly, and a couple of his friends carried Jonas off. The crowd thinned until it was just Kepler, standing at the edge of the mat. She had her arms folded, jaw set and mouth carved in an scowl like she had some shit up her nose.

"You down for round two?" I asked, my voice hoarse from the fight.

She turned away and sidled off back toward her own group. They were still lining up for sim time. I watched her go, and when I was sure she wasn't going to look back, I fell to the ground and rubbed my thigh, wincing. Jonas had done a number on it. I didn't know if I could stand. But I had to, because no one was going to help me up.

I WAS LYING in my bunk, reading a tome called A Brief History of Mechanized Warfare: Third Edition, which was anything but brief, when the door opened.

I was sharing my room with seven other guys, mostly human. Sometimes the division was clear cut, other times there was a mixing of races — humans just not quite human anymore. Some with longer ears, others were taller, some had white eyes, some black. Some had noses that were wide and flat and others had scales. It was a real mixed bag, but that was the Federation way. *All people, one Federation* — and all that shit.

" —and then he got him in a choke hold with his legs, and nearly killed him! Jonas was—" A guy named Saxon, who everyone called Sax, stopped himself mid-sentence, clocking me in my bunk. He cleared his throat, pushed his glasses up his nose, and went quiet. The guy he was with peeled off and headed over to his bunk at the far end of the room. I restrained a smile. Word was travelling fast. That'd piss Jonas off, no doubt. He was one of Kepler's buddies. He always seemed to be buzzing around somewhere or other, but he wasn't much for conversation. I saw them together sometimes, but I kind of figured he was the big brutish type, and she was kind of high strung. She was smart — as a fucking whip. Him, not so much. I saw how he looked at her too, but that wasn't my business. It didn't seem like it was reciprocated. Still, he'd jumped at the chance when she'd put the word out she wanted someone to be my sparring partner.

I put the book on my chest. "Sax," I said quietly, swinging my legs off the side of the bed. It hurt to talk. My cheek was swollen, my nose bruised. Jonas had gotten some licks in. He liked to go for the face.

Sax looked up from his trunk, but said nothing. They didn't bother with me, really — concerned about how it'd make them look — but it'd been four months, so we were like familiar enemies, rather than strangers.

I took a breath. "How's the studying going?"

"Fine," he muttered, searching for something in the bottom of his case.

Small talk obviously wasn't going to work. "You had your number for the exam yet?"

He sighed, giving up on the search. "Fourth, you?"

"Ninth."

He smirked. "Lucky you."

"Why's that lucky?"

"That's Kepler's troop. They always kill it, every time. They win by a fucking mile. No one can even compete." He leaned back, staring at the wall with something like admiration in his eyes. "She's... she's just focused, you know? Like a laser. You can't teach that. She's gonna fly through Basic and'll be an officer before we make our first mission."

I bit my cheek. What was it with this girl? Everyone treated her like royalty. If anything, she was a total fucking bitch. I shrugged. "Oh well, we'll see."

"I'll trade with you if you want," he said suddenly, standing up and approaching. He was a little weedy and had thick-framed glasses. Once he graduated Basic, he'd qualify for cybernetic implants, but that was only when he graduated. *If* he graduated. I'd seen his sim scores, how he handled himself on the mat. He wasn't exactly combat ready.

I smirked. "I don't think it works like that, but I'll ask, alright? Better you than me." I said it, but I didn't know if I meant it. I didn't know what it was about her, but I felt like we had unfinished business, that someone needed to put her straight, and take her down a few pegs. And I felt like the only person who'd be prepared to do that was me. Maybe I'd get a chance in the sim. I pulled the book onto my chest and put my feet back up. Sax eyed me for a minute. I could tell he was dying to ask about Jonas, but he didn't. He had an image to protect. I didn't hold it against him. I just kept reading.

# 9

I dreamt I was suffocating.

I was lying in the desert, alone, looking up at the stars, and then I felt the ground start to sink beneath me. It softened and dropped and then poured over me as I fell beneath the surface. It ran into my mouth and nose, blinding me, choking me. It stuck in my throat like cement and crackled in my lungs. The weight built up on my chest and pulled at my arms, dragging me deeper. I tried to call out, to scream, to claw for the surface, but I couldn't. The stars disappeared and darkness folded in. My heart was loud in my ears and then it stuttered and seized. Hot and cold rushed through me in waves and my skin peeled away. My muscles tore themselves from my joints and my body folded into a tiny ball until my bones all crunched together under the crush of sand. Pain. Darkness. Fear. Pain. My chest. My heart. Pain.

And then I woke up, for the hundredth time, sitting bolt upright and gasping for air.

I turned, but no one had stirred, or they just didn't care. My bedsheets were soaked with sweat, as always. I sighed and rubbed my throat. It was stinging. I'd started sleeping with a water bottle next to my bed, but twice I'd woken up to take a drink, only to find it wasn't filled with water anymore. No one owned up to it, but it meant that I was back to heading off to the bathroom to quench my thirst.

I swung my legs off the bed and checked my watch, cracking my neck. It wasn't long before five in the morning. By the time I got back to bed I'd never find sleep before my alarm. Instead, I pulled on a pair of sweat shorts, laced up my running shoes, and headed out. I could grab a shower after a quick sim session and a run — maybe even get in some bag work.

I liked the Regent Falmouth best at this time in the morning. There was a lights-out policy at nine thirty, and though being in the halls after that wasn't allowed unless you were going to or from the bathroom, once it got to two in the morning or so, the monitoring stopped. It wasn't uncommon for recruits to get up to do some studying in the library or get in an early morning gym session — though that was usually around six or so. At twenty to five, it was a ghost town, which suited me just fine.

I was stretching out my shoulder when I walked onto the Upper Training Deck, unaware of the sound of footfalls echoing through the room. I yawned and stepped onto the training floor, a huge span of resin covered steel with various grids and lines painted on it, denoting formations, paths, and the running track, which looped around the outside. At the far end were the sim pods and an open gym. I shook out my left leg and got ready to take off when I stopped, catching sight of the person circling around and coming toward me at a run. I shook my head. I had to laugh. Who else was it going to be?

Kepler jogged to a halt and grimaced, breathing hard. She pushed the short brown hair off her sweat-slicked brow and narrowed her eyes at me. She pulled the buds from her ears and stopped her watch, throwing her hands to her hips. Her jaw was set like iron as she made to stride past, stopping when she drew level with me. "What're you doing here?"

"Came to get a quick run in," I said flatly. I wasn't in the mood for a verbal joust.

"Track's taken."

She and I were the only ones there. "Couldn't sleep either, huh?"

She rolled her eyes. "You think you get to the top of the class by just sleeping in?"

"That's not what I meant."

"Look," she said, pulling up her watch, "I've still got a long way to go, so if you wouldn't mind..."

"Pissing off?"

She shrugged and put her ears buds back in, setting off again. Exams were coming up. She was pushing harder. I had to admire it. For a second I considered running, seeing how I'd fare against her. She was fast, that was for sure. She was built like a runner; narrow, strong shoulders, muscular midsection, long, defined legs. I couldn't stop watching her as she circled around, but I had to. If she got back and I was still here, well — she already had it out for me; the last thing I wanted to do was piss her off any more. If she was only mildly pissed off with my presence as it was, I didn't want to anger her further. I was sort of hoping eventually she'd just get bored of trying, or maybe develop some sort of slow-burning guilt for trying to bully me out of the Corps, though I wouldn't have put money on either.

I turned away with Medical in mind. They had a Physiotherapy Gym there that'd be empty. I could probably get some time on the running machines or benches before the first appointment came in.

I got about five steps before the door at the end of the corridor opened and Jonas sidled in. My eyes closed and I couldn't help but sigh. Of all the luck. He was in running gear too. Obviously come to join Kepler on her morning routine, and I'd bumbled right into it. He was the last person I wanted to see — especially without anyone to stop him from ringing my neck and I didn't think Kepler would be much help.

I tried to ignore the voice in my head that said turn and break for the door on the other size of the Training Deck, and kept my head down instead. With any luck, his want to not speak to me would outweigh his want for revenge, or maybe he'd be so hellbent on falling in next to Kepler that he'd let me go. I figured neither was going to be the case, and that he'd probably run me down if I bolted. Whatever way you spun it, I was cornered, even with two hundred meters of space at my back. I held onto just the dimmest flicker of hope, but when I drew near, he stepped in front of me. It was all I could do not to barge into him.

He stared me out, his bottom lip quivering, nostrils flaring, then looked toward the crosscut of space he could see at the end of the corridor, and back, but said nothing.

"Do you mind?" I said quietly, gesturing so that I could pass.

He shoved me. I knew it was coming, but I made no attempt to block. Maybe he'd sock me a couple times but let me off easier if I didn't put up a fight. If I did, then I'd have staked my life on his he would have killed me. Hell, I was.

I hit the ground and slid on my ass. I watched as he advanced and got to my feet as quickly as I could, just in time to drop my elbow to block a right hook.

"You think you're funny, huh?" he grunted, winding up for another one.

I was taking up ground pretty quickly, edging backward as he came forward. "Look, Jonas, I don't want any—" I blocked another blow, realizing he was going to keep hitting me. His pride was bruised, and he wouldn't be satisfied without his pound of flesh, especially not with Kepler watching. He'd already been shamed in front of her once. I didn't know how far he'd go to *impress* her, but I wasn't looking forward to finding out.

"— trouble," I finished, dragging in a hard breath. "I'm not going to fight you," I grunted, swerving backward to avoid a jab.

"No? You were happy to get your cheap shots in yesterday." He was grinning.

"What was I supposed to do, let you give me a beating?"

His knuckles nicked my forearm and stung. I stomped the pain down. Now wasn't the time to lose focus.

He didn't answer, because there wasn't an answer. An answer meant that it made pragmatic sense, which this didn't. This was emotion. He'd come here to get in good with Kepler, maybe sell her a story that the sun was in his eyes, or that he'd had some bad shrimp the morning of the fight. Either way, he was here to make good with her, and running into me, in his mind, was a fast way to do that. If he kicked my ass right then and there, then she'd see how tough he was and fall in love with him, and they'd live happily ever after. I could see the process in his head. I could see the gears turning.

My feet hit the resin and squeaked. "Jonas — think about this. If you kick my ass, you're going to land yourself in some serious fucking trouble."

He laughed. "Oh yeah? You're a snitch now, too, as well as a cheater?"

"No, but if I turn up with a broken nose at breakfast, someone might start asking questions."

"You think anyone gives a shit about what happens to you?"

"You want to risk it?" I tried to sound confident, but it came out strained and hoarse. My heart was hammering in my ears and I could see my raised hands shaking.

"Humph." He stopped and rubbed his knuckles. "Better stick to body shots, then." He rushed me before I had a chance to react. That was his way. I needed to watch out for that. I still hadn't learned.

My feet left the ground and I felt the corner of his shoulder hard against my ribs and gut. He pushed down and twisted toward the ground. I landed on my back and all the wind shot out of me. I felt his thighs against my hips and by the time the stars cleared from my eyes, he was on top of me. I covered my head instinctively and set my jaw, wishing my arms shielded more of my face than they did.

The first blow got me in the chest, the second in the ribs. I tensed and my arms widened. The third found my nose and darkness lashed in my vision. My eyes streamed and pain deafened me. A blow came every second or two, the ears, the arms, the shoulder, the head. I tried to curl up, to hit him in the back with my knees, but it was no good, he was too big and my legs tapped pointlessly on him. It was over when he was done, and not before. I just wasn't sure if that was going to leave me dead or not. But that thought was punched out of my mind as quickly as it came in. I could taste blood suddenly. My vision was dark, my head screaming. Pain throbbed in every part of my body and the weight of his pressed down on me. Sickness twisted in my guts and I whimpered. Everything disappeared. My heart throbbed. I could feel it in my eyes, my ears, in my throat. The weight. The pain. The darkness. I couldn't breathe. I couldn't do anything.

There was noise in the distance, like I was underwater, and people were yelling above the surface. I could hear two voices. I could feel myself jostling, but I couldn't open my eyes.

I felt a breath creep into my throat, cold and wet, and then I coughed, violently, rolling over. The world swam into focus and I saw blood speckle the floor from my spluttering. My breathing felt wet and heavy. One of my eyes was already swelling shut.

I curled my legs into my chest and came to the realization that Jonas wasn't on top of me anymore. I didn't know how long for, though.

The voices still hung in the air. I strained to listen to them. One female, one male, arguing. I tried to look up, but I couldn't. I couldn't move. Footsteps rang out. I curled up tighter in case he was coming back.

I sensed someone over me and tucked my head against my chest, protecting myself as well as I could with my arm. I felt fingers on my elbow and wrist. I couldn't fight it. I didn't have it in me. My arm twisted out and I rolled onto my back, pressed there by rough hands. I tried to speak, but I couldn't find words. Everything hurt. My face was throbbing, my shoulders felt uneven, chest sore and tight. Cracked rib, maybe. Maybe ten of them.

"Jesus Christ," I heard the female voice whisper. My eyes opened for a second and I saw Kepler strobe above me between the blotches of darkness. I felt her fingers on my neck and watched her watch me for a second. Then she was at the base of my skull, pulling up my eyelids, moving my lips down and up.

She sighed and hung her head, sitting on her knees next to me, sweat dripping off her brow, her skin tanned and glistening in the halogens. She had a halo around her head, her whole visage painted in soft focus. My eyes swam.

"He really did a number on you," she said, her voice distorted above the ringing. "But it doesn't look like anything's broken —

though I can't speak for your cheek." Her finger touched my face and pain exploded in my head. I coughed again, retching on it. It felt broken. "He hasn't knocked any of your teeth out either. So at least you'll be able to eat." She turned down the corners of her mouth and sighed. "Maybe."

I tried to look around for him, but I couldn't move my head.

"He's gone, don't worry." She pushed herself to a stance and stepped away. "I pulled him off you." She chose her words carefully. "I'm not... I mean... I didn't want this to happen, alright?" It sounded like she was pissed off at me. "I wanted him to toss you around in training, rough you up. I wanted you to quit. But I didn't want this. I didn't want him to—" She cut herself off, her voice tight. She looked at me for a second, and out of the corner of my eye I saw her bite her lip. I watched her distantly, focusing on dragging breaths into my lungs. It was all I had the strength for. "Jonas can get a little carried away. He's hot headed." She cocked her head. "He's a Polgarian, though, so what can you expect? What's worse is that he's practically in love—" She cut herself off, maybe remembering who she was talking to, or wasn't. She resumed her haughty air and pulled her shoulders back. "You know, you really fucked up my training this morning." She reset her watch and hung her head. "I'll get him to lay off you, but stay out of his way. Stay out of both of ours."

Her footsteps died away and I was left there on the floor, bloodied and battered. When the door clanged shut behind her, I felt a tear run across my cheek. I curled back into a ball and sobbed for a while.

When the pain subsided enough for me to crawl to my feet, my face was on fire. I got to the bathroom and found someone else in the mirror. Someone with puffy cheeks and blood-red lips. I filled a basin with cold water and dunked my head in it, letting off as horrific a scream as I could muster. The bubbles popped against my ears and stung the open cuts on my skin. I fucking hated Basic, and I fucking hated the Federation. I'd been keeping it bottled up but now it was exploding out of me. Out of my mouth as the scream, out my eyes as tears, and out of the cuts on my skin as blood.

Every night I dreamt I was dying. And every day I was inching closer to the real thing.

I pulled my head up and watched the bloodied water run off my nose and drip into the pool, bursting under the surface in pink clouds.

Seven percent was starting to sound pretty good.

## 10

I was carefully sucking something close to oatmeal off a teaspoon when Saxon slid in next to me in the Mess. I stopped eating and looked up. Saxon never sat with me — in fact, no one did. I ate at a table at the far end of the room, on my own. Not that I really cared. I wasn't into the whole male-camaraderie thing like most of the recruits were. I'd always liked my own space. Found solace in it. Peace. Safety. They were all so tightly knit — having come up through the academies together. It was a hard shell to crack for an outsider.

Sax watched me intently through his thick glasses, hands still around his tray. I'd barely sat down when he came over, and my face was getting worse by the second. In another hour I doubted I'd be able to eat at all.

"What?" I muttered.

"Your face," he said, his mouth widening into an excited grin. "Everyone's talking about it."

"Everyone's talking about my face?"

"No, everyone's talking about you — Jonas. How you both agreed to meet up for a rematch before breakfast, and now it's one apiece." He was bubbling.

I ground my teeth together, pain lancing through my jaw. "Not exactly how I'd describe it."

Sax cocked his head.

"He jumped me. I didn't want to fight him. Kepler pulled him off me. He would have killed me." The words tasted sour on my tongue.

"That's not what he's saying." He looked over toward where I guessed Jonas was sitting, and then back.

"Well, he wouldn't." I tried to spoon more oatmeal into my mouth.

"So there's not going to be a decider?" Sax seemed disappointed.

"Only if he corners me again." I dropped the spoon. It was too painful. "I've got no intention of fighting him, because I've got nothing to prove." I sighed. "We're all probably going to die on our first mission anyway, Jonas included. There's a fair chance he'll catch a bullet the second he hits the ground. It's just how it is. Don't know why anyone wants to make their time before then any worse. I certainly don't." I rubbed my weary eyes gently. The early wake-up and getting my ass kicked were both catching up to me.

Sax opened his mouth, but closed it again without speaking. He nodded. "I get it." A strange smirk flickered on his lips for a second before he got up from the table. He clapped me on the back and a jolt of pain leapt through my ribs. "You know all that stuff... You know like the pranks — the hazing? You know that was just a joke, right?"

I turned and stared at him through my one good eye for a second. I wasn't sure if it was pity, or fear maybe — but something had changed. I nodded. "Sure, whatever helps you sleep at night," I growled, hoping he might take the hint and fuck off.

He smiled at me for a moment, forcing it up his cheeks while he stared at mine, bloodied and bruised, and then made his way back to his table. Some of the people he was sitting with turned to face me as he approached, then started whispering. When Sax sat with them, they huddled over the table like hens at a grain pile and cast looks at me. I stared at the cold oatmeal in front of me, listened to my lips throb, and felt sting of a headache creep into the base of my skull. I rubbed my forehead and got up. I wasn't anyone's sideshow, and I certainly wasn't getting into any sort of back and forth regarding this ongoing feud. I was trying to lay low, and so far, was doing a shitty job of it. I'd cut back on the smart-ass remarks, or maybe just realized they weren't as funny as I thought. I'd done my best to stop interrupting people, and I'd been trying to do well in my classes. I didn't know what else I could do other than leave. I stared into my gloopy oatmeal and thought about slamming my face into it and inhaling. The thought passed, thankfully.

I DUMPED my tray and headed for the door. I checked around quickly, but I couldn't see Jonas. I doubted he'd been pulled up for it, but I couldn't see him. Probably off somewhere regaling people with how we'd met up for round two and he'd given me a thrashing. At least one part of it was true.

I threw open one of the doors and stepped through it, grimacing at the thought. The scab on my lip split and began to weep and I swore, touching my finger to it. This was going to be a pain in the fucking ass. It'd never heal, especially with training not slowing down.

I made my way to the bathroom and ran the cold tap, reaching for a paper towel to sponge the blood off my chin. I had my head in the sink when the door opened. I stood up so quickly I almost fell over. The thought of Jonas walking in almost burst my heart in my chest.

I turned on my heel, hands rising instinctively, but it wasn't Jonas, and he wasn't coming at me. Kepler was standing against the door, leaning back, arms folded, one knee raised and foot planted on the steel. She had her tongue pressed against the inside of her cheek and she was scowling, as always. "You must have a fucking deathwish," she scoffed.

"What, you're going to take a swing at me now too?" I dropped my hands and fished the soggy towel out of the sink, hurling it into the bin.

She shook her head, pushing off and coming towards me. "Not me, dipshit. I want to see you bounced out of here, but not dead. Seems you don't share my sentiment though."

"I don't know what you're talking about," I muttered, breezing past her. The last thing I was in the mood for was a lecture. My head was starting to pound.

She put her hand on my chest to stop me, but it wasn't the dominating, rough gesture that I'd expected. Her fingers touched the front of my jumpsuit and I paused. She had her head side on, her eyes full, and without any of the bite they usually carried. "If you keep pushing him, he'll kill you. Polgarians aren't wired the same as us. They don't like to let things go. If I hadn't have been there this morning, then—"

"What the hell are you going on about?"

"Jonas." She furrowed her brow and I couldn't help but study the minute lines of her face, her smooth olive skin.

"What about him? That's fucking done. You won't see me trying to pick another fight with him. I never want to see the guy again." I sighed. I could feel my lip bleeding.

"Then..." She trailed off and shook her head. "Everyone's saying you're gunning for him."

"What?"

"I just heard it. Sax — is it Sax? The kid with glasses, came back over to his table, saying that you were going on about putting a bullet in his back the first chance you get. As soon as you land on your first deployment, that you're—"

I cut her off, swearing. "Shit." I rubbed my face with my hand harder than I meant to and tried to stifle the wince I knew I was doing a shitty job of hiding. "That's not what I meant — I mean — It's not what I *said*."

She arched an eyebrow and let her hand fall from my chest. "Well, it's what everyone's saying. These kids are all fresh out of the academy, it's the first time they've ever had any autonomy. They all grew up thinking they're better than the normal corps. They don't know what it's like out there — they've been fed propaganda to get them riled up. They're all dying to go out and kick some ass — spill some blood for the Federation. They're ramped up to see some now. They're just trying to stir some shit up for entertainment."

"And you're not?"

She looked offended. "Listen, Maddox, I didn't have to come in here, alright? I did it because I thought you'd gone and done something as stupid as publicly sworn revenge on a Polgarian on the very same day he nearly killed you."

"Oh what, you're concerned now, huh?" I gestured to my face. "Things getting a little too real for you?"

She screwed up her face and squared on to me. "I never wanted this. What Jonas did—"

"Was a direct result of your actions. You waltz around here like you're king of the fucking shit heap, fucking with people's lives. You don't think I'm worthy of being here? Tough fucking luck. I'm passing the exams. I'm scoring high enough to earn my place. You want me bounced out? You know as well as anyone, Miss-Top-of-the-Class, that landing in the regular corps is a fucking death sentence. You slit my throat right here, or you get me thrown down there with the rest of them, it's by your hand either way. So don't you give me that high and mighty routine."

She scowled, her pupils flitting back and forth across my battered face as she searched for a retort.

"Ask yourself," I said, dropping to a whisper. "How long did you wait, honestly, before you ran over and pulled Jonas off me? How long did you watch him pummeling me before you felt that little twinge of guilt in your guts?"

She pursed her lips, her eyes still searching my face for something. "Your lip is bleeding," she said after a second, quietly, with something between concern and loathing in her voice.

I wiped it off with the back of my hand and walked away. "I'm not fucking surprised."

# 11

By the morning of the sim, my face was practically healed. I'd gotten myself up to Medical after realizing I couldn't eat lunch, and was met with a little animosity. The doctor on duty sighed, no doubt sick of stitching up recruits that had 'gone a little hard in training,' which is the cursory remark he made to explain away my face. He didn't ask for specifics, and prodded me a little less gently than I would have liked. He gave me a face-sleeve that I had to wear for a couple of days, packed with little nanobots and stem-gel to expedite the healing process. I'd expected some painkillers, but the Federation medical advancements were obviously a lot further ahead when it came to the military, in comparison to what was available on the colonies.

I gave everyone a wide berth for the days I was recovering, taking my meals right at the end of the mess periods, spending my downtime in the library, and getting my training in in that golden period between the patrols stopping and breakfast. I'd spent the last few nights reading up on what to expect for the Sim-Exam. In a word, it wasn't pretty.

The full immersion simulation was a totally visceral experience.

Groups of recruits were all put in a shared simulation, but were hooked up to nerve stimulating electrodes, an IV drip, and were given a sedative. The process lasted over twelve hours, but inside, it'd feel like weeks. This was a full exercise, in full gear, except it was all in your head. No one knew what to expect — the missions changed every year, and there were rumblings that this year's would be a doozie. Rumors circulating through the recruits, all trying to hedge their bets by studying exam patterns through the years, eavesdropping near officers' tables and open doors when they could.

We shuffled onto the upper training deck in a throng of bodies. I hadn't risked speaking to anyone since Kepler cornered me in the bathroom, in case they tried to twist my words like Sax had. I hadn't seen Jonas since, either, but then again I'd been actively trying to avoid him. The ship was pretty huge, and even though the training section for the Mechanized Corps only occupied a part of it, it was still a mess of corridors and levels. If you wanted to stay out of someone's way, it was pretty easy. All you had to do was check a class schedule, and every corner you came to.

I could feel my heartrate rising as we all filed in. The floor had been filled with sim pods all lined up in neat rows. There were hundreds of them — enough for every recruit there, by the looks of it. The training deck, which was practically a hangar, was totally filled with them, and recruits were already beginning to file through the corridors.

Meyers, the officer I'd met on my first day, was standing on a set of steps, directing the traffic. "Find your number — that is your pod. Do it quickly, do it quietly. This is an examination," he called. "If you have not taken your issued medication, it's now too late, and you will be failed."

I stared at the piece of paper in my hand. There was a number and letter printed in it, 11E. I could see the pods all had their denotations printed on the side. They were arranged in lines, ahead of each other. Each row was a letter, each column a number.

"When you reach your pod," he continued, "climb inside and take your chair immediately. The examination starts in eighteen minutes. Anyone not in their pod at that time will be failed."

Everyone balked at that and picked up their pace. It wasn't even eight in the morning yet, and everyone was still shaking off the dregs of sleep. I made my way past Meyers to row E and then edged down towards Pod 11.

When I got there, most of the recruits were already climbing in. I looked up and down the line. I could see Kepler about three pods down, facing away. When I turned to face the back, Jonas was grinning maliciously at me from fifty feet away. I sighed and tried to seem indifferent, climbing inside.

The full immersion pods were different from the others. Instead of a headset, omnidirectional treadmill, and fake rifle, this time, it was a reclined seat. I slid onto it and listened to the plastic groan under me. On the headrest was a helmet on a runner that pulled down over the head and the arms of the chair had tubes that you put your hands into, with haptic gloves on the other end.

A screen lit up in front of me, displaying the message, 'Please remove your shoes. Bare skin contact necessary.' I cocked an eyebrow and pulled my boots off, tossing them into the corner. I planted my feet on the stirrups and felt the cold lick of steel on naked flash. My feet started to tingle. There was current running through the pads.

The message changed. 'Place your head back and await imaging.'

I obliged, shoving my hands into the tubes. The helmet descended until it covered my face, and then tightened over my head until the outside world disappeared. There was no sound or sight and my breathing sounded hollow in my ears. I swallowed hard and felt them pop in the pressurized helmet. Something cool touched my temples and warmth started running down my spine. The words 'Neural Link Active' appeared in front of me and a wave of nausea washed through my guts.

A sharp pain in my wrist made me cry out, but the sound died in the darkness. That was the IV going in. The same tingle ran through my fingers and I realized I couldn't pull them out of the gloves.

My heart was beating hard now, and a strange noise had kicked up, like running water. I tried to breathe, tried to calm myself, but it was no good. I was trapped in the darkness, totally at their whim. I blinked and my body lurched, like the floor fell from under me. I was spinning, all my blood moving into my face, my fingertips. I made a long, low gutteral noise just short of a retch, and then was pulled out of consciousness.

THE SNOW WAS FALLING SLOWLY through the birch forest.

The trees snaked into the air overhead, gnarled by the fallout and frozen in time. I blinked a few times, picking out the distant wispy branches against the tumultuous sky overhead, seething in shades of brown and gray like an upended ocean.

My first breath was soft, no more than a gentle gasp. The ashy snow hugged me from beneath, cold and damp against my jumpsuit. I wiggled my elbows and my hips to make sure I was all still there, and then sat up, feeling the cold, stagnant air in my lungs. The hairs on the back of my neck stood up and I shivered.

A fire crackled gently, paltry and small in a depression dug in the permafrost. Rushed hands had scraped back the blanket of snow and tossed a couple of dried sticks into the depression. Around it were logs, daypacks, blankets spread on the ground. Mounds of snow kept some of the wind out. Night was closing in, but beyond the camp, the outlines of cooling towers stuck out of the earth like tumors. There were eight bodies around the fire in all. Five were still, lying in Federation winter gear, gray pilot jumpsuits with a thick cloak and woolen collar, heavy boots and pocketed trousers packed with extra rations. They were like the dead, still and dusted with snow.

Somehow, I'd managed to roll half off my sleeping mat and out of my cloak. How, I couldn't say. I rubbed my neck and then pulled up my sleeve, searching for the needle mark, but it wasn't there. Shit, this was a simulation.

My brain stuttered as I looked around, felt the chill in the air, smelt the death hanging off the trees. It felt so real — much more than the training sims. In those, you never got a sense of air pressure or touch. The rifle always felt lighter than it should, the explosions less dangerous, no more than blasts of air coupled with bass notes generated inside the pod. This was different. This was in my head, my nerves. I shivered, but I wasn't sure whether it was the cold or not. I'd read up on Full Immersion Sim training. It was the most effective way to prepare recruits for battles. Pain was real. Danger was real. My mind was plugged into the machine, my hands and feet hooked up to electrical stimuli that teased at the nerves and skin. I ran my fingers over the woolen collar, felt at the fibers of the fur there, rubbed them between my fingers.

"It's real," came a familiar voice.

I turned back to the fire and my eyes fell on Kepler. She was leaning forward, elbows on knees. In one hand, she had an energy bar, in the other she had a stick that she was prodding the fire with. There was one figure opposite, wrapped up in their cloak, but I couldn't see their face.

"What?" I said, quietly, conscious that I'd wake the others.

"It's real, the collar, what you're feeling."

I furrowed my brow and pushed myself to a stance. "This is a simulation."

She smirked, green eyes glittering in the firelight. "Yeah, but that doesn't mean it's not real." She watched the flames intently.

"That's exactly what it means," I sighed, sitting myself down on a stump across from Kepler's log. "None of it's real."

She shrugged. "Depends what you regard as real. If real's what you see, and hear, and feel, then this is real. You feel the air, it's cold. If you stuck your hand in the fire, it'd burn you. You'd feel the pain like it was real." Her hand moved quickly and her pistol leapt from her thigh holster, aimed at me, center mass. "If I shot you now, in the gut, you'd feel the bullet go in, you'd feel the hot blood running over your hands as you tried desperately to stop it. You'd feel the creeping sense of dread and terror that life was slipping away, regardless of where you think you *really* are." The pistol raised. "If I shot you in the head, you'd die. The others would wake up and find you dead, with a bullet in your skull. And are you willing to bet your life you'd just *wake up* if I did? If so" —she dropped the pistol and spun it effortlessly, offering me the grip — "then shove this in your mouth and pull the trigger, and spare us all the pleasure of your company."

I stared at it, and then at her, unsure whether she was just having a bad day or if this was her *game face.* I said nothing. She chewed the energy bar slowly, and then holstered her gun.

"That's what I thought."

I cleared my throat and shifted on the log, warming my naked hands on the flames. The person across from me had a hat on — a woolen cap pulled low enough to cover their eyes. Their collar was done up and nearly touching it. I could see them shivering. "What's, uh," I started, aware my voice was thin and hoarse, "wrong with him?"

Kepler stopped chewing. "Simulation sickness."

I'd read up on it before the exam, and on how to combat it. The only way was through desensitization. Sim training hardened you to it. I'd been putting in my hours.

"She'll come around." Kepler sighed, crumpled the wrapper and tossed it into the fire. It crackled and spat flames into the air.

Sim sickness was the mind rejecting the simulation. It was the refusal to accept one reality over another. Those who couldn't compartmentalize the transition suffered like that — shakes, nausea, fever. It was basically withdrawal. It usually passed quickly, but it looked rough all the same. I stopped staring and went back to Kepler. "How long have you been awake?"

She checked her watch. "Two and a half hours."

I shook my head in disbelief. "Two and a half... But—"

She read my mind. "Time dilation. In full-immi it's cranked up to eleven. The twelve hours we're down will feel like weeks, months maybe." She shrugged and poked the fire. "If we last that long."

I opened my mouth to comment but decided it was best just left at that. She didn't seem like she was in a great mood. I studied her bottom lip for a moment. She kept licking it. She looked a little drawn. Her hand was shaking. I didn't say anything, but I would have put money on it that she was feeling a little bit of sim sickness herself, and just wouldn't admit it.

She snapped the stick between her fingers and threw it into the fire, standing up quickly. She grunted under her breath, and then kicked snow over one of the nearby sleeping recruits. "I wish they'd just get on with it already. You know, I was second up — she was first," she muttered, nodding to the shaking mass of cloak to my left. "Dunno how long for. She was sitting in the snow when I came to. I built the fire right away, but she was practically freezing, couldn't stand on her own. I was probably only a few seconds behind her going under. You can't have been more than a couple behind me. And now we're stuck waiting for these idiots." She kicked more snow.

"Do you know what our objective is?" I asked, trying not to worsen her mood.

She scoffed. "No. I don't know if we will know. I don't know anything about any of this. All I know is that nothing's going to happen while they're sleeping. When they wake up, then *maybe* something happens — we get orders, or there's some environmental shift or occurrence. Who knows?" She returned to the fire and tossed a couple more twigs on from a small pile in the snow. The flames died a little. "This is just a fucking loading screen. And we're going to have to sit here until they go under, eating into our rations and freezing our fucking butts off." She sank onto the log and buried her head in her hands, grumbling.

I suddenly had the urge to hug her, but I resisted it. Maybe it was the cold. That's what I told myself. I doubted she was the hugging type, anyway, and I didn't feel like getting punched so soon after my face had healed. I didn't know what it was — maybe just a glimmer of humanity from her. Either way, it was good to see. It was almost... *Nice.* She was her hard old self, but for a second there was something under the shell, something human in her. It resonated with me. I was scared. I had been since the second that dropship swept in over Genesis and tossed me. I was scared that everything was going to change, and end. There hadn't been a moment where I didn't feel like I was counting down to death. And with everyone around so sure, so casual about the whole thing, like we weren't hurtling through space toward some distant rock that was more than likely going to be the place we'd die, it was grinding me down. Seeing this wobble in her, the most sure of all, was reassuring, and just for a second, I didn't feel scared. I didn't feel alone. I clenched my fists and willed myself to stay where I was and stop staring at her, but I couldn't.

"Where are we?" I asked after a couple of seconds.

She looked up, and then at the trees, and then the stacks, and then back. She shrugged. "Don't know. Could be somewhere real, could be built for this. Not like anywhere I've ever been."

"Have you travelled a lot?" I was curious — I didn't know a damn thing about her.

She sighed and I felt a harsh remark coming, but she didn't give it. She glanced at the shivering recruit across the fire, and then her eyes settled on me. Maybe she just wanted to kill time, maybe it was to take her mind off the cold. Either way, she gave in. "Yeah, I guess. I grew up on the Falmouth. It's the only place I've ever called home. It's always moving somewhere — to pick troops up, or drop them off. It docks with this station or that one, goes into orbit around planets, meets with other ships — so yeah, I've been around."

"Have you seen many planets? Been on them?" I couldn't keep the excitement out of my voice. I'd only ever been on Genesis and it was a ball of dust.

"A couple. When we could. Most of the places the Falmouth goes are warzones — go figure. Not exactly the perfect places to hop in a dropship and cruise on down to the surface." She looked wistful in the firelight. "But there were times — some good times."

*"We?"*

"Me, my dad — my brothers." She smirked for a second. I didn't want to ask why she hadn't mentioned her mother.

"I don't have any family," I said quickly, without meaning to.

She stopped poking the embers with a stick and stared at me. "None?"

I gestured to the white section on my head. "Tuber." I shrugged.

"Guess you can't miss what you never had, right?" I tried to laugh it off, but she was too decent to join in. It died in the evening air.

"I've got three of them — brothers, I mean." She shook her head. "All older."

"All enlisted?"

She nodded. "Yeah. One's a pilot, one's an engineer, and the other..." She trailed off and stared into the distance.

I didn't have to ask. Those statistics they gave us weren't made up, that was for sure. I let her go on when she was ready.

"My father — he's still around. A lieutenant colonel now. Last I heard he was on rotation on a destroyer in the Leeam System. *Peacekeeping*. That's what they call it." She tsked. "It's just a show of bravado though." She snapped the stick and tossed it on the flames. It was the last one. "It's basically just flaunting their firepower — the Federation — showing the donkey the stick. And it's a big stick. No one needs to get hit by it to know it hurts." She shrugged. "Peacekeeping."

"Big shoes to fill."

She stared at me, wringing her hands. "Something like that."

The last of the twigs crackled. The temperature was falling with the sun. "I'll get more firewood," I said, standing up.

She rose to her feet too. "Don't worry, I'll go."

"It's fine, I don't mind."

"Seriously, I'll do it." She clenched her fist to stop her hand shaking.

I took a breath and looked up at the darkening sky. "Let me." She looked gaunt, pale. "You said yourself it could be a while. Get some rest."

"I'm fine," she said flatly.

"I'm not saying you're not. But this is an exam, right? A test? You want to be at your best — we *need* you at your best. So take a minute, grab some sleep, get yourself straight." I pointed at her hand. "And get that under control."

She pulled her fist behind her back but didn't say anything.

I nodded to her and turned away, heading toward the woods. I heard her sigh and then take her place on the log. "Maddox?" she called.

I paused. "Kepler?"

She pointed over the group of sleeping recruits to a pile of rucksacks. "There's a hatchet in each of our packs." She smiled, her hand dropping to her lap. "And call me Alice."

# 12

I tracked back through the snow with an armful of firewood to find that the exercise had been pointless.

Everything had been soaked by the snow, so it'd taken well over an hour to gather anything remotely dry, and now it didn't matter either way. I dropped what I was carrying, cursed myself for wasting the time and energy, and stretched my back.

Alice was standing among the recruits, all of whom were awake. She'd snuffed out what was left of the fire and buried it under the snow. Everyone was gearing up, pulling their rucksacks on, checking their weapons. Alice was ready to move out. She looked up as I approached. "Maddox, good of you to finally show up." She smiled wickedly at me.

We were back to this, then. I nodded to her and watched as her expression softened a touch. She returned it, barely. It was hidden. Hidden from anyone else in case they saw she had a modicum of leniency in her. This was her show, and whether she was wearing epaulets or not, there was no doubt who was in charge here.

I shouldered my rucksack and tightened it. "Where are we going?" I asked.

She turned and pointed through the trees, toward the stacks. Now that the day had faded from the sky, a dim glow was visible in the distance, thrown from some unseen source.

"That's all we have to go on?"

"What more do you want? A big fucking sign?" Some of the other recruits chortled at the remark.

I preferred her when she was on her own. A lot less bravado. A lot less attitude.

Jonas sidled out from the shadow of one of the trees. "You could always just stay here where it's safe, you know, if you're scared." He smirked at me and the chorus laughed again.

For a second, a deathly silence reigned, and then the bullets started flying.

THE FIRST ONE ripped right through the middle of us, slicing the air just over my right shoulder, and parting two of the recruits next to the campfire.

The second impacted a birch about ten feet to my right. The trunk exploded in a shower of splinters and wooden chunks. The sound of the shots rippled through the forest and everyone dived to the ground for cover. The snow stung my fingers and slid down my collar as I crawled sideways, the bullets still flying. I watched another hit a tree and blow a hole in it the size of an orange. Slow firing rate. Very high caliber rounds. Not anti-personnel. No, anti-vehicle. I listened, straining my ears over the shouts from the recruits and my own heart. I could hear thudding, distantly. What the hell was engaging us? I racked my brains. I'd taken in so much information in the last few months and it was spinning around my head, clothes in a dryer, tumbling without any sense. I forced myself to focus and dragged myself next to the other recruits, who were all lying face down in a huddle. These were long distance rounds, coming from deeper in the forest. What could be in there? It wouldn't be handheld — that was for sure. The thing would have to be huge to carry something of that caliber. A shiver ran down my spine at the thought. No, the terrain was too rough, the snow too deep — nothing would be out alone, either. If there was a force roving the forest, there'd be lots of gunfire. And any militarized unit worth their salt would get closer anyway — creep up to maximize the chances of a successful encounter. Long range engagement was more likely to be something automated — scanning. We'd tripped its sensors maybe — the noise, or heat signatures, and it'd let loose. Tank? No — the trees were too dense. Drone? No, the angle was too flat, it wasn't flying. It was slow moving, heavy. The thudding. What did it mean? Something bi-pedal? A spider walker maybe? Yeah, could be. I listened harder, ignoring the yells of the recruits asking what the hell we were going to do. Thud-thud, thud-thud. Four legs. Must be a spider walker equipped with an anti-vehicle cannon, maybe an .82, or something bigger. Another trunk exploded and the tree collapsed on itself falling with a crack. A plume of snow rose into the air and swirled around the bullets as they punched through the cloud.

Alice was lying a few feet away, facing me. Everyone was yelling. I caught her eye and saw something there I didn't expect to — fear. We looked at each other for a second, and I knew that no one was going to do anything. Everyone was waiting for an order that wasn't coming. If I yelled, nothing would happen — no one would listen. Not to me. It had to be her. They'd listen to her.

I reached out and took a fistful of frozen ground, dragging myself forward until I was face to face with her. I gripped her wrists and held them, felt them shaking in my hands. "Alice, listen to me," I yelled above the din. The thudding was louder, the bullets closer.Her bottom lip was shaking, face dusted with snow.

"It's a walker — a spider. One cannon. Anti-vehicle, large caliber. It's not that close — if it was, it'd have hit true with one of the first rounds. We need to get out of here. We have to move. If it gets here and we're lying down, it's going to obliterate us, one by one."

"What do we do?" she croaked, unable to find that verve she usually carried.

I clenched my jaw. There was only one thing to do. "Run. On your order, we get up and we run. Everyone splits up, breaks formation.

We RV at the foot of the stacks." I swallowed, hard. "It's all we can do. Run. And hope."

She bit her tongue and stared at me, looking for another option in my face. She didn't find one. After a second she nodded, a little at first, and then more. "Okay. Yeah."

I smiled and let go of her wrist, going for her hand. Her fingers closed around mine and gripped hard. "You can do this, alright? We're getting out of here."

She returned the smile and nodded, more decisively this time before drawing a breath and turning her head. "Okay, on my mark, we get up, and we run for it!"

"Run for it? You're crazy. We'll be torn apart!" someone yelled, their face buried in the snow.

"Then stay here. Die. Everyone else — on my go. We head for the stacks, RV there, okay?" Her voice was thickening, hardening as she found her rhythm. She looked at me again, a flicker of a smile of thanks playing on her lips, and then she yelled. "Now!"

We all scrambled to our feet in one tangle of bodies and split in different directions, peeling away from the makeshift camp. Alice ground her heels in and headed sideways. I followed automatically, with three or four others in tow. I could hear Jonas' heavy panting and swearing behind me, along with the others. Alice was leading, picking her path, and we stuck right on her ass. She'd been training — that was for sure. She was fast as hell. I could barely keep up. That advantage I'd had when I'd first come on board was gone. If she kept up like this, I was going to be left behind. I gritted my teeth and sucked in hard, ashy breaths, pumping my legs through the snow as hard as I could.

Alice peeled right toward the stacks, visible through the trees. I skidded in the snow and followed her, slingshotting around a tree. I heard someone grunt behind me and then tumble into the snow, but I didn't look back. A second later, I was jerked backward. I lost my balance and tucked my shoulder, throwing myself into a roll. Jonas streaked past, hand still outstretched, face stricken with fear. He'd shoved whoever was behind me and grabbed for my pack. Good thing he hadn't gotten a decent grip.

I pushed myself up and kept moving, the bullets still flying. Two more people overtook me before I picked up pace, following the gray packs in front. I could see Jonas up ahead, elbows high, charging forward like a bull. I tried to make up the ground but couldn't. I'd lost my momentum and my bag felt heavy. I considered dropping it, but it had everything in it — food, clothing, weapons, combat gear, a sleeping bag and tarp. Without it I'd be frozen before dawn. I pulled myself along on the trees until I found my footing and then got the hammer down, my feet churning, boots soaked.

I watched in the dying light as Jonas made up ground on Alice. She was running hard, and the bullets were flying faster. The spider was gaining ground on us, no doubt pissed we'd made a break for it. Its fire had picked up, concentrated on us. I couldn't tell if another had joined the chorus. Splinters rained all around. The deep chugging of an engine pierced the night. The throb and hum of hydraulics. The boom of its steel shod feet puncturing the ground with each fall, gears churching as it trudged through the forest. Where the fuck were we and what the fuck was going on? I could feel my heart beating out of my chest, my vision strobing in black and color, my muscles aching, lungs burning.

I watched Jonas pull level with Alice and then in a moment of stillness, throw an elbow into her. He could have argued it was accidental, or that she jostled him, or that she stumbled, but I saw. I saw his head turn — I saw him cast a glance down at her feet, at the narrowness of the path they were threading through the trees, and then I saw him lean, pull his hand across his body, and throw his elbow into her ribs. She took it hard, crooked sideways, let her bag twist over her hip, lost her balance, and then clattered into a birch. Jonas had at least forty kilos on her and they were carrying the same kit. Hers must have been near half her bodyweight. The fact she was carrying it at all was impressive, that she was motoring like she was was astounding. But, strong as she was, it was physics. The bag was heavy and the momentum was too much for her.

The sound of her hitting the tree was dull and deep, like the kick of a drum. The bag rose over her shoulder and her feet shot out behind her, throwing powder into the still air. She somersaulted and landed face down in the snow.

The bullets kept flying and three bodies streaked past. Jonas was in the lead and the two he had in tow kept running. None of them made an attempt to stop. I could hear Alice grunting, swearing in the snow, trying to get out from under her bag. I didn't think before I slung my bag off my shoulder and dived into it next to her. She'd plunged in up to the shoulders and driven the snow into a mound around her head.

I sank my fingers into the fabric of her rucksack and pulled, hard. I slipped and slumped backwards, breath ragged in my throat. The tree next to us caught a bullet and groaned under the strain, waving. A engine howled, too close. The tree showered us with ice. Alice swore. I took one of the straps and yanked. She yelped in pain, but there was no time for gentle. *Come on, get the fuck out of the snow!* My hand found the shoulder strap and I gave it everything I had. She slid free and keeled backward onto me. The wind leapt out of my lungs and she kicked her legs to get free of the white coffin. I pushed her off, throwing her bag over her hip. She twisted to her knees in front of me, on the path that the others had tread. Her eyes met mine and I saw the fear there again, her eyelashes and hair caked in snow. Her hat was gone, lost in the powder. There was a moment of stillness as she stared at me. The cry of the hydraulics and the thump of the feet were right on us. The ground shook with each fall. I dared not look over my shoulder. Her face said it all. Her eyes moved from my face and went sideways and up. Twenty feet, maybe thirty, staring up the barrel of the cannon that had chased us to death. I felt something colder than snow run down my spine. My breathing stopped in my chest, my diaphragm refusing to move.

I felt my jaw flex, looked at the bag on her back, at her feet, that they weren't under her. She couldn't make it — she wouldn't. If she stood, it'd put a round right over my head and into her, dead center mass, and blow her apart. Her eyes were wide, mouth open. She was frozen, and I wasn't thinking.

I followed her gaze, judged the angle, and felt my fingers curl in the earth. The cold stung them, the frozen ground like broken glass on my palms, but it didn't matter. My boots scraped in the snow and I leapt upward, between her and the barrel, mouthing the only word I could — *run.*

I took a step and a half, and then felt my chest explode in a shower of blood. She twisted on her heel and moved. The tree she'd run into was cut in half and it tumbled between us, blocking the path.

She took up ground, and I blinked, keeling sideways. With each flash of consciousness, she faded into the distance. My breath had stopped. My heart had stopped. There was nothing but cold, and then darkness.

I hit the snow, and it swallowed me up.

THE HELMET SLID up off my face and I opened my eyes, my chest throbbing, heart hammering slowly against my ribs. I lay in the dark, listening to it. Thud. Thud. Thud. I wondered if it would stop, but it didn't.

My mouth was dry and I felt a cool trickle of sweat run down my cheek. When I wiped it off, I realized it wasn't sweat.

The needle slid out of my arm and I pulled them out of the sleeves, wiping the tear from my eye. Dying sucked.

I sat up and looked around the pod. The door was sealed shut and a button was glowing dimly next to it. I shuffled over to it, my legs aching, and jabbed it with my thumb. Light bled in around the edges and it opened up, gull-wing style to reveal the Upper Training Deck of the Regent Falmouth.

I sighed and stepped down, staggering on the steel steps.

"Maddox," someone called.

I turned to face them. It was Meyers, the officer who had been directing recruits earlier, the same one that had sent me with Kepler... *Alice...* on the first day. I wondered suddenly if she'd gotten away, if she was alright, there in the snow, in the dark. I turned and stared back at the line of pods, all still closed and sealed. She wasn't dead yet. I swallowed and tried to keep another tear back. My mind was reeling, my chest still throbbing.

Meyers approached, smirking, a pad in his hand. He pulled it up and tapped on the screen. "Fourteen seconds. I think you just set a new record for quickest death ever." He tapped some more. "Says here you didn't even make it to your mech. Kicked it in the staging area." He dropped the pad to his side and shook his head. "Well, I can't say I'm surprised."

"Did I fail?" I asked quietly, still not kicking myself that I'd stopped.

He took a slow breath. "They'll review the footage — we'll talk to the others when they're out, make our assessment based on your conduct. But, well..." He smirked again. I wanted to slap it off his face. "Fourteen seconds."

I nodded and held my tongue.

I could hear him laughing as he walked away.

I didn't know which pod belonged to Alice, and I didn't know that it mattered anyway. She was in there, somewhere, in one of them, in the forest, or inside a mech, taking fire, giving it. I let my eyes rest on them for a while, just in case her door popped. I couldn't tell if I wanted it to happen or not.

I decided I didn't, but I still didn't regret helping her.

# 13

I got off the training deck and realized that every single recruit was still in the exam. I was kicking myself that I'd managed to get myself killed so quickly. I wondered whether that thing was even trying to hit us, or if I had somehow managed to throw myself into the line of fire, protecting her from a shot that wasn't even going to land. No, Jonas had thrown her off. It was going to take her apart. There was no doubt about that.

I sighed and stepped onto the plain white platform that I'd gotten off at four months earlier. I didn't know that I'd ever see it again.

I hit the call button on one of the pillars and the train came unnervingly quickly. It wasn't against any rules for recruits of the Mech Corps to head down to the lower decks; it just wasn't the done thing. No one from above ventured down, and no one from below ventured up. Not that it really mattered anymore. Fourteen seconds didn't seeming promising.

The train arrived and I stepped on, heading down.

My mind drifted on the way, and when it pulled up, I stepped off in a daze, unsure that I'd ever get on again.

I pressed through the corridors, and already the light seemed dimmer, the hallways a little less bright and shiny. I followed the sounds of voices and rowdiness with nowhere to be for another eleven hours.

The corridors led me toward a mess hall not dissimilar from the one up top, except this one was a lot bigger, and a lot busier. The one upstairs housed a couple hundred at most, but this one was almost the size of our training deck. The Mech Corps occupied the highest decks of the rear and middle portion of the ship. The Regular Corps occupied the bottom sections of the front section, more than five times as much as the Mechanized Corps. The rear was all hangars housing dropships, equipment, and everything else. Behind that were the engines. The front upper decks were all private quarters — the families of the officers, and the civilians. It was up there, somewhere, that Kepler had grown up, with her brothers, her father. The academy was up there too, somewhere, though getting up there was an impossibility. The ship itself was a goliath. Running circuits around the lower decks took hours. They were built in space and never ventured into gravitational fields. They were just too large — floating space stations. They had a way of making you feel tiny.

I stood in the throng of the mess and people moved like a sea. Recruits, privates, officers. It was a melee — no one separated, none of the decorum on show above. Most of the people here were all like me — colony kids, tubers, drifters — everyone who would be scooped up off the surface of every dustball passed.

I looked around and saw people rough-housing — pushing and jostling, laughing, joking, shoveling down food. These were *my* people. The people I'd left behind. The people I'd soon be joining. I was framed in the doorway, in my Federation gray, and no one even looked twice at me. I felt my jaw twitch. This was where I belonged, and before the day was out, this was where I'd be again.

"Trading up?" came the only familiar voice in the room.

I turned to see Everett approaching, tall and tough, her hair pinned back tight as always. She was smiling, but there was sadness in her eyes, but not for her — it was an acquiescence. A look of abject welcome.

I smiled back, mirroring it. "Guess so."

She pressed her lips into a line and held her hand out. "It's alright, soldier. If it's worth anything," she sighed, dropping to a whisper, "it's more fun down here, anyway." She broke into a smile and I took her grasp, shaking.

"Humph, looks like." I shook my head. "I'm just a little annoyed I never got to pilot a rig of my own."

She spread her hands. "Aren't we all? And yet we go on. I've managed to survive. You will, too."

I thought about that seven percent. "Yeah, maybe."

"Come on, sit down. Get something to eat, you look a little peaky." Her smile was warm.

I nodded slowly and followed her. I felt meek all of a sudden, like a child following his mother. Guess four months of getting shunned and bullied would do that to you. A warm smile felt like a hug. I think I would have burst into tears if she'd actually hugged me.

She stopped near a table and turned. I looked down to find her hand on my chest, fingers long, hands weathered. "Hey, I know it hurts now, but it's okay. It's not so bad down here." Her smile wavered and her hand balled slowly into a fist. She knocked it gently against my sternum once, caringly, almost. "You'll get used to it."

I looked down, unable to meet her eye. "That's what I'm afraid of."

I HEADED back upstairs just before six. I figured I could pack and get out of my dorm by the time everyone finished the exam, and then slip down to the lower decks. Everett had introduced me to the admissions officer, a guy by the name of Hamer. He promised to put me up somewhere decent when I did get *hooked* as they called it, in what was known as a two-man, as a favor to her. A dorm with two beds in it. A little more comfortable than the larger rooms. She seemed popular — not as stuck-up as the officers on the upper deck. They were a little more grounded, it seemed. Living by that seven percent, it was hard to hold yourself above anyone else. Ninety-three out of every one hundred in this room would die on the next world they landed on. It was hard to look down on people when that was the reality. I'd thanked him for it, and her, and promised to keep my head down. They'd both wished me well, and told me they'd see me soon, and as I made the journey back upstairs, suddenly I didn't feel so shitty about it.

I was stuffing the last of my socks into my bag when there was a knock at the door. I looked up and froze, staring dead at the last person I expected to see.

"Alice," I said breathlessly, standing straight, a sock draped over my fingers.

She stiffened at her name. Everyone called her Kepler. I realized then that I'd heard her ask me to call her that less than twelve hours ago, but she'd asked me to weeks ago — maybe months. "Maddox," she mumbled, lingering at the door frame, half in, half out, her hand on it, fingers tight, knuckles white. She looked torn up.

"You're out early."

"We, uh — finished the mission — ahead of time." She was trying not to sound proud, but she had no reason not to.

I forced a smile. "You pass?" My voice sounded strained in my ears.

She nodded. "You?" She asked it, knowing the answer.

I didn't respond to the question. "What's up?" I held the sock in my hand, curling it in my fist before I shoved it into the bag.

"I..." She trailed off. "I just wanted to call in, and..." She didn't seem to have the words. But it didn't matter. I'd never see her again. None of it mattered.

"It's fine." I sighed. "I'm glad you passed. You'll—" I paused, staring at her. She looked uncertain, tired, drawn. The sim had been hard on her. I couldn't imagine how she felt after twelve hours under. It'd felt like I'd been up for a week straight when I came out after a few seconds. "You'll make a great pilot."

A smile flickered across her face. I looked away and kept packing.

She started again, but didn't come into the room. "That night, in the forest, it was... You stopped."

"What?" I pulled the drawstring on my bag tight.

"You stopped. Everyone else kept running. But you stopped. I tripped, and—"

"You didn't trip."

She furrowed her brow.

"Jonas shoved you. I saw it," I growled.

She stared at me, desperately willing herself to laugh it off. "Jonas was— "

"Hightailing it, like we all were. He shoved someone else, too, before that. Threw me aside, and then shoved you into that tree." I didn't give two shits anymore. He could fuck himself for all I cared, and there was no way I was going to let her go out there — for real — without knowing exactly the sort of person he was. "He was shit scared, and he put you down to save himself." I sighed. I thought I'd have a well of anger to draw from, telling her, but I didn't. I just felt tired of it all. I was looking forward to heading down, maybe to my death, maybe to a new life. Who could say?

She opened her mouth to speak, but nothing came out.

"I just thought you should know," I muttered.

She stared at the ground for a few seconds, and I took that as my cue to leave. I put my bag on my shoulder and headed for the door. When I reached it, she hadn't moved an inch. I stopped to see if she would, but she didn't, she just looked up at me, eyes shining. Humbleness didn't come easy to her, but it did suit her. She looked beautiful, framed there. Genuine. Real. Honest. I felt a pang in my chest that I'd never get to see it again.

"I'm going to go before anyone else shows up," I almost whispered. "I don't really think there's any need to hang around." I forced another smile, and even managed an abject laugh. "Guess you got your wish after all, huh?"

She turned to look at me, still not moving. "No, I didn't. You... you saved my life in there. If you hadn't, it'd be me that would have failed. I'd be the one packing my bags."

I shrugged. "Well, it wasn't, you didn't, and you're not. Honestly, Al —" I corrected myself. "*Kepler,* don't worry about it. I never belonged here anyway."

She swallowed and bit her lip. Whether she was looking for more words I couldn't say, but I wasn't going to stand around drowning in silence.

I got a couple of steps down the corridor before she called out. "Maddox, wait—"

I turned to face her and she stepped into the corridor, pale in the halogens. "What is it?"

"Thanks."

I nodded. "Don't mention it." I spread my hands. "My own fault, really, right? Nice guys finish last and all that."

"I was wrong about you," she said quietly. "I treated you like shit, and I... I was a real jerk about it. Got you bullied. Got you beaten up. Got you *killed.*" She shook her head and pushed her tongue against the inside of her cheek. "You know, down there, in the sim, there were times, you know, when things were crazy, where we needed to rely on each other, and every time, the guys I was with — soldiers — my troop — they weren't there. They weren't reliable. They wouldn't have done what you did. You threw yourself in front of that thing for me without even thinking."

"That's sort of my specialty."

She smirked. "It was stupid, you know that, don't you?"

"Oh yeah. I do." I sighed, thinking about what I'd resigned myself to, and for what.

"So why'd you do it?" She stepped closer to me now, lips a little parted. I could hear her breathing, shallow. She looked tired. She could barely stand up. It'd been a long day for me, and a long few months for her. I couldn't believe she was even here, and not laid up in bed recovering. The mental strain alone must be horrific, let alone the physical toll.

I didn't know that shrugging would really cut it. I drew a slow breath and thought about it. "I don't really think I have an answer for you. I know how hard you work for it. I know how much it means to you. When Jonas put you into that tree..."

She stiffened and looked at the ground for a second.

"I saw you go down, saw everyone run past, and knew that if I didn't do something you'd die, and that'd be it. You'd fail and it'd all be because of some prick like Jonas? Not a chance."

"And why did that matter?" she pressed.

"Because, Kepler, as much of an asshole as you've been to me over the last four months, I don't like to see other people suffer — that, and I know it's all an act." I grinned a little and watched her blush, trying to look harsh and failing.

"What the hell's that supposed to mean?"

"You've got a chip on your shoulder the size of a damn asteroid. You grew up on this thing," I said, gesturing to the ship. "Brothers, father — officers, pilots. You live and breathe this thing. But you don't skate through on their coat-tails, you're out to prove something. It's just a shame that all you've ever been asked to prove is that you're as good as them. I think there's a lot more to you, Kepler. You just need to give it a chance to show through." I put my hand on her shoulder and squeezed. "You're going to go far, and I think you did more to earn the chance to than I've ever done. I'm a tuber, from some dust-ball in the middle of an unsettled system, born to terraform a planet that I'd never even get to breathe the air on. You — you're different, look at you. Made to be better." I let go of her shoulder and gave her a casual salute. "Forget about it, huh? Move on with your life, do something good with it. I'm going where I'm supposed to — where I belong." I turned on my heel and made for the door at the end of the corridor. "I'll catch you around, Kepler," I called, knowing I wouldn't.

"Maddox," she yelled hoarsely, her voice strained. I didn't try to read into what was making it that way. "Wait — don't go. I can... Uh, I can talk to them."

I turned, a few feet short of the door, to face her. "Who, Kepler? And what would you say? I had the news a couple of hours back. I was the only recruit out of three hundred and twelve who died during staging — you know that? I'm not fit to be a pilot."

"You are. You could be a pilot. You *should* be a pilot. You should have been there with us, the whole time. It's my fault you weren't. If I hadn't have—"

"Don't do it to yourself." I stared at her, looking at the genuine look of guilt painted across her features. “Kepler, I’m going to say this once, alright, and then I want you to go and celebrate with the others.” I let myself smile at her, framed in the white corridor. “It’s okay. I’ll be okay. Don’t hold on to this, alright? It happened the way it was supposed to.”

Her shoulders rose and fell and her fists clenched. She knew where I was going, and what was more than likely going to happen, and it was some solace that she gave a shit, that after four months someone gave a shit — but more, that it was worth it. That throwing myself in front of that shot wasn’t just a worthless act.

I left her there and turned back to the door. I approached but it didn’t open automatically. I pushed the button, but nothing happened. I pressed it again, and this time, instead of opening, it turned red. I jabbed it again, but nothing happened.

“What’s wrong?” she called, still lingering.

“I dunno,” I sighed, looking back. “Door’s busted. It’s probably nothing.”

The words had barely left my mouth when the corridor descended into a red haze and then rocked violently. The floor tilted to forty-five degrees and then lurched, throwing us both into the wall with a crack.

A siren split the air and I scrambled forward toward her. She’d hit hard on her shoulder, her head. My bag had been on mine, filled with socks and clothes — it'd broken my fall. She wasn’t so lucky. I bounced from floor to wall as the angle deepened.

I cleared a doorway and skidded to a halt next to her. She was already on her knees. She stared up at me in the red light, blood trickling from her forehead. “Jesus, Alice,” I yelled, pressing my palm against it. With my free hand I reached for the bag still on my shoulder and swung it around. I grabbed the shirt that was on top and pressed it to the cut. “Hold that there, keep pressure. Are you okay?”

She nodded quickly, her eyes closing as she winced.

“What the fuck is going on?”

“I — I don’t know.” She screwed her face up. “It’s... Uh...” She squinted, listening to the siren. “That’s the emergency siren — all hands on stations. It means… Uh…”

“Attack,” I breathed. “We’re under attack.”

As I said it, all the doors flung open at the same time.

“What do we do?” I asked, our eyes meeting, our faces a few inches apart.

She swallowed, hard. “I don’t know.”

## 14

There was only one reason that all the doors would open like that. Emergency evacuation. They all clamped shut to minimize damage and the spread of fire or to contain a hull breach. When they all opened at once, it meant that the ship was going down. But the question of exactly *where* it was going down to, and why the hell it was going down at all were still tabled.

I slung my bag to the ground and pulled a fresh shirt from it. I tore it into strips in the throbbing red haze and wrapped it tightly around Kepler's head, staunching the bleeding with a clean sock pressed as wadding. She grunted and winced, but I ignored her. This wasn't any sort of time to be gentle. The ship had twisted almost ninety degrees now and deep groans and rumbles were reverberating through the hull. Whatever was attacking us was laying waste, that was for sure. Hell, I didn't even know we were near anything.

I pulled Kepler up by the arm and laced it over my shoulder. Her fingers squeezed at my collarbone and took a fistful of jumpsuit. She held on, her legs unwilling to go under her in any real way. Her eyes were like saucers and the blood was still pouring. She was concussed — maybe worse. I had to get some help, but there was no one around.

I sucked in a hard breath and staggered forward, my back screaming as I strong-armed her along the uneven wall, crooked sideways to support her. Every doorway we reached was a thigh high hurdle to be cleared.

I told her to hold tight before sweeping her legs up and stepping over the first, ignoring the sharp edges of the frame as they cut into my thigh. She curled against me, her hair on my cheek, the smell of the sweat on her skin sickly sweet and stale in my nose, her breath tight against my neck. I could feel my heart in my hands, white against her back and legs. But I had to keep going.

My chest burned and by the third hurdle, I set her down, panting. "We've got to get higher — out of the corridors," I squeezed out between breaths.

She looked at me through bleary eyes. "I... I don't... I can't..." She was getting worse.

"The Training Deck, it's huge — we can make up a lot more time crossing that. We can drop down to the escape pods from there. It'll take forever going on like this." I didn't believe the words as they came from my mouth, but Kepler was still reeling. I just hoped she'd come around a little by the time we got there.

The floor rocked with each passing explosion, still a distance away — the other side of the ship from us, but getting closer. The force pushed us level, and then back sideways, swaying like one of those old Earth ships on an ocean of water. I swallowed hard and made the call. I couldn't carry her the entire way. At least on level ground she could stagger and I could catch my breath.

She sat on the side of the doorway, pressing her fingers slowly to her head, and I knew that she wouldn't walk on her own.

"Sorry, Kepler," I said quickly, kneeling. "This isn't exactly how I pictured this happening."

She looked at me quizzically as I reached for her neck. "What are you doing?" she asked slowly, but not making any attempt to push me away. I unzipped her jumpsuit down to the waist. Under it she was wearing a white tank top. Yellow stains had formed under the arms and around the neck. I almost forgot how long a day it'd been for her. The whole thing seemed so far away now — so unimportant.

I grabbed her hand and sleeve in two hands and pulled it over her fingers. I felt them hook around mine and squeeze, and I had to pull them free. I was doing my best to smile at her, though I don't think she quite grasped what was going on. I pushed her arm out of the sleeve entirely, and then slipped the other one off so that her jumpsuit was around her waist. She was holding her arms out like a mannequin, stiff and unmoving.

I swallowed, trying to keep the quiver out of my voice. Jesus, how hard did she crack her head?

"Alice, can you hear me?"

She nodded slowly.

"Alright," I said, looping one of the sleeves over her shoulder. "I'm going to need you to get on my back, alright?" I turned around and edged backwards until she parted her knees around my flanks. She instinctively put her hands on my shoulders and I guided them with a mixture of haste and care until they met in front of my chin. I watched as she touched each hand with the other like they were someone else's. I meshed her fingers with mine until they held on their own and then pulled the sleeve over her shoulder and my own, pulling the other under my ribs. I tied them together as tightly as I could over her wrists and across my chest, and then took hold of her thighs, pulling her off the frame and onto my back. I tightened the knot again and hoped that combined, she'd stay on my back long enough for us to make up some ground.

She pressed her head between my shoulders and I felt the coolness of her blood seeping through my shirt. I forced myself to ignore it and pressed on.

The ground levelled by the time we got to the main hallway that led up to the Training Deck. I staggered to the corner and paused for breath.

"I can walk," Kepler whispered in my ear, making no effort to loosen her grip around my neck or lift her head from my back.

"It's fine," I wheezed, wondering whether or not to step out. I could feel the floor shifting, this way and that. We had to.

I hadn't seen anyone since it had started. Everyone would have been in the mess, or the Training Deck. The escape pods were on the other side — they would have headed that way at the first sign of trouble, directed by the officers present. I was away from it all, and Alice had come to find me. We were alone, then, on this side of the ship — stranded and left to fend for ourselves while everyone else escaped. There was no sign of Jonas or any of the others who were falling all over themselves to soak up a bit of her light. And I think that said it all.

I swallowed and stepped into the corridor. It was wide and long, and opened out at the end in a staircase. It rose up to a mezzanine of sorts, splitting around the base into two further corridors. Above it, on a shelf, were emblazoned in huge gray letters 'All People. One Federation,' and below it the words 'Upper Training Deck.' I made for the stairs as quickly as I could, the letters painted blood red in the emergency lighting. I tried not to look at them as they tilted and swayed above me. I could feel Alice's dead weight shifting as the floor swayed. The explosions rumbled and shuddered through the hull, throwing me sideways and threatening to topple me.

I reached the stairs and lifted my foot. It felt heavy, my muscles filled with acid, tired and strung out. My chest was burning, my eyes watering and bulged. I could feel my heart hammering in my ears and throat and I was wondering how long I could go on. The stairs stretched up above and then in front, and then above, and then in front as the ship tilted and rocked. A cold sense of dread was creeping up through my heels and pulling me down. Alice's thighs were loosening from around my hips and her weight was becoming heavier, her grip looser. Her breathing was shallow in my ear and I could feel her blood dripping onto my shoulder. I dared not put her down to check, but I could tell she was drifting from consciousness. I needed to get her somewhere safe — somewhere I could get her help.

I gritted my teeth and grunted and took the steps as hard as I could. I got halfway when an explosion echoed, closer than before, and the whole ship shuddered and recoiled. A horrifying groan echoed through the halls and the sounds of tearing metal reverberated through me. The gravity shifted and dipped as the ship rotated and the stairs went from an incline to a decline. Whatever had hit us had hit us hard, and rolled us. We were flipping, and fast. My eyes widened and I made for the rail, throwing myself with everything I had.

A draft pulled on my clothes and buffeted in my ears as I lurched and as my fingers met cold steel, a strange and strangulated sound of desperation escaped my lips. The wind kicked up like someone had turned on a huge fan in the distance. But I knew it wasn't that — it was the opposite. The wind was blowing, it was sucking. All the doors were open, the ship had rolled, and now the hull had been breached.

The metal sighed and wailed like whalesong and the ship continued to turn. The steps pulled themselves out of reach and I scrabbled at them with my feet, Alice dangling off my back as the floor became the wall. I was gripping the rail with everything I had, but if it inverted completely, I'd never be able to hold us up, and the ceiling was at least thirty feet above. If we fell, we'd be toast. I'd break something — and Alice? I didn't want to think about it.

I stared at the floor as it tilted away, polished tiles slick and beckoning. In the distance I could see the double doors to the Upper Training Deck, open and dark, like the mouth of a Terraterrion space squid, agape and waiting.

"Sorry, Al," I mumbled, spitting through my gritted teeth. I let go and aimed my heels at one of the steps. They caught hard, and sent us tumbling. The fabric ripped. Her hands came free, and then we impacted. All the wind was beaten out of me and my back cracked against the floor. The heat against my elbows told me I was sliding. I could feel the tiles under me, each join another beat against my shoulders as I tried to angle myself. Alice was ahead, jumpsuit trailing behind her like a train, ragged and split at one shoulder. She was spinning, half on her side, head bloodied, eyes closed.

The door came up fast and she sped through it, onto the deck and the space that lay beyond. "Alice!" I yelled, stretching out. It was no good; she was dead weight, slipping away. She'd come off my back in the fall and had pulled away. I couldn't catch up.

I swore and looked desperately around, the doorway approaching quickly. I planted my hand on the floor and it squealed in the darkness, twisting me over. The friction screamed at me, hot and stinging on my skin. I got my knees against my chest and folded myself toward the frame, kicking off it as I passed.

The burst of speed sent me sprawling and rolling, but it was something. I tucked into a ball and sped down the deepening ramp. All of the SimPods had come off their mounts and tumbled into the far wall, lying now in a broken pile of aluminum and smoke.

Alice was ahead and spinning. I reached out, making up ground. What I proposed to do when I got to her, I didn't know, but if she clattered into the pods at the speed she was going, I didn't know what the hell would happen.

We were at forty-five degrees and holding, making up ground fast on the heap of shrapnel ahead. "Alice!" I yelled. She didn't answer — didn't move, didn't react.

I stretched out my hand, reaching in the dark, her body shapeless in the gloom.

The ship rocked again and an explosion ripped through the hull, close enough to echo through the doors. The wind picked up more, sucking at us as all the air was dragged out of the corridors.

The angle changed and everything began to shift, tipping back the other way. We were getting pummeled. The angle flattened and we slowed. I went from tumbling to sliding to crawling to running in seconds, leaping down the incline before it moved again.

My heart was singing in my chest, my breath tight, my knees and hips raw. But it didn't matter. Sweat poured off my face and fear clawed at me in the wind.

I jumped, two-footed and gangly, and crashed to the ground on top of her, enveloping her in my arms. She groaned and mewled.

We rolled to a halt and I heaved her up with everything that I had. "Alice!" I shook her, half dragging her, half pushing her to her feet. "I need you to walk! I need you to get the fuck up, right now!"

My hands were on her back and then under her arms as I shoved her forward, stiff-legged and weak.

"If you don't, we're going to die, and I'm not about to leave you here."

She flopped and staggered and as the floor began to fall away from us again I drove my shoulder into her gut and lifted. I heard the breath shoot out of her in the windrush and made for the door, loping along with her elbows banging against my back.

We skirted the trashed pods and made for the door before anything upended again, following the windrush. We made it through and I laid her against the corner behind it, sinking to a knee, letting out a low, gutteral whimper. Ahead I could see the words 'Emergency Exit' emblazoned above a doorway. The doorway was shut, the doors closed. Beyond, I could see a fire raging, glowing through the portholes. They'd snapped shut automatically when the hull had breached but the blast had buckled them. They stood crooked in the frame and a slit of yellow was visible between them, air rushing out, fueling the flames burning in the semi-vacuum beyond. They raged and crackled.

I beat the floor with my fists, screaming.

"M— Maddox?"

I twisted round, the wind whipping across my skin and through my hair. "Alice!" I crawled towards her, sliding on my knees. "Are you okay?"

She smiled weakly, her eyes barely open. Her hand hovered in the air, gingerly making a point, and then rose.

"What is it, Al? The fire?" My voice cracked, tears forming. Another explosion reverberated in the background and the wind picked up. The doors were parting. I swallowed back the fear but it wouldn't budge. It stayed in my throat like a hot lump.

She shook her head. "N— No..." Her hand raised further and I followed it to a steel door to our right. Next to it was a plaque that read 'Stairs' with a down arrow, alongside the words 'Lower Hangar East.'

I broke into a smile and a tear ran down my cheek. It got to the stubbly line of my growing beard and stopped, wavered, and then left my skin, sucked into the air in the vacuum.

The droplet disappeared between the doors and sizzled in the flames. By the time it did, we were already through the door and heading down.

# 15

I slammed the heel of my free hand into the pad and the door dragged itself open, spitting sparks.

The hangar beyond was in flames and the heat rolled over us like a wave. I shielded my face with arm and turned Alice away from it. She had her arm around my neck and I was hauling her along. The stairs had been hard, and most of the time I'd had to drag her over the steps, limp-legged.

I pushed forward into the wall of choking smoke and smog and squinted around. Tilt-wings and other small transport ships were in pieces, churned and toppled, in flames. A huge, gaping hole was spread across the rear wall, the metal around it all gnarled and bent outward like steel ribs. The hangar itself was huge, despite being an auxiliary entrance for smaller ships. It was completely open to the coldness of space, protected by a sonic airlock — a stream of sonic waves that kept the air separated from the vacuum — but let things pass in and out freely, like ordnance. Whatever was being fired on the ship had come straight through and decimated the hangar. The airlock hung, translucent like a curtain, and beyond it, a war was raging.

It was impossible to hear the battle from beyond the veil, but in the space outside, ships were swirling in a deadly melee. A planet, green and indigo, swept with clouds, hung half in view, and from the surface spewed cannon fire and rail pulses. They leapt off the planet and out of view, and then seconds later, the ship shuddered under the impact and sparks exploded from the ceiling, or a plume of flames erupted from the gaping hole in the wall.

I choked on the smoke and edged forward, looking around for any means of escape. Every ship that wasn't totaled had already been taken, and everything that was left was a smoking wreck. I bit down on my tongue hard enough to draw blood and swore. Alice felt heavy on my shoulder. She coughed on the thick air.

I kept moving. It was all I could do. The floor was starting to shift again.

Ships buzzed like wasps outside, streaking past the airlock, laying fire into each other. Ours, and... Who knows? I didn't have time to scrutinize it. We had to find some way off the ship — an escape pod, or... Or....

My eyes settled on the far wall and I froze. None of the ships had been tethered, but there, along the back wall were dozens of F-Series mech suits, lined up and harnessed to the walls.

I turned from them to the gaping hole in the wall, and then to the airlock. The projectile had come straight through — but if the next one hit the hull near to it, and the airlock was disrupted, the entire hangar and the rest of the ship would spontaneously decompress and we'd be sucked into space.

I swallowed and tightened my grip on Alice's ribs, hiking her higher onto my hip. It was our only chance. I started moving fast, pulling her along with everything I had.

I circled the wrecks and made for the back wall, keeping one eye on the airlock, and the other on our footing. The ground was tilting as the ship was battered, and the thrusters fought to push it back level.

The F-Series loomed, twenty feet tall, and I headed for the closest ones, praying that they'd open. Between each one, a set of steps led up, near vertically, to a platform that serviced the one on each side. I grunted and scooped Alice onto my shoulder as I had before. She didn't make a sound. I wasn't sure if she was even conscious anymore.

I took the rail in my right hand and held on to her with my left, her head lolling across my aching back. I planted my feet in the rungs and heaved her upward, throwing her the last span onto the platform. She landed hard and lay flat as I pulled myself up, chest heaving. Against the walls were switches. I didn't check what they were, I just threw them all. Lights buzzed to life and the F-Series found power. I stepped over Alice and approached the one on the left, reaching for the hatch release. I closed my fingers around it and twisted, pulling the handle upward. It hissed and a spurt of compressed gas shot out of the body. The hydraulics lifted the steel hatch with a whine and I watched it. "Come on, come on!" I yelled, urging it up with my hands.

I had no fucking clue how I was going to get her in there. It took me two attempts to pick her up again. She'd gone totally limp, eyes closed, breath shallow. What I hoped to achieve with it, I couldn't say — but if the airlock blew out, at least we wouldn't have our eyes boiled in our skulls in the vacuum of space. Once we were rigged up, we could go from there. We could try to find our way off the ship — look for a leaving transport, head for the escape pods... The F-Series would provide some protection at least, and if we were blown out of the hangar, at least the F-Series had directional thrusters. It was a small hope — a splinter of it and no more, but it was all we had.

I cradled her in my arms and hefted her feet up over the lip, growling as I forced her legs in, pushing her over the crest. She tumbled into the cockpit with a heavy thud.

The fires raged around us and the floor had sunk again. I ignored it and swung myself onto the front of her F-Series, reaching in to straighten her up. The steel cut into the underside of my arms as I forced her straight and looped the harness over her shoulders. She didn't have a helmet, or any of the other safety gear, but there was no time. I clamped the harness shut over her chest and yanked it tight. She yelped a little in shock, but didn't look up or move her arms. I took a deep breath and stared at her, wondering if it was all useless —

if she was bleeding into her brain, or if she was just going to slip into a coma and die — or whether the F-Series would be any protection at all when the ship was torn apart. I ignored the thought and threw myself upward, closing both hands around the hatch. It gave under my weight and I dragged it down, slamming my feet into the body of the F-Series and forcing the hatch to seal. I watched as Alice disappeared, swallowed up inside the steel body, not knowing if I'd ever see her again.

The second the hatch engaged, the harness decoupled and the F-Series dropped two feet onto the hangar floor and toppled forward. I threw myself sideways towards the rail and reached out, feeling the shoulder of the F-Series clip my calf as it fell past me. My hands clattered into the metal and my legs swung against it. Pain lanced through my shins and knees and I let out a low, guttural grunt.

Alice's F-Series clattered to the ground and slid, face down along the floor, back toward the fiery corpses of the ships that had amassed in the corner. I scrambled for purchase and surmounted the steps, my breath ragged, back screaming. I yanked on the hatch release of my own F-Series and clambered in. I sank into the chair and flicked the switches in front of me, bringing it online. I'd done it so many times in sim that it was all familiar, but totally alien at the same time too. My hands were shaking so hard I could barely get them to the right places. The screen initialized and lit up, scanning the room. The hatch hissed closed as I clamped my harness together and the couplings disengaged. My hands pressed into the gloves and assumed the controls and a message popped up on the screen in front of me. 'AI Assistant Initializing. Please wait.'

"Wait?" I yelled. "I don't have time to wait." I yanked on the controls and the F-Series pushed forward off its mount, landing hard on the ground. I lurched down the slope awkwardly. This was nothing like the simulations. The recruits who passed the exam would have had weeks of hands-on training in the full immersion simulation. I'd had none.

'AI Assistant Online. Welcome to the F-Series Federation Mechanized Unit.' The words stung my eyes, burning white against the fiery hellscape in front of me.

"Welcome," the voice said. It was male, friendly, but calm. "Please enter your pilot authorization code to assume full control."

"I don't have a code!" I shouted, forcing the mech straight, fighting the incline.

"Scanning biometric profile."

It wasn't giving me full control. The handling was sluggish and most of the HUD options were grayed out and locked off. There was no telemetry, no weapons access, no external comms. I was a goddamn statue. "Don't scan biometric profile! Save Alice!"

"Airman Maddox, James Alfred. Current status: in review. I'm sorry, Airman Maddox, you are not authorized to operate this Mechanized Unit. Please disembark when safe, or I will be forced to report you."

"Report me?" I squawked. "Have you seen what the fuck is going on?"

As I said it, a rail pulse lit up the hangar and swept away, carving the side of the hull into two chunks.

My cockpit crackled with static and a voice cut through the din. "Attention all crew of the Regent Falmouth, this is Acting Commander Volchec. We've come under insurmountable fire. The ship is compromised and we're dropping out of orbit." The voice paused and sighed, the fear and strain palpable. "Abandon ship." Volchech's voice was quiet and hopeless. "I repeat — abandon ship."

The airlock stuttered, fizzled, and then failed. The dim blue hue that let us know that space was out there and the air was in here disappeared, and then everything went sideways.

Everything that was inside the airlock, burning and smoking and sliding and exploding, all left the ground at once and flew toward the door. The force nearly snapped my neck as my F-Series was slingshotted into the vacuum of space and jettisoned from the Regent Falmouth.

"I'm detecting major structural damage to the hull and vital systems of the Regent Falmouth," the AI announced flatly.

I watched through the screen as it spun into view, criss-crossed with rail marks, scorched and black, and punctured and bled like a pin cushion. Debris flew everywhere and ships zoomed and flew between it, fighting and picking one another off like bugs in the distance. I wondered who was flying them. Who got out. Who didn't. Who would survive, and how. Everett. Did she make it? Would anyone?

"You don't fucking say! Engage thrusters!"

"You don't have sufficient—"

"I think we're a little past that, don't you?"

The AI went quiet for a second, as if deciding. "Granting temporary control. Full capabilities online. What would you like to do?"

I pulled up my hands and straightened them in front of me, jabbing at the holographic options suspended there. The thrusters kicked up and pulled me out of the spin. Though the F-Series didn't have aerial capabilities like the A-Series or S-Series, they did have directional thrusters for faster ground movement, and in space, that was enough to get you moving.

"Equilibrium restored," the AI announced. "Though I'm detecting the gravitational pull of the planet Draven. We do not have sufficient thrust to escape. Would you like to send out a distress signal?"

I grunted and searched the screen frantically, but there was nothing but debris everywhere. "No. Find Alice!"

"Who is Alice?"

"The F-Series. The F-Series that was in the hangar! Scan for it, or look for it, or something!" I howled.

"What sort of scan would you like me to run?"

I couldn't believe it was asking me that. "How the fuck should I know?"

"This is why only trained pilots should operate Mechanized Units."

"Seriously?" If it had a neck I would have wrung it.

"Scanning."

For an AI it had some sass. I mean, Sally had some, too, so maybe it was a pattern. Who the hell was programming these things?

"For your information, it will be approximately twenty seconds until we reach the stratosphere of planet Draven. The chances of surviving reentry at this speed are very low." It was telling me I was going to die, but it didn't sound concerned at all. I wasn't sure if that was reassuring or terrifying. I didn't have time to think.

"Have you found her?"

"Not yet."

"Well then, keep fucking looking!"

"Your vitals indicate elevated stress levels. Calmness is an essential quality of a good pilot."

"If you—"

"Scanning."

I ripped the controls up and watched the hands of the F-Series rise in front of me just in time to block an incoming piece of hull careening towards me like a steel log. It impacted my hands and forced me backward. I could already feel the heat building up inside the cockpit, the cooling fans whirring incessantly with the friction from the atmosphere.

"I detect one signal matching the signature of a Federation F-Series."

"Where?" I yelled, wrestling the log away. The debris was glowing around me as it all rained down onto Draven.

"Two kilometers and moving away."

"Show me!" I called, routing all the power we had into the thrusters. The screen in front of me displayed all of the twisting, hurtling debris lit up and everything was outlined and shaded in red. In the distance I could see a tiny green blip, tumbling toward the surface. A reticle appeared around it and zoomed in. An F-Series was tumbling haphazardly, beginning to glow.

"Raise her on comms," I commanded, slamming my thumbs into the thrusters and powering forward. The suit began to judder under the force, the air battering at me as I weaved between the chunks of falling ship.

"I am getting no response," the AI said back. "It appears that her ignition system has not been initiated."

"Keep going."

"The chances of survival are very low, and falling. Without control of her suit, she will burn up on entry. I recommend putting your thrust into a vertical vector to reduce our descent speed."

"Don't you fucking dare." I could see flames building along the bottom of the screen. "How far?"

"One point two kilometers, but it is futile, she will—"

"Keep going!"

The AI quietened down and instead brought up the figures for me on screen — the hull temperature, the distance to Alice, a dotted line tracing the path. Below her was the curve of the planet, cut out against the endless canvas of space, the faint glow of an approaching dawn lingering beyond the horizon. Above, the Regent Falmouth was exploding into a million pieces. Ships and steel rained down all around us and I had to keep adjusting not to get obliterated by them.

We broke a kilometer and I could feel the atmosphere clawing at me. Every bolt in my suit was shaking and my eyeballs were rattling in my head. Sweat was pouring off my temple and the screen was white with fire. All I had to go on was the glowing reticle. I kept it in the center of the screen and kept the thrusters pinned.

The distance counter rolled into triple digits and a vague visage of a figure swam into view.

My arms stretched out and she flew closer.

The AI spoke up. "Hull integrity is failing. The temperature is too high. We must reduce speed immediately or—"

We impacted like colliding stars. An almighty crash rang through the rig and I snapped my arms shut around her. We were spinning, locked together. The camera dome on top of my rig's body was pressed against hers. I was in the dark, in an oven, roasting alive. The air was soup and my lungs burned under the taste of it. I gripped hard with one hand and peeled away, looking for an out.

"Reverse thrusters, slow us down!" I screamed.

"I am. We are unable to slow down. We are moving too fast, and our load is too heavy. I recommend releasing to increase chances of survival."

Load? He meant Alice. "Find me another option."

"There is not one. You must release the cargo to improve your chances from the current chance of success."

"Which is?"

"Zero percent."

I swore and looked blindly around. There was nothing. Nothing but debris. Shit. Wait. The debris. "Redirect thrusters to this vector." I tapped the screen and the reticle moved.

"I don't recommend—"

"I wasn't goddamn asking! Do it."

He didn't say anything else, but I felt us start to shift, barely noticeable through the indomitable vibrations. We floated left, straight into the path of a chunk of hull.

"Collision alert."

"I know!" I reached up over my shoulder as I had done a thousand times in simulation and felt my fingers close around the grip of the Samson Automatic Rifle holstered to the back of the F-Series. I pulled it down and levelled it at the debris, pulling the trigger.

The bullets ripped out of the barrel and into the slab of steel. I directed them to a corner and it began to twist. "Reverse thrust!"

We slowed and the debris closed in on us. I twisted over as it drew level and took the corner in my hand, swinging us above it. The shaking quietened and I slammed Alice down, pinning her against it. My hands spread out and I forced it level, riding it down through the layers of the atmosphere. I held my hands there, watching them smoke. The readout on my HUD told me the surface of it was way above safe temperatures, but it didn't matter. Nothing did now. If it didn't work — if the chunk of steel didn't do enough to disrupt the air so that we didn't burn up, then it was all pointless.

I couldn't breathe, couldn't speak. Everything was shaking. My hands were numb, my back in pieces, my feet tingling and ringing like bells. My skin was burning, eyes stinging. I closed them. Clamped my teeth shut. The blood boiled in my skull. My ears threatened to burst. I couldn't tell if I was screaming or not. I couldn't tell if

I was conscious or not. My mind was churning, blending thoughts into mush.

And then there was silence and space. The gentle whistling of air.

I felt coolness rush between my feet. I opened my eyes. The screen was devoid of flame but cracks snaked through it. A warning sign was flashing and smoke was trailing through the display, but ahead, beyond it was the green and lush landscape of a planet. Distant and dramatic, but not bathed in fire, and not seen from outside the atmosphere.

I swallowed hard and shook sense into myself. Alice. She still needed me.

I kicked the debris away and watched as it sailed, smoking, through the air. Debris still rained down like meteorites all around us. We weren't out of the woods yet.

I took hold of her suit and turned her over. She was still unresponsive. As was my own AI. The words 'Onboard Systems Failure... Rebooting...' still shone red in my eyes. I watched my fingers work through the letters, spidering along the carcass of her F-Series for the manual override I knew was there.

Chutes. She needed chutes. I'd studied hard, and good thing. If I hadn't, I'd have never known that there was an override, let alone where to find it. I pulled the panel on her back, between her shoulders, up and closed my fingers around the handle and pulled, hard.

Studying never accounts for the real thing. The second I pulled the handle, the chutes exploded in my face. Like an airbag, they blew me clean off her body and into the sky.

The jolt somersaulted me into the air and I watched as she decelerated under a canopy of white, drifting into the sky.

The systems failure message disappeared and was replaced with one twice as bad. 'Altitude Warning: Deploy Parachutes? Yes/No.'

I was spinning, fighting the closing doors of darkness as the centrifugal force dragged me away from the light. I reached out, fighting it as hard as I could, with all I had left, and tapped the button.

There was a jerk, a crack, pain, and then darkness pulsed. Something warm trickled down my nose and a bloody patch appeared on the screen in front of my eyes. I lifted my hand to my head, but it felt numb and heavy, like a crab claw. My eyes lolled and I sank back, dragging in thick, heavy breaths.

I could see Alice above, a white dot against a brightening sky, and behind her the destroyed remnants of the Regent Falmouth entering the atmosphere.

I tried to stay awake, but I couldn't.

I blinked once and felt the blood in my eyes.

I swallowed some of it, felt it on my lips and dripping from my chin.

And then there was nothing.

# 16

When I came to, the sky was black with smoke and the air was still, the stench of death hanging like a corpse from a tree.

I sucked in a sharp breath and sat up, slamming into the tightened harness across my chest and rebounding back into the chair. My breath rattled in my throat, the air stifling. I was on my back, the screen on in front of me, spattered with dried blood, displaying the dark clouds above, but otherwise everything was quiet.

I unbuckled myself and hit the button to open the hatch. It hissed and cool air rushed in. It spread to reveal a foot of cloud, but that was it. The motors whined against something and then quit.

I sighed and reached for the bottom of the hatch, levering myself awkwardly up into the gap. I managed to get my head out, and then worm onto the top of the body, pulling my legs free.

The air was cool, but my skin still felt hot and dry, my mouth parched, my stomach aching. I didn't know what time it was, but the sun was up, obscured behind the smoky clouds. I knew it must have been a while since we crashed, judging by the sting of hunger in my guts. My brain felt foggy, still, and the events that had unfolded felt like a distant dream. I rolled sideways and off the F-Series, realizing I was lying in a crater. The chutes were tangled in the trees above, swinging loosely. I must have hit them and snapped the cords, fallen the rest of the way, and impacted. I stared at the F-Series, half buried in the soft earth, and then at the surrounding trees, gnarled and thick with dark trunks and strange, vine-like leaves that smelled of rotting fruit. The ground was covered in moss and sloped away. I could hear water running nearby, but otherwise, I had no sense of direction or bearing. The air was still, and nothing was moving above — no ships, no artillery, no fire — nothing. Was the battle over?

Why the hell was everything so murky? I blinked a few times and shook my head. It was hurting like hell. Splitting, in fact. I touched my fingers to it and immediately recoiled from them. "Fuck!" I half yelled, falling backward away from the pain. I stumbled and bounced in the moss, deep aches leaping through my back and legs. I gingerly felt my head again and traced the ridges of what had to be a near bone-deep gash. It ran from my hairline down to my right eye. It wasn't a cut — an impact welt that had hit so hard the skin had burst. I screwed my face up and felt the blood caked around my eyes and mouth. No wonder I couldn't think straight.

I gasped suddenly, the events of what had happened suddenly solidifying. Alice. Where was Alice?

I looked around, panicked, but there was nothing but goddamn trees. I swallowed air I was breathing so hard, and took off down the slope, kicking over trunks and through the brush.

I found the stream and tried to clear it. My foot sank in up to the knee, but it didn't matter. I scrambled up the bank, clawing in the loose earth, and burst out of the woods onto a rise. The landscape ahead was torn apart.

What would have once been rolling fields and forest was now a cratered, burning crash site.

The Regent Falmouth had fallen out of orbit, reentered the atmosphere, and crashed into the surface. It was in parts, like a dismembered whale, beached on the planet. Troop carriers weren't designed to enter any gravitational fields, let alone land on a planet. Whatever had laid into it had torn it apart anyway, and as soon as it hit the atmospheric shell, it was completely destroyed. Everyone who was still on board was likely dead. My jaw clenched hard as I stared down at it, nothing moving except the flames slowly licking at the hull. Smoke curled off it, spouting from every orifice, drifting into the sky and amassing in a thick ceiling a few thousand feet up.

What in the hell had attacked us? Who would even dare attack a Federation carrier? Who *could?*

I screwed up my face. What did I know? I knew that we weren't supposed to be in battle — not yet. We were headed to one, but that was months away. So what the hell happened? I remembered fire coming off the surface, and from ships. What the hell was this planet?

I stared around, looking for any sign of Alice — for any sign of anything — but there was none. The battle was done, and there was no sign of either the Federation or whoever had the steel balls to attack them.

I smacked my parched lips and searched the landscape for any hint of where to go next. I needed water, I needed food. I touched my head and winced. I needed medical attention. But venturing down to the crash site wasn't something that reeked of a good idea. If we'd been attacked, then it was by someone who either wanted what we had, or by someone who wanted to put us down because we were the Federation. They were hardly short of enemies across the universe. But I suppose that's what happens when you want to subjugate and colonize every galaxy you come across. They brought peace, order, trade, technology — but there was resistance. There was always resistance. Rebel forces and factions. Some small. Some large. They'd been documented in the Federation histories and written about in their books. I tensed my jaw and stared down at the crash site, sprawling and scorched. My fists clenched at my sides and I stared down at my jumpsuit, blood spattered, filthy from scrambling up the bank, and stretched out of shape from Alice's fists curling into it.

I felt a pang in my chest and the world wobbled. Alice. Where was she? How the hell was I going to find her? I turned back to the forest and stared up at the ancient trees. As I did, everything seemed to freeze. What little breeze there was died and all the hairs on the back of my neck stood up. Something flashed in my peripheral and I dived forward instinctively.

Whatever it was whistled above me, glinting in the dim light, no more than a few inches from the back of my neck.

I rolled forward and leapt again, my heels flicking dirt behind me. Ground spewed between my feet as an object pierced the earth, hard. I landed face down and scrambled forwards, but before I could even get to my feet, pain ripped through my back and I was crushed against the soil.

I gasped for air, pinned down, hands clawing all around me. My back popped and threatened to break under the stress. A gurgled noise escaped my lips, and something cold came to rest against my throat. I froze. The feeling of a blade there, it was unmistakable. I dragged in a slow breath and waited for it to turn in to me and slice across my jugular, but it didn't come.

I could feel my heart pumping against my ribs, my cheek pressed against the moss, a tear worming its way through the dried blood.

Footsteps echoed in my head, cutting through the melee of thoughts, slow, methodical. I saw boots, military grade, appear in front of my face. The stopped a few inches from my cheek and paused.

"Well," a guy laughed, his accent off-world thick. "What do we have here?"

I swallowed.

The guy crouched and I saw the gray trouser legs of a Federation pilot sink into view. A rifle clacked as he rested it on his knee and I felt the blade loosen against my skin just enough so that I could lift my head. I looked up at the pilot with the rifle slung across his lap. He had about ten years on me, wiry, his face lined and stubbled with rust-colored hair. He cocked his head. "Am I talking to myself?"

"I... uh," I stammered, swallowing.

"What d'you reckon, Fish? He look like Free scum to you?"

Gears whirred above me and hydraulics hummed. I heard the telltale hiss of a mech's hatch opening and then the clang of boots on steel. A strange rippling noise cut the air and a second pair of boots landed next to the first, light and agile, spinning to face me. I craned my neck upward, feeling the blade still hanging next to my throat. The pilot had disembarked, and I could see the outline of a mech behind me out of the corner of my eye. Its foot was planted on my back, stuck there. It was smaller than the F-Series, by a long way — maybe half of the size. It hadn't been there a second ago. I mean, it had, but it hadn't. I couldn't see it. I hadn't seen it sneak up on me, blade drawn. It was a T-Series. A Tactical Series Federation mech — they called them Panthers, and they used them for covert ops. They were equipped with stealth cloaking tech to help them stay hidden. Safe to say that it worked.

I looked from the human to the new pilot and paused. It was humanoid, but had blue skin — a domed head and wide lips. Its eyes were black and its nose was two slits that flared with its slow breaths. It looked amphibious, and had fins above its collar. They flickered as it stared back at me. It made a quiet gurgling noise and the rusty-haired guy snorted. "You're telling me."

I didn't understand. It was just a noise.

"I'm Federation!" I called, as loudly as the earth against my cheek would allow.

The guy with the gun pressed his finger to his lips. "Shh, shh. You don't want to alert anyone else now, do you?"

I fell quiet.

"I asked you a fucking question," he growled.

"No, no, I don't."

"I'm going to ask you this once, boy. Are you Free?" His voice was stiff and flat, and his finger flexed on the trigger of the rifle. I had a feeling if I answered wrongly he wouldn't think twice about using it on me. Was I *free?* What the hell was that supposed to mean?

"I don't understand."

He laughed quietly, genuinely amused. "No? What's not to understand? You either are, or you're not." He reached down and pulled on my collar. "You're wearing Federation Grays, but they're a bit filthy, *bloody*... So the question is whether they're yours or you pulled them off some dead Feddy... Or *killed* one for them. So which is it?"

"They're mine! They're mine!" I whimpered, pushing my face into the moss.

He sighed. "You sure as hell cry like a Federation pup. What Battalion are you in?"

"I'm not," I squeezed out under the boot of the Panther. "I'm a recruit!"

The guy stood up and bit his lip. "Recruit?" He stared into the distance for a second. "What the hell's a recruit doing down here?" He was asking himself as much as the one he'd called Fish. "How'd you even get here?" He looked at me again.

"We were on the ship — it went down, and... And we..."

He sighed, making a cyclical gesture with his hand for me to hurry up.

I cleared my throat, spitting out dirt, and chose my words better. "There were two of us. We couldn't reach the escape pods — we took two F-Series, and—"

"House Cats?" He scoffed. "You're not trying to tell me that two green-ass recruits rode two jacked House Cats right down to the surface?" He shook his head. "Nah, I don't buy it." The rifle was in my face again, suddenly. "Truth, now, or I put one in your head."

"Please!" I mewled. "It's the truth, I swear! It was our only chance! She was going to die!" I sobbed suddenly, uncontrollably.

He kept the rifle on me until the fish-man took the barrel in his hand and pushed it down, staring at the first guy. He grumbled and then dropped the gun to his side. "Fish says you're not shitting me." He scoffed and laughed. "In that case, I think it's time you got the fuck up, 'cause this is a story I've gotta hear."

THEY LET me up and watched as I brushed the caked blood off my jumpsuit.

The one he was calling Fish climbed back into the T-Series and lifted the foot off my back. He walked around to face me, but didn't disembark.

The taller guy, the human, rested the rifle over his shoulder and put his other hand on his hip. He was in a pilot's flight suit, and the name across his chest said MacAllister. I looked at it briefly, and then at him, wiping the tears from my cheeks. I could feel them flushed, even through the dirt and the blood.

"Look," I said quickly, "I really have to go — I've got to find Alice."

He arched an eyebrow. "Alice, eh? That your girlfriend?" He elbowed the T-Series humorously, but his elbow clanged off the steel, but Fish didn't react.

I sighed. "No. She's... she's a recruit, like me. But we got... separated. She's *somewhere* out there." I cast my hand around in a wide circle and MacAllister followed it, smirking.

"And she was in an F-Series, too? You both were?" He shook his head.

"Yeah. Her chutes popped before mine. When they did, I hit my head," I said, gesturing to my bloodied face. "When I came to, I was lying in a hole, and Alice was..."

"Gone." He nodded and stuck out his bottom lip. "Alright, well, here's what you do."

I leaned in.

"You pick yourself up," — he smiled — "you dust yourself off," — he lifted his hands — "and you move on." He pushed his hands toward the horizon, smiling broadly.

"What? *Move on?* What the hell are you talking about? Didn't you hear me? She's out there, somewhere, and—"

"And she's already fucking dead, kid." MacAllister hung his head and squeezed my shoulder. "I hate to be the bearer of bad news, but she's dead. It's a damn miracle you didn't burn up on re-entry, and I'd love to hear all about it over a cold beer, but I've been a pilot for a long time now — and I've never heard of *anyone* surviving before. The fact that you did is one in a million, and you really think she did too?" He smiled abjectly at me.

"Yes," I answered firmly.

His smile faded. "Look around, kid. Look at where you are. Look at what's happened. That's a Class 1 Federation Carrier — you know how much firepower it's packing? You know what it takes to bring one down? And they did it. We were just passing by" — he moved his hand through the air — "this planet, supposedly uninhabited by intelligent life, save a few mining colonies here and there, and then suddenly..." He closed his fist. "Fire. Explosions. Death. We scrambled as quick as we could, but turns out that this planet was home to a hidden Free Stronghold." He scoffed and shook his head. "They could have just let us fly by. We never would have even known they were here. But they just couldn't pass up the opportunity. They waited until we were right on top of them, and then they hit us with everything they had. Surface strikes, air strikes, you name it. And that's the result." He flicked his wrist at the crash site.

I swallowed and gritted my teeth.

"I was in a tilt-wing, gunner. We'd scrambled to fight back, but it was too little too late. We got clipped in orbit, managed to make it down to the surface, rigged up, bailed out... And now..." He turned away and stared at the horizon. "We're getting as far away as possible. The Free are sweeping through here every hour or two, looking for survivors from the crash, rounding up those they can, killing the ones who fight back."

"Killing them? Why? What did the Federation ever do to them?"

He grinned. "Shit, what are they teaching recruits these days? The Free and the Federation have been at war for centuries. *Freedom fighters against the great oppression...*" He laughed. "What, ain't never heard the slogan?"

I shook my head. "No." This was wasting time. Too much time.

"What I'm saying is that the battle's lost. The day is lost. But the war isn't over. The Federation will be sending reinforcements. The Free are rounding up everyone they can, stockpiling all the resources they can. When the Federation arrive, they'll look to ransom off the troops they have for credits they can use to fund their crusade. When that happens, the Federation are going to roll over them in a fiery fucking wave. The Federation don't negotiate, trust me. You're going to see Federation destroyers in the sky, and then everything's going to be turned to ash. When that happens, you want to be as far away from here as you can." He jabbed me in the shoulder. "Mark my words. We're getting out of here, and you're coming with us."

I held firm. "No, I'm not. I'm staying."

"Are you fucking stupid, kid?" His tone lowered.

I didn't know that it was a question that required an answer.

"If you stay, you die. Don't you get it? It's just that simple."

I set my jaw for a second and stared him in the eye. "Like you said, it's just that simple."

# 17

I breezed past MacAlister and Fish and back up toward the stream and the forest.

"Hey, kid, you're not serious?" MacAlister held his hands out, rifle stretching into the air.

"I'm not going to just abandon her," I called through gritted teeth. "Or the others." I paused and took a hard breath, turning. "And neither are you."

MacAlister snorted and looked at Fish. "Yeah, sure, like we're going to stick around. Dunno about you, but I like my head attached to my body."

This guy was a bit of a prick, but time was short and if things were as they said, I was going to need all the help I could get. Fish in his T-Series would be a valuable asset. He'd almost taken my head off, and I had the distinct feeling that he wasn't trying very hard. And MacAlister? Well, he'd been a pilot for ten years, and survived the crash himself. He was obviously hard enough to do so, and didn't seem afraid of a fight, despite wanting to run from this one.

I dug deep into my albeit limited bank of Federation knowledge and came up with something that made Mac pale a few shades."Desertion is a corporal offense punishable by ejection." The words spilled out of my mouth, out of my control. All I could think about was Alice out there, somewhere, dying or captured, and I'd be stupid to think that I'd be able to do it alone. Hell, before today, I'd never been in a real mech. So fighting an entire army capable of bringing down and destroying a Federation Troop Carrier would be, as MacAlister put it, suicide.

MacAlister's demeanor changed and he stared at me with cold eyes. Silence reigned for a few seconds. I saw the fists of the T-Series clench and attempt to rise, but MacAlister reached back and quelled him, not leaving my gaze.

He broke into a grin and laughed falsely. "Ah, you had me going there for a second!" He shook his head and slapped his thigh. "Good one, kid. You take care now." He nodded to me and waved, and then turned away. The T-Series stayed there, staring at me and I tried to hide my shaking hands by curling them into fists.

"I'm not joking," I called after him. "There are Federation troops in trouble, and they need our help."

He paused and I watched his shoulders fall. He pulled the rifle up to his shoulder and turned, pinning it on me. He trudged back level with Fish and stopped, cheek rested on the butt, the sights trained on me. I spread my hands, feeling the catch in my throat growing.

"I don't think you quite understand the gravity of the situation," he growled. "There's absolutely nothing to stop me from putting a bullet in your chest right now, and just walking away. You saw me stop Fish doing it a second ago, didn't you? That was your chance, kid, and I don't know why the fuck I'm giving you another one, but I am."

I swallowed.

"Walk away, now. We'll go our separate ways, and you can go on your little crusade, but you never saw us." His voice was even and gave the sense that he really wasn't fucking around. "So I'm going to ask you once, and if I'm not completely convinced by your answer, I'm going to pull this trigger and be gone before you hit the ground." He drew a slow breath. "Did you see us?"

I chewed my gums, mulling the decision over. "I'm going, either way. And I need your help."

His grip tightened on the rifle, fingers flexing. I had no doubt he'd be more than prepared to put a bullet in me.

"But if you don't want to come, for whatever reason, then... I'm still going. I can't just walk away — not when people need me. Not when people are counting on me. You're the ones who're going to have to live with it. But I won't rat you out, you have my word on that." I sighed and turned away, screwing my face up, expecting to hear a gunshot ring out and feel the cold spread of death between my shoulders, but it never came.

Instead, I heard the rifle clack as it was lowered and then MacAlister whisper the words *goddammit* under his breath. I breathed a sigh of relief and kept walking.

"Kid," he called. "Wait up."

HE BIT his lip and stared down at it. "And there I was thinking you were bullshitting me about riding this thing down to the surface." He whistled and then spat into the undergrowth, staring down at the F-Series lying in the crater. The hatch was still half open and bloody handprints showed the path where I'd crawled out. The crater itself was pretty big, sunk into a bank between two trees. The Front Line Series, or F-Series, was just over eighteen feet tall. It was about as basic as mechs come. Zephod steel plating, inbuilt grenade launcher, no aerial capabilities, and a loose rifle — cheaper to change if it got damaged. The whole thing was built as cheaply as it could be.

"Fucking House Cats." MacAlister laughed and kicked the shoulder plate of my rig. It rang in the forest like a gong.

I stared down at it. It was black and charred. Half of the plates were missing — peeled off on re-entry. The antennae were gone, and the camera dome, set on the top of the body, was cracked. The rifle was lost, too.

"Well, this thing's fucked." MacAlister turned away. "Doubt it'll even spin up. It's a shell, and it's cooked. I'm surprised it wasn't destroyed completely during the fall. Must have been a hell of a ride."

"It wasn't a picnic," I sighed. "So what now?"

"Give it a whirl, see if this bitch will stand." He hung his head. "Going in on foot is an even *worse* option than going in rigged up, as if that was even possible, so I'd say climb in, and see what happens."

I nodded, wondering whether they'd stick with me the whole way, or bolt the first chance they got. He watched me climb onto the charred body of the House Cat and shimmy into the cockpit. I twisted myself down into the hole and lowered onto the seat. It stank of sweat and burnt plastic, but I must have too. I reached up and pulled the hatch closed above me, strapping myself in. I was on my back and I could feel my heart beating in my throat, the blood heavy in my head. I became distinctly aware that I hadn't eaten or drunk anything for a long time, and that all I'd had was unconsciousness and a head injury rather than any actual sleep. I rubbed my eyes and drew a few slow breaths before flicking the switches off and on to reboot the system. The screen went dark in front of me and then flickered to life again. I stared up at the tops of the trees above, swaying gently against the charcoal sky, the trunks black and dusted with ash.

The words 'AI Assistant Initializing. Please wait,' appeared on the screen once more, and this time, I did. MacAlister had been pretty explicit about the state of affairs. I'd filled him in on what exactly had happened, and he'd been pretty straight with me. By now, she was either dead — bled out or killed on impact. If she'd survived that, then it was likely that she hadn't died between then and now, unless the Free had found her and killed her. If that hadn't happened, then she was likely out there somewhere in her own F-Series, either kicking ass, or still unconscious. Either way, her demise wasn't likely something that was going to be time sensitive. It was weird. I had the urge to go balls to the wall, running round blindly, yelling her name for fear she was going to die if I didn't. But then there was the pragmatic side of my brain that was telling me that doing that was only going to get me killed, and if Alice wasn't dead, and she was fine — which was a real possibility — then I'd be slitting my own throat for no reason. We needed to be careful, and we needed a plan. For that we needed information, and that would take time and effort.

'AI Assistant Online. Welcome to the F-Series Federation Mechanized Unit.' The words glowed against the sky.

"Finally." My eyes were stinging and my brain fizzing. It'd been a long day, and it was about to get longer.

"Welcome back," the AI said.

"Would you believe me if I said it was good to be back?"

"I'm told that I'm a scintillating conversationalist," it replied dryly. "So yes."

I smirked. "By who? Have you had many other pilots?"

"I am a newly installed system. It was merely anecdotal. A result of my humor programming."

"So I'm your first, then, eh?" I pushed my hands into the gloves. Sally flickered in my mind for a second and I wondered if she'd found a new 'former yet, or if she'd been sent to the crusher. Both made me a little sad.

"Yes, though I'd hoped for a more seasoned pilot. Surviving past my first mission is something that I'd very much like."

I laughed. "You know what? Me too. You got a name?"

"I have a designation."

"Well, if we're going to do this together — and probably die together, then I'd like to be able to call you something. You choose."

"Processing," it said quietly.

"Well, while you decide, my name's Maddox. James Alfred Maddox."

"It's nice to meet you, James, even if you aren't a pilot."

"I got us down, didn't I?" I chuckled.

"I have decided."

"Lay it on me."

"My name will be... Greg."

I pinched the bridge of my nose and shook my head. "Greg? You can choose any name in the universe, and you choose Greg? Why?"

"I like it."

I laughed. Fucking AIs. "Alright, Greg. It's good to meet you. Now, shall we get the fuck out of this hole, or are we going to lie here all day?"

## 18

We trundled down out of the woods.

Fish was in the lead, in his T-Series. He had just sort of popped his hatch and turned toward Mac, who told me he preferred Mac to MacAlister, and stared for a second or two. Mac then nodded and said *okay,* and Fish closed it, and then took off, melting into the trees in a shimmering cloud as his stealth cloaking tech kicked in.

"What the hell was that?" I asked, heaving myself out of the crater. All the gears and hydraulics shuddered and whirred, throwing off the soot and carbon. My voice echoed in the cockpit.

Mac shouldered his rifle, small through the towering lens of the House Cat. "Fish's an Eshellite. They communicate mostly through body language and subtle gestures. You get used to it." He shrugged a little, his voice coming through loud and clear, patched into the F-Series' comm system. Greg had linked us up when it was back online. Apparently after transitioning into the Mech Corps, every pilot got a Federation commlink implant behind their ear that did close-range comms and let them hear the voices of other pilots right in their ear. The thought kind of freaked me out, but I didn't let that slip.

"Oh," I said, trying to sound like it was something obvious that I already had an idea about. Fish hadn't even made a sound since we'd met and it'd been nearly thirty minutes. Mac had talked *a lot.* "Not a very talkative bunch?"

Mac grinned. "Not really. They're an amphibious race, but they don't have vocal chords like us. I mean, they can make noises, but it's hardly English. They can breathe air, but they can also survive underwater. Something about submersible lungs that siphon oxygen." He waved his hand. "How the fuck should I know? I'm a soldier, not a biologist. It's mostly the little things, movements, ticks, the way they position themselves. Most people miss them altogether and assume they're idiots, or just can't understand." He scoffed. "The Eshellites are a clever fucking race, I'll tell you that much. Usually don't make a sound because they don't think most of what we say warrants a response. But they understand everything, and they see everything."

"So how does an Eshellite get in with the Federation as a pilot?"

"Same way we all do, I guess. A little bit of luck, and a lot of bad timing. Eshellites aren't exactly the most caring species, and they're cold-blooded — literally and metaphorically. They don't get flustered and they're a helluva lot faster and more reliable than humans. Makes them perfect for wetwork." He stepped quietly through the brush down the hill and I followed as gently as I could, but I couldn't help but feel that I was making lots of noise.

"Wet-work?"

"Tactical stuff. Assassinations. Search and Destroy. That sort of thing."

I nodded and pulled myself off comms with Mac. "Greg, can you pull up some info on Eshellites? And on Fish if there's a service record? And you know what, on Mac, too if you can."

"Here's a summary of the species," Greg said, pulling the information up on screen. I scanned it as he took me down the hill.

When we reached the edge of the trees Mac motioned me to stay hidden in the shade and pressed himself against the outermost trunk, staring out across the ridge I'd walked earlier. The stream ran in front of us and a grassy pasture rose into a moor of sorts, building to a series of undulating peaks on our left. To the right, the valley swept down to the crash site, cratered and mauled by the wreckage. It was still smoking.

The stream splashed out of nowhere and water drenched the bank. Fish materialized in front of us and stared at Mac. The cam dome on top of his T-Series moved up and down and he turned away.

"Alright, kid," Mac said quietly, stepping out. "Coast's clear, for now. Let's go get my ride."

Mac took off at a jog, clearing the stream and hiking up to the top of the bank. He took off at pace, halfway between a jog and a run and stalked like a wolf across the pasture. I watched him go, disappearing into the distance, a gray speck against a sea of gray, cut out against the smoke-filled sky. A splot on a darker splot. I looked up at the ebbing clouds. "Greg, what's your telemetry system like?"

"I'm outfitted with the standard Federation telemetry system, or FTS, capable of short-range calculations. Why do you ask?"

"Can you plot the course we came in on?"

"That proves difficult, as the planet has both rotated and partially orbited this system's star since this morning."

"Can you plot the course we took after we entered the atmosphere? Say from twenty thousand feet?" I narrowed my eyes at the colorless sea above.

"That I can do. Calculating."

A few seconds later, a white line appeared in front of me. It appeared from the top of my screen and shot into the sky overhead, continuing as a dashed line through the ceiling. I turned around and followed it as it curved into the trees we'd come from. "Alright, can you map Alice's trajectory?"

"It may take longer, but I can try."

"Do it. We're not going anywhere." It was true. We were waiting for Mac to go and get his rig. He'd bailed out along with Fish, and they'd managed to eject their rigs, too. Fish was a pretty small target, even in the T-Series, and with the stealth tech, it was a no brainer to keep the added protection and firepower. Mac, on the other hand, was a HAM Series pilot. HAM stood for Heavy Artillery Mech Series. I'd never seen one before but I heard they were big, bloated, and packed enough firepower to down a dropship without breaking a sweat. And, when surrounded by a fleet of House Cats, they could do it. But out here, alone, with no protection — he'd be a sitting duck.

"I have finished the calculations," Greg said.

A second line popped up next to the first, rising into the sky, except this one originated over the rise that Mac had disappeared over. "You've mapped her landing site?"

"No. Unfortunately, while reviewing the footage, I discovered that we lost sight of her. However, I was able to estimate the location with a reasonable degree of accuracy."

"What's reasonable?"

"A ten square kilometer range."

"Ten kilometers?" I scoffed. "I'd hate to see what broad is."

"A hundred."

"I wasn't asking." I sighed. "Alright, well, let's go then."

"Wait."

"For what?"

"Pilot MacAlister is approaching."

"Oh?" I looked up. Greg was right. Mac was coming, and fast. He was sprinting down the hill toward me, waving his arms.

"Hey! Hey!" He was yelling.

I froze, but Greg didn't. "I recommend we retreat. I'm detecting large sonic readings. Five hundred meters and closing."

I dragged in a ragged breath and felt my heart kick into overdrive. Greg assumed control until I pushed into the gimballed cages under my seat and moved my legs. It was almost symbiotic — the relationship between pilot and mech. I moved but he kept me going, keeping me balanced, choosing where my feet went so that I could focus on what mattered. And right now, that was running the hell away.

Mac closed in on us, but then fell behind as I took off. I could feel the ground shaking under my feet, and wondered what was closing in on us. By the way Mac was running, and screaming, it was something mean.

Engine roar cut through to the cabin and the ground was engulfed in shadow. Something swept overhead and peeled upward. I barely caught a glimpse of it, only the afterburn as it swept up into the ashy clouds. "What the hell was that?"

"My best guess is that it's a Federation E-68, a heavily armed type of fixed-wing multi-directional jet aircraft, commandeered by the Free forces in the area." Greg sounded calm. It wasn't rubbing off.

"Just keep running!"

"You are in control."

"I was talking to myself." My feet hammered the ground, flicking up earth.

Mac's voice crackled in the cockpit. "Jesus Christ! Did you see that?"

"It was hard to miss!" I yelled back.

"Then where the hell are you going?"

"What do you mean? You said to run!"

He dived forward and rolled to a knee in a hollow, shouldering his rifle and turning to face the sky. "Like hell I did! Get your fucking act together, you've got to take care of it."

"Take care of it?" I scoffed.

"I believe he means the Free craft," Greg added.

I ignored him. "What do you mean take care of it?" I called back, grinding to a halt and turning back to face him.

He offered up his rifle. "Well, this damn pea shooter's not going to do shit is it? You're packing a built-in forty-mil full auto grenade launcher. So do something about it!"

I opened my mouth to retort but I knew he was right. There was no sign of Fish, and Mac's rifle was designed for mid- to long-range engagements with infantry — *human infantry.* I swallowed hard and felt my hands shake inside the haptic gloves. It was on me, but I was totally out of my depth.

"I detect elevated adrenal levels and a spike in heart rate. Are you alright?" Greg asked casually, bringing my vitals up on screen.

"Fine," I spat through gritted teeth.

"Your blood oxygen levels are dropping. I recommend taking deep breaths."

"I'm fine!"

"Nervousness is normal in newer pilots. Fear is a natural response to—"

"I said I'm fine!" I yelled, reaching forward and tapping the buttons to activate the grenade launchers. I felt them lock in on the arms, loading the grenades into the barrels. Two figures popped up on my screens. An eight burned on the left and the right, pulsing gently in green.

"You have sixteen rounds in total. Would you like me to initiate active targeting?" Greg asked.

"Uh, yes," I growled. "That'd be handy — it's not like I've ever shot grenades at a goddamn plane before."

"It appears active targeting is unavailable. Our antennae and auxiliary feed cameras were damaged during reentry."

"What the hell does that mean?" I started strafing, remembering my training — keep moving, don't stay still. The F-Series was packed with four-inch steel plating, but a tracer round or rail pulse would rip through it like cotton wool. It was only designed to deflect incoming projectile fire, glancing blows from small caliber arms, and to protect from blast damage. The House Cat was, for all intents and purposes, cannon fodder, designed to be marched in en masse and overwhelm the enemy forces with sheer brute force. The Federation weren't going to waste good money on something they knew was just going to get ripped apart. I sighed and pushed that thought out of my mind.

Greg chimed back in. "It means that you must aim manually. I won't be able to advise on matters of targeting, nor will I be able to track the craft as it comes in. It is likely, however, that it is circling around for an ordnance run."

I set my jaw. "Fucking great."

"It is not great. The odds of survival are not in our favor."

"I was being sarcastic."

"I was not."

I sighed and pulled my hand out of the glove, massaging my pulsing temples. "Is there anything you can do?"

"Yes." Greg dinged like a microwave and a small crosshairs appeared on the screen in front of me.

I sucked my cheeks. "Thanks." As I moved my arms, each equipped with a launcher, the reticle split into two and they moved freely around the screen, giving me some idea of where I was shooting.

Not a second later, the cloud ceiling burst and the plane swept down and levelled out, coming in fast. It was sleek and wide, like a disk, with jets on either wing, and a pointed nose like a beak. Fins stuck up above and below, making it look like a flying shark zooming toward us. Something glowed on its belly and then minigun fire lit up the ground, charging us down in a line of exploding earth. I dived to the side and Greg kicked me in the ass with the thrusters. The world inverted as my heels flipped over my head and then turned the right way up again as I landed on one foot and one knee, grinding in the dirt. My head swung forward and stopped an inch or two from the screen, the harness choking me.

The plane peeled off the ground and took to the sky again. Mac raised his arms and yelled the words, "What the fuck was that?"

I ignored him, but shared the sentiment. "What the fuck was that?"

"The Federation Standard F-Series is equipped with dash-boosting. A burst of thrust to evade incoming fire," Greg stated, his voice sounding just a little tired of having to explain everything.

"A little fucking warning would be nice!"

"If I had not engaged them, we would have been, how do you say it, *toast.*"

"Are you making jokes?" I pulled us back up to our feet and headed back into the field, ready for the second round.

"Would you like me to reduce my humor settings?"

"We'll talk about it later," I grumbled, rubbing my cricked neck. I tightened the harness as much as it would go, but I still felt loose.

"A pilot's helmet is essential during combat, and is held via a suction vacuum to the headrest, in order to prevent neck injury. I would not recommend future engagements without one."

I was focused on the screen in front of me. The crosshairs waved gently as I kept the grenades trained on the spot where the plane had popped out last time.

"It's unlikely that it will strike from the same vector twice."

"If you don't have anything helpful to say, shut the fuck up," I grunted at Greg. He fell quiet and reserved himself to whatever it was that AIs do when they're not berating their pilots.

I could hear the jets rumbling somewhere above the cloud ceiling and I dragged in ragged breaths, trying to ignore my heartrate, which despite reading one thirty in my peripheral, felt like it was vibrating against my ribs. I tiled my feet into the cages and felt the thrusters push against the ground. "Alright, let's fucking do this," I muttered, trying to tune out the quiver in my voice. My fingers felt sweaty in the gloves, but there was no time for self-doubt now. If I let it in, it was going to get me killed. Not that I thought anyone had any confidence in me as it was.

I waited for the engine not to change as the plane swept around for its descent above, and then jammed my toes down and engaged the thrusters, leaping forward into a hard run. I needed to get close if I was going to have any chance of tagging it, and I hoped that a flat-out charge would be the last thing it would expect. I think it was the last thing anyone expected.

Mac yelled, "What the fuck are you doing?"

Greg asked, "Would you like to know the chances of success in a head-on engagement?"

The only thing that escaped my lips was a muffled, gargled noise that resembled the sound I'd heard a Gargax Hippo make once on a video I'd watched in bed while on Genesis, which seemed like a lifetime ago.

The plane popped into view, trailing cloud, and opened fire. I raised both arms, strafed right and then back left until I was right under it. The barrel of its gun swung wide and laid into the ground and I emptied my chambers into the air overhead as it flew by. The first nine and last six missed, but one, right in the middle, fizzed out of the barrel and exploded on the exposed underbelly in a shower of fire and shrapnel. The plane tilted and then spiraled, shedding half a wing and one of its tail fins. I covered my head instinctively and ground to a stop. The ground shuddered under the impact and the plane disintegrated and flipped, its nose digging into the meadow and pitting it over. Mac popped his head up from his hollow and waved at me, gesticulating in the distance. The air rippled next to me and Fish appeared, one of the long blades affixed to the forearms of his Panther protruding. He turned to look at me, and the blade retracted with a hiss, as though I'd taken down the plane a second before he was about to do the same. I sighed and gave him a thumbs up with the huge metal hand at my disposal. He didn't return it and instead sidled casually toward Mac, who was already high-tailing it toward the plane.

I jogged to catch up and boosted past Fish, leaping the last twenty meters or so and landing in a skip next to Mac. I reached up and popped the hatch, crouching as I did. It opened with a worn-out whine and I hauled myself out. Greg had fallen silent. Maybe he didn't like being wrong. Maybe he was calculating the odds of it.

I dropped to the ground and sprung forward next to Mac. He fired me a quick smirk, approaching the plane. "That was some fine shooting, kid." He stuck his bottom lip out. "Though the screaming was a little much. A little dramatic, maybe."

I shrugged, finally feeling my heart rate slow. "Eh, guess I just saw red."

He laughed. "Maybe there is some fight in you after all. Saw *red,* hah — and your middle name was, what, Alfred?" He paused for a second and stared at me.

I nodded.

"What do they call you, eh? Got a nickname? You survive long enough, you gotta have a nickname. Not going to be stuck calling you James the entire fucking day."

"Jim. My old work buddies used to call me Jim."

He chuckled and clapped me on the shoulder. "That's a terrible name. I think Red suits you much better." He waggled a finger at me. "People will think it's because your middle name is Alfred, but we'll know better. It's because you've got a hell of a temper… And because you yell like a girl."

I opened my mouth to respond, but he was already walking. Red. Huh, I guess it could work. So long as Mac didn't tell people the real reason. I sighed. I didn't really have the energy to argue. "What're you doing?" I asked after him as he approached the cockpit window, rifle raised.

"Gonna see if this fucker's still alive."

"And if he is?"

"Humph, then Fish and I are going to show you what being in the Federation's really like."

Fish appeared next to me, as was seemingly his way. He'd disembarked his T-Series, too, and stood watching Mac edge toward the window. He reached slowly down to his belt and pulled out a long, curved knife. He held it up in front of his eyes and ran his finger down the blade, checking that it was as sharp as it looked. He looked at it sinisterly as Mac opened the cockpit door and jammed the rifle in the face of the pilot.

Fish almost smiled, and his gills flickered. I wasn't sure I was liking where this was going.

He lowered the knife and walked toward Mac. I drew a hard breath, felt my heart kick up, and then followed.

# 19

I watched silently as Fish pushed the blade into the base of the Free pilot's skull, and then levered it upwards, severing his spinal cord with the sort of ease and precision that only comes from practice and repetition.

My blood ran cold and I turned away, taking only slight solace in the fact that Mac had cracked him hard enough in the head with his rifle that he'd been knocked unconscious.

"So interrogations are what being in the Federation is really like?" I asked, my voice strained as I tried to keep the vomit in my stomach.

Fish pulled the blade out and cleaned it on the guy's shoulder before putting it back into the sheath. He took no notice of my comment.

Mac sighed and came over, standing half in my face, half off, eyes hard and cold. "Dunno if you realize, kid, but this is war. We've been at war with the sons of bitches for centuries. Under different names on different planets. They're not an organized force, just bands of rebels and outcasts and criminals who wave the Free colors and think that makes their cause benevolent. All you've got to do is paint your fucking face and raise a middle finger to the Federation and you're one of them. They take every Federation life they can, when they can, however they can, just because. The only reason they're taking prisoners this time is because they need something to ransom and with all the shit that was on that carrier — well, it's something they think they can sell. Only, just like the Federation, they've got no intention of dealing. We call in backup, so do they. Federation come to deal, with no want to do so, and the Free don't, either. Blood's getting spilled either way. Either the Free take what's brought for ransom and then execute every last Federation soldier, or the Federation destroy the entire fucking planet. So, while you're quibbling over the life of someone who tried to tear you apart with a minigun not minutes ago, someone that would have happily watched you bleed out for their *cause,* you're saying that you'd rather us not have interrogated him, despite securing information that could save thousands of Federation lives?"

I gritted my teeth. "No... it's just... you didn't have to execute him like that," I sighed. "It's a little *cold-blooded,* don't you think?"

Fish perked up and narrowed his eyes at me, a low hiss escaping his lips. Mac motioned him down with his hands, eyes not leaving mine. "I think that was pretty fucking human. I told him from the start, didn't I, that it was going to hurt if he didn't give us what we wanted?"

I nodded, wondering how many hadn't given them what they wanted, and how many times it had to have 'hurt.' I touched my fingers to my head again and felt a wave of pain surge through my skull. Why did everything have to be pain? Why blood? Why war? I broke my gaze with Mac and stared down at the crash site. How many people had felt pain for no reason? How many innocent people had died? How many people that I'd known and lived with for the last four months? Meyers, Jonas, Saxon... Everett? Were they all dead? Wounded? Captured? I felt my fists close at my sides as anger welled in me, but I wasn't sure who I was angry at — myself, the Free, the Federation... all of them. None of them.

"And I could have," Mac went on. "Hell, I *have.* It's not my first go-round, and he could tell that. Which is why he talked. And because he obliged me, I gave him a quick and painless death, didn't I? So I'd say he got off pretty lightly, wouldn't you? Considering what he and his people have done to us already today, and intend to do in the next however many fucking years that'll follow this goddamn mess."

I swallowed. "Yes." I couldn't say otherwise, even if I didn't like it — which I didn't.

"You don't get it yet, Red, but you will." He half clapped me on the shoulder, half shoved me. "You'll be pulling fingernails with the rest of us in no time at all, just you watch."

He turned away and I watched him go to the plane to salvage what he could. I didn't know what scared me more — the fact that Mac and Fish could so easily take the life of a defenseless person, or that I didn't doubt in years to come, I'd be doing the same. I rammed the thought down and shook it off, approaching the open cockpit, ignoring the eyes of the dead man against the fuselage.

Mac stood up and turned to me, tossing a pistol my way. I caught it and stared down at the black slab of metal. It was cold and heavy. I swallowed. I'd never held a gun before — at least not a real one. I'd fired lots in virtual, and I'd fired them at lots of things, too. And I thought it'd be just the same. Point and click. But the idea of pulling the trigger and putting a bullet in someone seemed strange — wrong almost. Being in a mech was different. Removed. Like the simulations. I turned and stared at Greg's charred shell. It loomed like an obelisk, heavy and steel clad — a suit of armor to protect the pilot, and *shield* them not only from artillery and enemy fire, but from the reality of it all, too.

I swallowed and curled my fingers around the gun, looking up as Mac offered me two more things. In his left hand was a belt and holster for the pistol. In the right was a full-face pilot's helmet, domed and gray with camera lenses and visored sections across the front and a bulbous jawline. I looked from one to the other.

"Well?" Mac asked, jerking them at me.

I took the holster first, slotted the pistol into it and then took the helmet, staring into the dead lenses.

"It's frankly astonishing you've survived this far without one of these," he said, rapping on the helmet with his knuckles.

I tried to smile, to return his genuine one, given as an older brother might hand down an old porno mag, like he hadn't just interrogated someone and then ordered an amphibious assassin to push a knife into a man's brain. I put it on quickly so that I could let the smile go.

I slammed the helmet down and felt the foam squeeze around my head, seeing nothing but darkness. Mac reached over and flicked a switch behind my ear and everything burst to life in front of me. The Federation logo, a huge mech hand reaching out for a planet, burned in front of me and then faded. A message flashed up saying that there was no AI chip detected, and that I needed to insert one. The pilot must have pulled it before putting the helmet on. I doubted that a Federation AI would be very cooperative with a Free rebel at the controls of one of their ships. Mac gave me a thumbs' up. "You hear me in there?"

I nodded. "Yeah, I hear you."

"A pilot's helmet is his best friend, alright? It's not just protection, it's the difference between life and death." His face hardened. He was serious. I was getting a crash course in piloting, literally and metaphorically. "Get your shit together," he said, pointing at Greg. "We move out in thirty seconds, before this smoke attracts any unwanted attention."

I waited for him to turn away and then I slowly strapped the holster onto my thigh. My hands shook as I did. I clenched my fist to stop it, but it wouldn't. I was hungry, tired, bloodied, and more than anything I just wanted to go home.

All I'd ever dreamed of growing up on Genesis was getting off-world. Seeing another planet. Seeing *anything* other than red fucking dust and rocks, and I never thought in a million lifetimes I'd miss it. That I'd be thinking about my own bed in my hab, staring up at the ceiling plastered with photographs of other planets — of mountains, and seas, and lush forests, wishing I could see them. And now that I was here, standing on grass greener than I knew it could be, a hundred meters from forests I'd only imagined, with air cleaner than I'd ever breathed, I was craving the stale stench of Settlement Ninety-Three and the dry, choking, blinding red dust.

I sucked in a deep breath to calm my nerves and felt it whistle in through the helmet vents. The world looked shiny through the lens, distant almost. The camera produced a wider field of vision than my eyes could alone. My peripheral was wider, and the contrast pumped up to make things clearer — easier to pick out. Easier to shoot. It was almost like the simulations. Removal. Just that one step back from the real thing. Mac's words swam in my head. The difference between life and death. Maybe it'd be the difference between me pulling the trigger first and putting someone down before they did it to me. I couldn't say, and I didn't like thinking about it.

On autopilot I walked up to Greg's hunched form and climbed up and in. I slotted down into the seat and strapped myself in.

"You found a helmet," Greg said.

"Mac gave it to me," I muttered.

"I saw."

"So why'd you ask?" I asked flatly.

"My core programming indicates that humans find extraneous conversation soothing."

I stopped fiddling with the buckle and looked up. "Soothing? What am I, a baby?"

"I detect that your helmet has no AI chip installed. Would you like me to walk you through the installation process?" Greg started moving forward under his own steam, following Mac, who had already set off around the plane.

"What, so I can have you in my head as well?" I sighed. "No, I think I like the peace."

"It is much more than that. I'll be able to assist you with many things, including combat." He said it like he knew that was the part of this whole thing that was getting at me.

I didn't answer. Instead, I just pushed my hands into the gloves and slotted my feet into the cages, but didn't take control. Greg followed in silence, trundling after Mac. I resigned myself to thinking, distinctly aware of the pistol knocking against my thigh with every passing step.

# 20

When Mac sidled out of a copse of birch-like trees in his HAM, I was astonished I hadn't seen it earlier. From a distance it looked like a huge boulder, but upon standing up towered at over twenty feet tall, and almost as wide. The shoulders were thick and long, and it squatted like an ape, armed with a bank of launch tubes for small missiles. The arms were huge and armor plated, equipped with two mini guns that hung under the hands. I'd read about them, but seeing one in person was a lot more daunting. I could see why they were such a nightmare for the opposition. It was a moving fortress, and despite not being able to see it, I knew it had a rail cannon on its back that could punch a hole in a dropship from a thousand meters. Mac had looked like a spider climbing in, accessing the cockpit via a hatch between the legs, rather than on top like the other mech. The armor was just too thick to have a hatch on it, so instead he crawled up the ass.

"Could have used that thing when the fixed-wing came in," I sighed.

Mac's huge rig lumbered up the slope toward me, sidling from left to right as it hauled its massive bulk. "Well, I was on my way when it turned up."

I didn't answer. My head was pounding and we still had a ways to go yet. I couldn't get the images of the Free rebel being interrogated out of my head, or his execution. Fish had disappeared again, gone off to scout ahead supposedly. I still couldn't figure him. Mac said that I'd get a chip put in my head that would translate most languages, and that I shouldn't get too hung up on it. I wasn't looking forward to that — having something put into my head, and being linked up to the Federation mainframe. I knew they couldn't read my thoughts but I still didn't like the idea of having everything I said logged, translated, and broadcast.

The rebel had told us that patrols had been out scooping up all the Federation troops and machinery they could find, and were consolidating it at an outpost for transport back to their main base of operations. With only three of us — or two and a half, if you didn't count Fish as a part of our suicidal trio — which I didn't because he wasn't ever around for more than ten seconds — attacking that would be insanity. But taking down a gravilev transport en route to that base of operations — well, that was just crazy enough to work, and not crazy enough not to try. On the transport would be a crap load of munitions, mech, and of course soldiers. Maybe enough to take a run at base of operations, soften it up for the Federation's arrival. But the first problem was that there was no telling when it was coming. That, and that it was passing through a valley about five klicks each. And, on top of that, the HAM was a slow moving target, and with only me and Fish as backup, if a fixed-wing came upon us, or worse, a tiltwing or dropship, we'd be sitting ducks. HAMs usually rolled in with a fleet of House Cats around them, Specs and Aces, the aerial mechs overhead, and Panthers as backups. All he had for protection was a beaten up F-Series without a rifle. No wonder my head was splitting.

We came down off the ridge in silence, trudging toward the main crash site in the shadow of the trees. Fish popped up and told Mac that he'd found the valley, and a good vantage point to strike from. He also told me that there were some downed House Cats on the way, should I need to salvage anything. But by the time we got there, there was nothing left to salvage. They'd been picked clean, and apart from snagging a few emergency rations, being able to swap out some armor plating that had seen better days and grab a new auxiliary camera setup so Greg could finally do some targeting, there was nothing to collect. All the weaponry and other expensive components had been ripped out.

I moved on from the carcasses, wondering whether they'd had pilots in at the time they'd gone down, and if so where they were now. The hatches had all been opened — either pried or popped, and the cockpits were empty, but I still assumed the worst.

We moved like the dead, slow and quiet. Everyone was tired and it took us hours to reach Fish's vantage point, a rocky outcropping on the side of the valley, littered with trees big enough to hide Mac's walking castle. He disembarked quickly, as did Fish, eager to be in the open air. I didn't like it one bit. I'd never breathed it and it felt wrong. I liked the claustrophobia offered by the cockpit. It was like being back in my Blower, except for Greg. He was no Sally. I smiled, thinking about her for a second, wondering what had become of her. Was someone else sitting in her now, asking about previous owners? Staring at the word FUCK engraved on the seat and decoding it like I had done? Or had she just gone straight to the crusher? I guessed it was the latter, and that made me sad. Could AIs fear death? I stared at the darkening afternoon sky through the screen and almost asked Greg. I decided against it in the end. He was being quiet, and I needed it. I laid my head back against the headrest and felt the foam suck on it. It was a weird thing — when you pulled away gently, the helmet peeled away. When you jerked, it didn't. Something about a semi-porous smart material that did something with a vacuum. I'd stopped listening after the first few words. I hadn't even asked, but it was something that Greg thought I should know.

I'd gorged myself on the emergency rations pulled out of the downed fixed-wing and with something in my stomach, I could feel sleep coming for me with ragged claws. I didn't resist, and the next thing I knew, Greg had fired up the interior screen and was calling my name. It was time.

I SHOOK off the remnants of sleep and looked up.

"James, it's time."

I swallowed and sucked in a few deep breaths. I'd dreamed of nothing. Just a dark hole that I was in where no light and no sound could reach. It was paradise. Now, it was nothing but noise. Mac's gears whirring as he started up. Greg's voice explaining what was going on. My own heart hammering in my head. I didn't think I'd ever been in a worse mood.

"Are you ready?" Greg asked.

"How about some music?" I sighed.

"Music?"

"Yeah, you know. Singing. Guitars. Drums. Heartbreak. Melancholy. Music."

"I know what music is," he replied.

"So play some."

"What would you like to hear?"

"Got any Steppenwolf?"

"Searching."

I cracked my neck and pushed my hands into the gloves, flexing. My feet planted in the cages and I flexed them, feeling Greg shiver to full height. The music kicked up and we started forward. I did all that I could to push the thoughts of what was to come out of my head, but as I stood on the ridge, staring at the glowing lights in the distance that were quickly approaching, there was no escaping it.

The gravilev transport was a series of cars that utilized electromagnetic repulsion to stay above the ground, hovering over terrain and flying across the landscape. The repulsors were powered by a core in the front car. If we could take that out, we could derail it. Then it was just a case of getting down there and fucking some shit up. Though I felt like when Mac said that, he was being hyperbolic. There was no way to tell how many Free troops were down there, or what sort of firepower they'd be packing. All I knew was that I had no grenades, no rifle, and my hull integrity was hovering dangerously close to a point where I could see the ground beneath my feet. I was hoping for one of two things: either that there was a fresh suit

I could don, or that the armaments they were packing would be light enough not to tear me apart. I didn't feel very confident about either.

The transport approached and I heard Mac square up next to me. He leaned down to the ground and planted his knuckles like a gorilla. In a smooth motion, he lowered his head and his back began to split apart, the armor plates rolling over each other.

"What are you doing?" I asked.

"That lead car's got armor thicker than most Federation Destroyers. A Gravilev Core isn't exactly stable, so it'll be well protected. If we fire normal ordnance, it's just going to piss them off. We're looking to put them down, right?" he said, not really meaning it as a question.

"I guess so," I replied sullenly, turning back to the valley. But what about the other cars? The equipment, the troops? What if he missed and hit a car full of munitions and vaporized the entire thing? They were all questions that I wanted to ask, but knew would be met with no more than a cursory brush-off. Instead I sighed and watched.

In my peripheral, I saw the barrel extend, two-pronged, over the back of his head, and aim into the deep gouge in the landscape. A fizzing filled the air and the hair stood up on the back of my neck.

Greg piped up. "I would recommend moving away from Pilot MacAlister. A rail pulse can be quite bright."

I did so, turning my back on it. But, even still, when it popped, I felt my eyes sting. It sounded like metal being struck and after the whiteness faded, I stared down into the valley at the fireball below.

The transport, hurtling along like a huge black eel, had a hole punched right through the front car. The nose dove into the earth and the front car pitted, ripping itself free of the rest. It somersaulted into the air and then impacted, exploding in a huge plume of flame.

The other cars sank and ground to a halt, buckling and kinking. The noise echoed in the cool evening air, ringing against the exposed rock of the valley sides.

"I believe that's our cue," Greg said quietly.

I clenched my fists to stop them shaking, and let the music sweep me up. We pushed down off the side, stomping toward the carnage with a heavy gait, watching as Free troops poured out of the transport like ants.

I got my heels down and broke into a run on the flat. Something flashed to my right and Fish blinked into existence on my flank, already firing off shots from his wrist-mounted rifles. Free ground troops sagged and sank with every flash from the muzzle. He made it look so easy.

All around us, missiles ripped through the air, plunging into the ground in dark eruptions of earth and blood. Ground troops fired on the move, trying to outrun the missiles. They couldn't.

Bullets pinged off my hull, but I kept moving. I couldn't stop. Greg wouldn't let me. My legs pumped on their own, my arms held up to protect the camera dome — the most important thing.

The targeting system was in overdrive. Infrared was spliced with normal vision and enemy troops, clad in a mish-mash of military gear, flashed in white against the dark rocks, crosshairs locked on them, following as they streaked across the screen.

"Would you like me to provide enhanced combat assist?" Greg asked dryly. "You're not utilizing our full capabilities."

I gritted my teeth. I knew I wasn't, and I wasn't keen to. Killing in virtual was basically like playing a glorified videogame. But without any guns, my first real kill would have to be *by hand.* And I knew that, helmet or not, mech suit or not, doing that wouldn't feel removed. It was going to feel real, and there was no shying away from it. I had no idea who these guys were, but they were out here fighting for something they believed in, just like we were. Only I wasn't sure if I believed as hard as they did.

My heart was pumping, mind racing, but this was it. I was running hard and in seconds I was going to be on them. If we lost, then everyone would die. They wouldn't let this stand. We had to win, and that meant killing them. Every last one.

"Yes," I said sourly.

"Combat assist engaged," Greg said, almost a little pleased. It made me feel sick. But I didn't have any time to dwell on it before he blasted the thrusters and sent us flying.

We skipped into the air and soared toward the incoming troops, their small-caliber weapons pinging off the hull like hail. We landed with a crash, took two steps, and then lashed out. A Free rebel with a scarf covering his face flashed on the screen for an instant before our right arm lashed out. I couldn't tell if it was Greg, or me, or a combination, but either way, I watched in slow motion as the steel fist shot forward, connected with the face and chest of the soldier, and sent him flying backward in a crushed heap. He flipped through the air and bounced twenty-five feet away, tumbling backward like a ragdoll. The reticle disappeared from around him and honed in on another.

Greg turned me away so I couldn't look anymore, but I didn't need to see. He was dead, and that was all there was to it. A life snuffed out in an instant. My first. It felt weird. It felt empty, and cold. It felt like it was going to stay with me forever, but it didn't, because it got mixed in with a wave of them. A wave of crunching bones, flashing fists, broken screams and fountains of blood. Fish twirled like a dancer, blades flashing, limbs arcing through the darkening sky.

It was all a blur of bodies and punches, and kicks, and spines snapping under my feet as we tore through them. I felt like closing my eyes, but I couldn't. I couldn't shy away. It was in me now. The feeling. The dread. The weight of them all, and I knew that it would mount, and keep mounting, that this was who I was now. This was my life and there was no turning away from it, not anymore.

Something flashed on my screen and Greg whipped us round so fast that the seal on my helmet pulled like splitting velcro, holding me in place. A flash of gladness filled me and then dissipated as we made the full rotation to face the F-Series that had crawled out of the woodwork. The grenade it'd fired on me landed behind me and exploded. I didn't look back. Greg kept me honed in on the advancing House Cat, giving me all the information I could want — and more, including the heart rate of the pilot. It was fast. Adrenaline surging. Fear riding high. I knew the feeling.

Greg put three paths up on the screen, all arcing white lines leading to the F-Series. One high, one low, one wide. I narrowed my eyes, seeing it reach for its Samson Auto, and kicked my feet down.

We crouched, and then took off, low, dashing forward. By the time the Samson came over, we were on him. I wound up a punch and slung it low into its guts. It staggered backwards, steel scraping on steel, and stumbled. I went at it again, this time with a left. It countered and threw its elbow down, knocking my hand to the ground. I had my shoulder to it and lurched sideways in the seat, throwing my arms around like a hammer. It caught him in the hip and he twisted away. Greg boosted us into the air and we twisted, landing on its back. The hydraulics whined and groaned under the added weight and it went to a knee. Greg's feed deconstructed the hull in front of me, showing me the weak spots — where to strike. I reached down and sank my fingers into the gap between two plates. I levered one up and it popped — they were designed like that — cheaper, easier to fix — easier to fuck up. Wires swam beneath in a tangled mess. It didn't matter which I pulled; Greg's flashing head-up display told me they were all vital. I took a fist full and ripped them out in a shower of sparks.

It stopped struggling beneath me and folded down to the ground, the motors buzzing to a halt.

"It appears you have shorted the electrical system," Greg announced. "I would recommend finishing him off as quickly as you can. Pilots MacAlister and Sesstis still need assistance."

"Who?" I asked, sidling around the downed House Cat and reaching for its Samson.

"Pilot Inglock Sesstis. I believe you called him 'Fish.'"

I pulled it up to my shoulder and cocked it, tearing the belt from the shell of the F-Series. "What the hell kind of name is that?"

"It's not an uncommon name on the Eshellite homeworld," he announced. "Would you like me to show you the hull's weak spots?"

"Huh?" As I asked, he scanned the House Cat keeled over in front of me and showed off the pilot inside, trying desperately to open the hatch. I could hear the muffled audio coming through, too. Grunts and yells of anger and terror. Greg put a red crosshairs just below the hatch seal for me. "Firing repeatedly at this spot will penetrate the hull and eliminate the target."

"You're serious?" I was happy with putting it out of commission. The pilot wasn't going anywhere. And they obviously weren't very skilled at the hands of a mech, that was for sure. Though I doubted anyone had as rigorous a process as the Federation did when it came to pilot training.

"Yes. Any persons discovered to be in open support of the Free cause must be condemned to death."

"I'm not going to *murder* someone," I said flatly. "Free or not." They could be like me — young, dragged into a war they didn't want to fight, told to kill or die without another option on the table.

"You have killed eight people today already," Greg retorted, trying to raise my arm.

"Who were shooting at me." I forced it back down. Fire was speckling my hull, but it didn't matter. It was small arms, not enough to do any damage.

"This pilot was shooting at you."

"*Was.* He *was* shooting at me, but I don't see him shooting anymore." My teeth were gritted now as I fought the arm.

"It is our duty. Our mandate. If we do not comply, we are in direct violation of orders. This is not something I can allow, Pilot Maddox." Greg had reverted to full Federation bitch all of a sudden.

"I'm not just going to shoot someone in cold blood!"

But even as I said it, he rode the arm higher. I could tell I wasn't going to win the fight. If anything I thought he was just being polite. The pilots had control only because the AI allowed it. What AIs couldn't do was make judgment calls. They couldn't decide based on how things looked or *felt.* It was all cold hard numbers. Ones and zeroes. And this was why their default setting was to give pilots full control, except when it violated a direct mandate, apparently.

There was no use fighting it, so I went with it. I moved my hand quickly and rifle shot upward. Greg pulled the trigger, aiming for the weak spot, but instead rounds glanced off the hull and then into the air as my arm pointed skyward.

"That was not following protocol, Pilot Maddox."

"Yeah, well, I'm not really a pilot, so screw your protocol," I snarled. In front of me, the pulsing white figure of the pilot had frozen, hands pressed against the hatch, heart hammering like a drum. I kept our arm up but Greg didn't seem to care. He walked us forward and reached out for the hatch with our other hand. I watched uselessly as his hand closed around it and yanked upwards.

It happened before we could react. The hatch flew open and the pilot leapt out. In one movement, a blond girl planted her foot on the hatch rim and fired three shots square into our camera dome. The infrared had shown her, but not the gun in her hand. I swore in shock. Despite the shots actually going a few feet high of my actual head, the screen blacked out for a second and then reeled as the camera dome swiveled to protect the lens. Greg stumbled backward and I winced from the shock of the flash.

The camera feed died in front of me and flickered, strobing black and white. "Pilot Maddox," Greg said quickly. "You must comply with protocol."

Without another word the hatch popped open and the dying sun streamed in. I was exposed to the world, and I had no choice but to get the hell out. I unbuckled my harness as Greg sank to his knees and then onto his hands, and I spilled out of the cockpit, rolling on the blood splattered grass.

I could see the blonde ahead, streaking back toward the transport. I reached for my pistol and went after her.

# 21

She was hauling ass.

She was near my height and built like a gazelle. I didn't know if I was out of shape, or if she was more than human, but she was moving like a freight train, long legs hammering like pistons.

She pulled ahead, behind the Free line that was still marching forward, laying down fire, trying to shoot the invisible menace that was hacking them apart and the huge mech on the slope that was shelling them with mortar. They were too preoccupied to bother with me.

My pistol clacked in my hand as I ran, knees pumping. I was out of breath already trying to keep up, and she wasn't slowing down. I could barely breathe in the helmet, so I pulled it off, hearing it land somewhere behind me. It was better, but I was still outclassed.

When she reached the transport, she stopped and turned on her heel, her battered military fatigues flapping around her, and fired at me.

I hit the dirt and rolled sideways, watching as spurts of earth shot into the air inches from my flank. The fire stopped as she hit empty and I looked up. She gritted her teeth, eyes dark with makeup, and tossed the pistol away. She looked left and right, but the transport had buckled around her and there was no way through. I could see that a flatbed section toward the back had been carrying the F-Series, the tarp that was covering it flapping in the evening breeze. But she'd run right into a dead-end formed by three solid cars instead. She stopped at one side and then dashed to the other, realizing she was trapped. She swore loudly enough that it carried over the gunfire, and turned to face me as I approached, catching my breath. I raised my gun and stopped twenty feet short. It waved gently in the air. She wasn't moving now.

She stared me down with a look that could kill and then curled her lips into an ugly grimace. She held her hands out. "Well, come on then, you fucking Gray-Skin. Do it."

I walked slowly forward until even my shaking hand wouldn't let her leave the crosshairs. "Turn around," I muttered. I didn't know whether shooting her in the back would be easier, but I didn't think I'd be able to put a bullet in her staring at me like that.

"I'd rather see it coming," she spat.

My jaw locked and my finger quivered. She saw it.

"How old are you?" she asked, narrowing her eyes.

"Shut up," I said, jabbing the gun at her. She didn't look much older than me, if any, but I wasn't going to answer.

"How long have you been in the Federation?" She cocked her head and I swallowed. Her golden hair spilled onto her shoulder and down, exposing her high cheekbones, angular jaw, and a spattering of scars across her naked cheek. "Do you even know what planet this is?"

"On your knees," I commanded, feeling like I should say something if I wasn't going to shoot her.

"Did you volunteer, or were you conscripted?" She raised an eyebrow now, lowering her hands. "They picked you up, didn't they — from some mining colony or—"

"Terraforming," I said quietly, not lowering the gun. I didn't know if the nerve would ever come to shoot her, or if she was just going to bolt and I'd watch her go. I think she was just waiting to see if she was going to risk it. Maybe looking for her own nerve.

She smirked, pulling her lips onto the marked cheek. A dimple formed there. I ground my teeth, trying to keep the gun steady.

"They picked me up from Nordos-8 when I was eighteen. Put me in gee-tees, shoved a gun in my hand and tossed me into the nearest warzone." She shook her head and kicked at the earth. "Caught some shrapnel," she said, turning her head away and running her fingers down her neck, scarred like her cheek. "And as I lay there dying, bleeding out, everyone moved over me. I was calling out to them. Help. Help." She stepped forward and I watched her drag her fingers delicately over the purple ridges of scar tissue on her otherwise smooth skin. "But no one would. They were all just borrowing seconds until they caught a bullet or shell. I'd gone down quickly, and no one was going to risk stopping to help. I wasn't worth it." She stepped forward again. "But I didn't die. When I opened my eyes, the sky was filled with ash, and everyone was dead. I caught a glimpse of a dropship peeling away from the atmosphere. They didn't care whether I was alive or dead — where I was. I was expendable mass with no other purpose than to eat a bullet." She laughed, shaking her head, edging closer. "And if you think that you're any different, then you're a fucking idiot." She stopped and looked up, her eyes blue in the halflight, popping from the black smeared around them. "I walked that battlefield for days. I found a survivor, and then another, and then another. And we stayed together, driven by how much we hated the Federation and everything they stood for. It didn't take us long to find others like us." Her fingers closed around the pistol, gently, softly. I watched them. "And it didn't take us long to find the Free. Thousands of us. Millions. All across the galaxy, fighting for freedom from the chains of the Federation. What's your name?" She was close enough to smell now. Sweat and something sweeter, mixed in the most enchanting cocktail I'd ever smelt.

"James," I whispered.

"Is this your war, James?" Her voice was like honey.

I swallowed and shook my head.

"Then come with me. Help us. Join our fight — the one that really matters. You're on the wrong side, James." Her hand moved so quickly I barely saw it. It came up like a blade and hit me square in the throat. I gasped and threw my hands to it reflexively. She took the pistol with ease and then my vision strobed black, an intense heat emanating from my temple. Pain blinded me and I went to a knee, catching sight of the girl raising the butt of the pistol away from the strike. She'd hit me — twice. My chest clamped shut and I crumpled, registering only the cool touch of the muzzle against my forehead.

"Look at me," she said coldly, pushing the barrel into my skin. "Look me in the eyes."

I obliged.

"You're a goddamn kid. The Federation will take that from you if you let them. Get out while you can. I'm giving you a chance, but you'll only get one." She lowered the pistol and I choked on my own breath, my head spinning, a thin line of blood running down my face. In a swift motion, she swept her arm up across her body, and then slammed the butt into my cheek. The pain blinded me and I sprawled sideways, clutching my face, listening as her footsteps faded away. By the time I raked together the strength to look up, she was already gone.

I scrambled slowly to my knees and turned toward the battle, suddenly aware that the gunfire had stopped. Mac and Fish were walking slowly between the bodies sprawled on the ground. They left no survivors.

I struggled to my feet, rubbing my throat and touching my fingers to my head. I was sort of sick of getting hit in the face. I stared around but there was no sight of her. I loped, sucking in thin lungfuls of air, for the next break in the carriages. They were at uneven angles with space enough to vault the couplings and squeeze through. It's the way I would have gone. She obviously hadn't headed back toward Mac and Fish or they would have shredded her already.

No, she was smart — smart enough to take one look at me and know I wouldn't pull the trigger. Smart enough to take one look at the graveyard behind me and not run headlong into it. She'd fled. Lived to fight another day. And I'd let her. I'd let her get close and disarm me, and I should have been dead for it. It wasn't because she took pity on me, on how pathetic I was. Or maybe it was affinity. Maybe she saw herself in me and spared me because she thought I'd come around — turn on Mac and Fish and join their cause. But she'd hit me then, and not taken me with her. I clenched my jaw thinking about it. Would I have gone? No I couldn't just leave... couldn't abandon Alice and the others. Mac. Fish. Everett if she was out there. It wouldn't be right. But then again, would they think the same? Would they leave me if they had the chance? I didn't have an answer. At least not one I was sure about.

I jumped the linkage and landed on the other side, surrounded by untouched meadow, the sun setting over the hills in the distance. Everything was calm. Quiet. And there was no sign of the girl. The grass stretched on for maybe two hundred meters, but then turned into a dense wall of trees that led up the valley side. I looked at it, turning left and right, but there was no sign of her, and I had no idea which way she'd gone. If there was a Free base here, she knew the terrain, and she'd have the upper hand. If I went after her, I'd get myself lost, or ambushed. I waited to see whether I'd glimpse her, but everything was still. The way she moved, she'd have a huge head start anyway. Even if I set off in the right direction, I'd never close the gap. She was in the wind, and that was all there was to it. I sighed and rested my hands on my knees. "Goddammit."

My breath settled and my throat loosened after a few seconds and I stood up, pricking my ears. Something was banging. A dull metal clang. I turned back and headed toward the transport. Something was definitely banging.

I rested my hand on one of the trailers and listened. It was moving, vibrating with each thud. Shit, the soldiers. They were being transported, too. They must be inside.

I rushed back around to Greg and climbed in. "Did you kill her?" he asked.

I swallowed and strapped in. "Yes."

He was silent for a few seconds. I didn't know if he was reading my vitals, analyzing my speech pattern, or just plain reading my mind. Either way, it felt like he knew I was lying and was deciding what to do with it. After an age, he said, "Good," and closed the hatch. The screen flickered to life, having settled after being shot, and we moved forward, picking our way around the front car to the far side.

We reached the troop transport carriage, threading between the littered corpses, and headed for the shutter on the side. It was locked with a keypad that I asked if Greg could hack, but he told me it would be more effective just to shoot it out to prevent a possible distress signal being sent out and then rip the shutter up. I relented and levelled the rifle, putting two rounds into the keypad before going for the handle. It warped in my hand and I wrenched it upward, snapping the bolts holding it in place. It rose, flapping into a roll at the top like a window blind, and unveiled a carriage full of soldiers wearing Federation Gray. They stared wide-eyed at Greg for a second before shuffling toward the edge.

"Come on," I called, motioning them out and taking a couple of steps back.

They filtered out, covering their eyes against the sinking sun. Some jumped down, others climbed. Some had to be helped and were limping, bandaged, bloodied, or barely standing. I scanned the faces as they oozed out, hungry and tired, looking for any sign of Alice. "Greg, can you see her?"

"I'm scanning the faces for facial recognition, but I cannot see her yet."

"Can you do biometrics, too? Every pilot is coded into the system, right?" I could barely keep the strain out of my voice. I'd managed to push her out of my mind while everything was going on, clinging to the idea that she was alive, and just captured. But now that we'd freed the captured prisoners, she'd have to be here. If she wasn't, what did that mean? It would have to mean that she was either still out there, or dead. The way I figured it there was very little chance of it being the former. I swallowed hard and kept looking, my eyes aching I was straining them so hard. "Anything?"

"It is difficult as facial recognition is only accurate on full facial input. While everyone is moving it is—"

"I didn't ask for an explanation," I snapped. "Just find her."

"I'm trying."

"Wait—" I narrowed my eyes leaning out of my seat. "Is that her?"

"Where?"

"Alice!" I yelled.

She looked up, about three deep in the crowd. The side of her face was bruised below the bandage that had been wrapped around her forehead, and she was limping a little, but otherwise, she looked okay. She stared at Greg, a look of confusion on her face. She got to the edge and looked right at me. I was grinning, and it took a second for me to realize why she wasn't, too. She couldn't see me. Couldn't tell it was me.

I reached up and popped the hatch just as she started to let herself down, accommodating what had to be an injured knee.

I hauled myself out of the cockpit and Greg crouched for me. Our boots hit the ground at the same time. She stumbled, and I caught her.

She looked up, confusion and surprise coloring her face in equal parts. "Maddox?"

My smiled broadened. Even I was surprised how glad I was to see her. "Alice," I panted, out of breath for no reason. "I'm so glad you're okay."

I felt her arms on my shoulders as she pulled herself upright, but I didn't feel them leave. "I thought you were dead," she said, her voice hoarse.

I laughed a little, looking away from her pale green eyes, glittering in the twilight. "That makes two of us."

"What happened?" She shook her head. "I don't remember... Just snippets. I was coming to see you," she started, screwing her face up, "and then I remember... Fire? Was there fire?"

I nodded, my throat tight again. "Yeah, there was."

"And I was in an F-Series when I woke up. Did you...? I've got this flash of your face," she muttered, holding her hand in front of her nose, "staring down at me. And then nothing. I was waking up and they were cutting me out of it on the surface."

"It's okay," I sighed and nodded. "You're okay, and that's the important thing."

"Did you save my life?" she asked, tilting her head to look up into my eyes.

I didn't know what to say. I had, but I felt bashful all of a sudden. "Yeah," I mumbled. "Something like that."

She opened her mouth and was about to say something else when she stopped, smiled instead, and just said, "Thanks." Her arms closed around my neck and she hugged me.

I returned it and felt her press against me. I rested my chin on her shoulder and closed my eyes. "I'm happy you're okay."

She released me but kept one hand on my shoulder, putting some weight on it. "Me too, though they weren't exactly gentle. But we don't have time for that. What's going on? We heard the gunfire, the artillery. Is it a battalion, or just a squad of survivors? And how the hell did you fall in with them? And what the hell's that?" She gestured at Greg. "And what the hell happened to it?" It was still charred and beaten up. "What, are you a pilot now?"

"I just sort of... fell into it?" I shrugged, looking at Greg. "Like you, I came to, but I was in a forest, alone. I got out, and then ran into these two pilots, Mac and Fish—"

"Fish?"

"Yeah." I waved it off. "He's an Eshellite — it's weird. Anyway, we got ourselves together, managed to find a Free rebel, he told us about the transport, and..."

"Wait, there's only three of you? And you just *found* a Free rebel?" She cocked an eyebrow.

I laughed nervously. I was trying to play it down. It was pretty insane thinking about it. "Well, yeah, okay, so we *shot* him down. He was in a fixed-wing. I tagged him with a grenade, and..." I guided my hand to an imaginary floor. "Mac and Fish had a talk with him, and here we are."

"And you just thought it was a good idea to attack a transport, the three of you? Why didn't you wait for backup, or—"

"Because backup isn't coming to free the prisoners. Mac said that they'll try and ransom them back to the Federation, but that the Federation won't cut a deal. If they know there's a Free BOA here, they'll wipe it out, killing them all, Federation soldiers included," I said quietly, so none of the other ambling bodies would hear.

She swallowed, her expression hardening. "No, they won't." She looked down and swore, hopping a little on her good leg. "I didn't understand it then, but now it makes sense. Before we were put on the transport I heard two of them talking, saying how everything's crazy back at base because everyone's scrambling to get off planet ASAP. The Free forces are jumping ship. I couldn't figure why then, but it makes sense now. If this *Mac* thinks that the Federation will just try to destroy the base, then the Free probably do, too. So—"

"So they're baiting them. They're putting the Federation soldiers in the base and then getting the hell out..." The words died in my mouth. "So the Federation will kill thousands of their own troops, but no Free. Jesus Christ."

Alice looked grave. "Yeah, but what can we do?"

I clenched my jaw and sucked in a hard breath. "We can stop it."

# 22

"You want to do what now?" Mac's mouth hung open like the lid of a dumpster.

Alice's skin danced yellow and brown in the firelight, the sparks shooting into the evening sky. The sap-heavy wood was spitting and crackling, the flames licking at the cool air. Bugs circled in it. I watched them, waiting for Alice to expand on her plan.

She rubbed her head, her eyes moving to me before they went back to Mac. We were near ten kilometers from where the transport had gone down, deep in the forest in some foothills. All around us, other campfires crackled. We'd held off as long as we could, but no Free ships were circling and the temperature was dropping with every passing minute. The day had dragged on for a long time — longer than our normal circadian rhythms dictated. Most of the soldiers, almost a hundred strong, were sleeping, curled up around their meager camps, huddled together like children.

I looked at my hands and watched them curl into fists. "We have to."

Alice nodded. "He's right. If we don't, they're all going to die. You said yourself that the Federation are just going to lay waste to the entire base."

"Which is exactly why we should be going the other fucking way!" Mac scoffed, pointing into the trees.

He and Alice had been at loggerheads from the moment they'd met. Like two apex predators who suddenly had to share hunting territory. Alice sucked on her cheek, her knuckles white around her knee. "Well, I'm going." She shook her head and stood up. "You do what you want. You're the one that's going to have to live with yourself."

She stormed off, disappearing between the trees. Mac watched her go, and then turned to me, sighing. "You fucking rehearse that or is it just the line they're teaching in the Academy these days?"

I shrugged and shook my head, pushing off the log I was sitting on to go after Alice. I could hear Mac swearing to Fish behind me, who'd been his usual stoic self the entire time.

I blocked it out, trying to figure out what I was going to say. Alice was up ahead on a little rise, bathed in the moonlight streaming in between the trees. I felt my chest tighten as I approached. I couldn't call what was going to happen next. I'd cared about Alice — everything else had just been a line. I couldn't have given two shits about the Federation, in all honesty. I was just trying to survive, and for some reason, I'd gotten it into my head that that would be a damn sight easier with Alice, and a damn sight less horrible when it happened. Now, it just seemed idiotic to rush headlong back into a fight when I had everything I was looking for already.

I stepped up next to her and looked out at the trees, glittering silver in the shine of the moons that hung overhead, one near and one far, both glowing a pale blue. "Beautiful, isn't it?" I asked stupidly, immediately regretting having done so.

She tsked and folded her arms, kicking at a rock on the bank. "It's bullshit is what it is. They don't have any goddamn honor."

I nodded, laughing nervously. "Yeah, I know, right? I had to threaten them with reporting desertion to get them to help at all."

She turned to me and scowled. "That's even worse. You shouldn't have to *threaten* anybody. They should all want to fight for their lives, and for the lives of the others, and for everything that the Federation stands for."

"Which is?" I turned, asking quietly. "I grew up on a tiny spit of a dustball in the middle of nowhere." I sighed. "Reared parentless and raised to work my entire life, never seeing the fruits of my labor. Probably dying in the same spot I'd lived in for eighty years. The Federation did that — gave me a life just to take it away. And there are so many others like me — who've given, and given, and given, and never got anything back." The blonde flashed in my mind and my voice softened and broke a little. "So I don't blame them. It's easy for you, because you've got something to fight for, that thing inside you that makes it all make sense. But most of them don't. We're all out here, borrowing time for no reason."

She turned and stared at me in silence for a few seconds, her mouth twitching at the corners. I couldn't tell if it was curling up or down. "So why come at all? If they were ready to run, why did you come back? Why convince them to come back?"

I looked down and exhaled slowly. "I wanted to... I didn't know if you were alive, and I had to know. It started off heroically, and for a second, I thought *yeah, maybe I can do this.* Be a soldier. Be a pilot, you know? But it wasn't noble or brave. It was hard, and it was cruel, and I don't know if it's something I'm cut out for." I still couldn't meet her eyes.

"So you came all this way," she said, her voice hard and cold, "and now that you've got a taste of blood in your mouth, you're shying away?"

I looked up. "No. That's not what I'm saying."

"Then explain."

"I don't want to kill people for no reason."

She scoffed. "It's not for *no reason.*"

Somehow it'd turned into an argument. "There doesn't seem like a good one flying around to me. Unless I'm missing something obvious."

"You are." Her eyes narrowed. "We're fighting for order, for stability. For peace."

"And they're fighting for freedom." I could feel my blood rising. "They're fighting for something they *believe* in. They don't want to be under the boot of the Federation. And they don't have another option. It's roll over, or it's fight back. Because the Federation aren't giving a goddamn inch, and they're not fucking asking, are they?"

She was seething. "You sound just like them."

"Can you blame me?" My voice sounded incredulous in my ears and I couldn't stop it. Everything I'd ever thought about her was spilling out and I couldn't stop it. "It's been easy for you. Growing up on the ship, with a family, with friends, with prospects. You don't get it because you've never felt the weight of their oppression crushing you. Crushing the life out of you. You've never felt *owned,* have you?"

Her fists curled at her sides. "I grew up a prisoner, just like you. You think I had any choices? Huh? You think I could just *go off* and do what I pleased? No. My death warrant was signed the second I was born, just like you. And it hasn't been easy, like you said — it's been a damn fight. I've had nothing handed to me. I worked my ass off, and have for as long as I can remember. I haven't ever had another option. It's been this or exile, so don't you try to fucking tell me that I've never felt the weight of that chain around my neck, because I do. I have, every single day since I was born." She was shaking, her eyes glittering, jaw quivering.

The anger flooded out of me and drained away all of a sudden. I took a slow breath and met her gaze. "Then what the fuck are we arguing about?"

She grimaced and shook her head, turning away to face the moon again. "We're arguing about whether or not you're going to let thousands of innocent soldiers, just like me and you, who haven't asked for this, and don't deserve this" — she took a deep breath and then sighed — "die."

I bit my lip.

"Because if we do nothing, they will die. And if we run, then they will die. The only way they might not is if we do *something.* If we get in there, and we free them. If there's an armada incoming, they're going to run their scans, find that there are thousands of bodies inside the base, assume they're Free rebels, and they're going to obliterate the entire thing. And a call from us isn't going to do shit. So our only option is to get them out." She nodded, confirming her plan.

I looked at her, a little enamored. All I was thinking about was running. She was thinking about everyone else. "Alright." I said it without thinking but I didn't regret it.

"Alright?" Her features softened in the moonlight.

"Let's save them." I watched her, my eyes tracing the lines of her face in the halflight. I watched them morph, slowly, into a smile, and then she nodded.

"Okay."

WE MOVED out at first light. When we got back to the fire, Mac was tossing twigs into it, a scowl carved into his face. He'd looked up and upon seeing the determined half smile on Alice's face, sighed and rubbed the bridge of his nose. He beckoned hyperbolically. "Come on then, lay it on me."

Alice took her spot across the fire from him, holding back a smirk. "Lay what on you?" she asked airily.

"The rousing speech to get me to want to lay down my life for the Federation."

She laughed a little. "There's no speech, MacAlister. It's your choice. I'm not forcing you, but Maddox and I are going, and we're taking everyone who wants to come with us, because if we don't thousands of people are going to die."

"You and Red?" He raised an eyebrow, gesturing to me.

She cast me a quick glance. "Red?"

I shook my head. "Don't ask."

She squinted at me for a second and then back to Mac. "Yeah, me and *Red*... We're going to try."

"And all you'll succeed in doing is dying as well." He snapped the twig he was holding and hurled it into the flames in a shower of sparks. I watched intently as they dueled. She wasn't about to back down and I didn't think Mac had the intelligence or the stamina to outwit or beat her.

"Maybe. We could die, sure. We could die right here, right now. The Free could hit us with an orbital strike as we talk."

I watched a couple of soldiers around the nearby fires, who were listening in, cast their eyes upward. I smirked a little.

"Or," she went on, "we could die in our sleep as a fleet of mech roll through, burning the forest to cinders. Or we could die making a run for it, fleeing to try to save our own skins. Or we could make it out, get caught by the Federation, and then be executed for desertion. Or we could die trying to save a thousand lives. We all die, MacAlister. It just boils down to how you want to go. Doing something that matters, or not."

He chewed his cheek, looking from me to Alice and back. I shrugged at him and he swore. "For fuck sake," he muttered, shaking his head at himself. "Alright then, let's hear this master plan of yours. Not like I've never gone to sleep thinking I'm dying the next morning, anyway."

She grinned, leaning forward. I did too. "Alright," she said. "The BOA is a little way away, over the next rise, not far. I overheard some of the Free rebels talking about it, and we haven't seen any ships take off yet. That means that they're getting everything together for a mass exodus."

"You can't know that," Mac cut in.

"Look, I do a lot of studying, alright? I've been reading recounts of the Free war since I was old enough to hold a book, and my dad used to read them to me before that—"

"You can't learn everything from books—"

"But you can learn a *lot.*"

I stayed quiet. I'd been cramming as much as I could for the tests and classes, but four months of work can't compare to a lifetime of acquired knowledge. I didn't know shit about the Federation military before I was conscripted, and it seemed now like I still didn't know shit, not compared to Alice and a seasoned pilot.

She continued. "And your assumption that the Federation

wouldn't come to bargain was based on what you knew. And my assumption that the Free are going to get off world all at the same time is based on what I know." She sat back a little and narrowed her eyes, thinking about her words before she said them. "The Federation will have pulled in ships from all over the galaxy ahead of sending their destroyers, which are no doubt en route. If there are some smaller Federation vessels up there, they're patrolling near-space, waiting for the big boys to arrive. The Free aren't going to send a single ship up on its own. It'd get torn apart by whatever's roving. Class two or three attack ships, maybe a couple of bombers — nothing capable of a big enough orbital strike to destroy the base, but enough to take out a fleeing Free ship. So what do they do about them?"

She paused for a second and the fire crackled. No one offered up a response.

"Well," she went on, "the Free are going to want to make sure that they take out the Federation ships before they can get word to the fleet of what's happening. If they don't, then their whole plan goes to shit. So, yeah, I'd say it's a fair bet that they're getting everything ready and then they're going to launch with *everything* they have as hard and as fast as they can. They're going to punch a hole big enough to get out and when the fleet arrives, they're not going to know the difference." She finished and leaned forward, pressing on her knees with her hands.

Mac set his jaw and stared at her, weighing it up. "Say you're right, and I'm not saying you are, but if you are — what would the plan even be? It's not like we've got enough of a force to take the entire base on. They'd be thousands, at least. We'd get mown down before we got close, and then everything would go on as normal — they leave and the soldiers still die. So what's the plan? March us all into the firing line? Overwhelm them with sheer numbers? That's the Federation's usual play, but newsflash, Kepler, it doesn't fucking work." Mac swore and then spat over his shoulder.

I swallowed, staying quiet. The blonde had said those words, almost verbatim, but I wasn't about to chime in. I thought about her

— about whether, if we did lay siege to the base *somehow,* she'd be there, shooting back. Whether she'd die for her cause. Whether it was right that anyone should.

"No, that isn't my plan," Alice sighed. "The Federation may not value lives, but I do. No, what we need to do is slip in fast and quiet, and hit them where it hurts. They'll be crazy getting everything ready to go, so hopefully we can get close and slip inside before they know what's happened."

"And how do you propose we do that, exactly?" Mac arched an eyebrow, shifting from devil's advocate to downright asshole.

"Well, we've got a T-Series, don't we? And an Eshellite? Masters of stealth and all that shit. He can just slip in and find us an entry point, radio back to tell us where, and voilà." She turned her hand out, pointing to Fish.

Mac turned to the Eshellite on the log next to him and waited for an answer. Fish looked from him to Alice and back, raised his chin a little and then gargled quietly.

"You've got to be fucking kidding me!" Mac practically yelled. "You agree with her?"

Fish gargled again.

"You're fucking crazy, the bunch of you!"

"And after we're in," Alice pressed on, "we split up. Free the prisoners. Sabotage their hangar. Keep the Free there, trapped in their base, get the soldiers out, and get clear of the blast zone. After that..." She trailed off. "I don't know. If we make it that far, we'll figure something out."

Mac scoffed and shook his head. "That can't be your fucking plan. Please tell me that we're not actually considering going through with this?"

No one came to his defense.

Alice sighed and looked at me. I smiled at her and she smiled back for a second before looking back at Mac. "Well, unless you've got anything better, then it's the only plan we've got."

## 23

The sun was just creeping over the horizon, flooding the sky with streaks of red and gold, and dew clung to the dropping grasses that spilled into the plane off the tree-clad slope.

We'd ditched our rigs about fifty meters back and snuck up on foot, me, Mac, and Alice.

Fish had gone ahead to scout, as usual, in his Panther. One second he was there alongside us, and the next he was gone. I was sort of getting used to it already, though.

Mac hung his head and sighed. He looked tired and strung out. He looked like we all felt. Sleep hadn't come easy and hunger was gnawing at me harder than ever. We'd salvaged what we could from the transport, but what little there was — mostly the Free's own rations, along with whatever the soldiers already had — didn't stretch very far between that many of us. I chewed my cheek instead, the lethargy clawing at my eyelids.

Alice was stoic, hardened almost. I was out of my depth and floundering, but she looked like she was exactly where she needed to be. The sim had obviously prepped her for this. She'd spent months on that op, at least in her mind, so this was just a continuation. One hell into another. I didn't know if she felt like this on the first day she had in there, and I didn't think it was really the time to ask. All I knew was that of the four of us, I was the only one who'd never been on a live op before, never gone to war before, and never piloted an F-Series in the heat of battle before — and if I was betting on who'd die out of us first, then it would have been me. I gritted my teeth and pulled my eyes away from Alice. I'd taken that bullet for her, sure, but noble as it was, it felt like I'd really fucked myself by doing it, and that was twisting in my empty guts like a hot iron.

We were waiting for any sort of signal from Fish that he'd made a hole, but we had yet to see anything. From our vantage point, lying in the grass just at the edge of the trees, we could see the Free base. It was a long, wide operation ringed by what looked like concrete and steel walls, and run backward into the side of a hill. We could see sentries patrolling the walls outside and guard towers manned by riflemen and searchlights. Everything inside was abuzz and transports and trucks whizzed around on the tarmac we could see through the fence portions. It was a mishmash of buildings and runways. Some ships sat ready for takeoff, being loaded or fueled, and in the distance we could see huge hangar doors agape and flashing with warning lights, the noses of colossal transport ships sticking out in the light of the dawn.

"If he doesn't get back soon," Alice muttered, "we're going to have to move."

"Move *away,* I hope you mean," Mack grumbled.

"Move up, MacAlister." Alice cut the air with her hand, gesturing at the base. "We've got a mission to complete."

"I don't know if you've realized, Kepler, but there's four of us. Well, *three* now if Fish has been captured and killed, which is pretty fucking likely considering what you sent him to do." He mumbled something under his breath but I couldn't hear it. "No, if Fish doesn't get back by the time the sun's up, this mission is a bust. We fall back, regroup, and try to reach out to the Federation. Send a distress call, or stick to the original plan, and get as far away from this place as we can."

"You do what you want, MacAlister. Red and I are going in." She turned to me and smiled, nodding.

I didn't have the heart to tell her that I thought Mac was right. If we didn't have an in, we'd never even get close. The sentries would alert them, and they'd scramble every fixed wing and mech they had. We'd maybe last a few minutes, expend what little ammunition we had left, and then we'd get flattened, whether we had the training or not. The Free rebels had the numbers to do it, and no matter how plucky or lucky we were, we'd get torn apart. Instead of saying that, though, I just nodded back.

"You guys are fucking nuts. Every minute we waste sitting here, the armada are closing in. Do you know what the blast radius is from a full-powered orbital strike? You know how far away we'll need to be so that the shockwave doesn't rip us apart?"

"Just go, Mac," Alice snapped. "If you're right, we'll be dead anyway and there'll be no one left to rat you out as a deserter."

"Fucking hell, why do you two always have to go there, huh? I don't know why the fuck having common sense is suddenly *desertion.* I've stayed alive this long by making smart choices and not by rushing into every fight headstrong and full of false notions of victory."

"Cool it, Mac," I said, aware that he was talking louder than anyone sneaking up on someone should.

"No, I won't fucking cool it. This is bullshit, and you two can shove your suicide pact up your asses. See if you still feel like heroes when you've got bullets in your guts. I'm out." He pushed up onto his knees and scrambled backward onto his feet, turning to walk away.

"Mac," I called softly. He didn't stop.

"MacAlister!" Alice called, a little louder. He still didn't stop.

"Mac, for fuck sake, will you just wait?" I half yelled.

This time, he did. He slowed and drew a breath, putting his hands on his hips. "What is it?" he said.

"Will you just turn around?"

He shook his head and did.

Fish was standing between us, suit hatch popped behind him, mech shadowed by the overhang of the trees.

"Fish?" Mac asked, surprised.

"Well?" Alice chimed in, looking at Mac. He was the only one who could understand him.

Mac laughed and then spat between his boots. "Jesus Christ," he breathed. "He says we're in."

FISH HAD MAPPED THE PATROLS, which circled the compound from one side to the other, and then doubled back, stopping at the mountain wall. One passed by every two minutes or so, but there was a curved section of wall that provided a blind spot while the patrols were approaching from either side. One patrol wouldn't see the approach due to the wall, and the other would be moving away as we came. Then, though, they'd double back, and by that time, we'd need to be within a hundred meters of the fence.

"We'll have to be quick," Mac sighed. "I don't think I'll be able to get the HAM in there that fast, though. The F-Series can really motor when they need to, but I'll attract too much attention and be left out to dry when the patrol circles back."

"You said that that eastern gate was unmanned, right, Fish?" Alice asked.

"No, he said he killed the guards on the eastern gate," Mac corrected her.

"Right, well, that's sort of splitting hairs, don't you think?"

He shrugged.

"Anyway," she continued, "that gate's close to the base entrance, right? But the hangars are on the other side. Why don't we just split up? If you guys can create a distraction, draw their attention to the far side of the base" — she looked up at Mac and Fish — "we can slip in the back, find the prisoners and get them out, and then we'll hit them from behind. All you have to do is—"

"Stay alive until that happens." Mac scoffed. "I didn't think this plan could get any worse."

"Look, it's all we've got, alright? Fish got us our hole, we're getting those soldiers out, and we need you to do it. I can see some ships on the runway there — if Fish can slip in and plant some explosives or something, get one of them to go up, it'll put them in a frenzy. You can fortify yourself on the far side of the base, hit them with a rail pulse, put one right into the support strut above one of the hangar doors, bring the whole fucking thing down. Trap them inside."

Mac narrowed his eyes, thinking, but didn't speak.

"They'll all come out, guns blazing, thinking it's an attack. And while they're all running the other way—"

"You slip in the back." Mac bit his lip. "Fucking hell, I can't believe I'm actually considering this."

Alice shrugged. "Hey, it's a good plan."

He laughed. "Well, I don't know that I'd go that far."

We geared up as the sky began to flood with yellow, the sun yet to creep over the horizon.

# 24

Mac and Fish gave us the most cursory of nods, and then set off around the base, sticking to the trees.

Alice and I stayed behind, watching the distant walls as the guards circled them slowly, rifles slung across hips. We could see the tower Fish had cleared, but wondered how long it would be until the guards were discovered. We didn't think very long. From what he'd said, Fish had unlocked the gate there, but left it closed. All we had to do was *push.*

"I don't like this," I mumbled, not taking my eyes off the base.

Alice sighed. We were both rigged up, sitting with our hatches open. We'd managed to fix up the F-Series that the blonde had been piloting, replacing some of the wiring, and had gotten it running again. Alice had even managed to find the pulled AI core and reinsert it, though hers seemed to be a lot more docile than Greg. I wondered why that was, but I didn't pry. The last thing I wanted to do was get into a verbal joust with another AI while Greg was too much for me already.

"You're not supposed to like it," she muttered back. "It's war."

I swallowed and cast a glance at her, her features hard and set, eyes narrowed. I could see the pulse in her neck hammering slowly. Boom. Boom. Boom.

I peeled my eyes away from it and turned them back to the task at hand. All we could do now was wait. Either Mac would get into position or the guards would find the dead bodies and raise the alarm. I honestly couldn't have guessed which was going to happen first. And I definitely couldn't have called it that it was going to be neither.

Mac's voice crackled over the comms. "Shit!"

"What is it?" Alice asked hurriedly.

"We're too late."

"Talk to me, MacAlister. What are you seeing?" Her voice was strained and her pulse had quickened.

"We're on the northern rise — shit — the fucking transport is wheeling out. Christ. I've got to hit it from here. You've got to move. Now or never." We could hear the clanking of the panels shifting around him as his mech began to squat, the rail canon growing out of his back. I looked left, seeing the glow of the muzzle in the trees. They weren't even a quarter of the way around. Shit. If he fired from there, every Free ship and troop would scramble to this side of the base.

Alice's hatch snapped shut. "Move!"

I sank back into my seat and rammed my helmet on. "Let's go, Greg," I snapped, pushing forward into the pedals.

He lurched forward after Alice, who was already running across the meadow, and slammed the hatch closed. The screen lit up, and red reticles began flying all over the place as he located and marked out guards. "Set a course for the eastern gate," I barked, jamming my heels into the thrusters. They kicked us forward, landing us next to Alice, who was pounding across the meadow. I could hear the engines of the transport ship beyond the walls spooling as it dragged itself out through the hangar door like a huge slug.

"Ten seconds!" Mac yelled in our ears.

We mistimed it, by a lot. The guards could see us coming, but it didn't matter. The whole plan was shot. "Greg, target th—"

"Targeting," he said back, reading my mind.

Red reticles pulsed over the four guards rushing at us, two from the left, two from the right. They went to their knees, firing their rifles. Soundwaves popped up on screen over one's head as he started radioing for backup. Alice must have seen it too because she cut them both in half with a stream of Samson fire. I sucked in a hard breath and squeezed the trigger, feeling Greg guiding my muzzle toward the other two. Earth and blood sprayed into the air as the bullets tore through them and the ground around them. Guilt fired through me and squeezed what little food and water I had in my stomach up into my throat like the dregs of toothpaste being rolled up from the bottom of a tube.

"They would have called for backup," Greg said quietly as we ran toward the gate. "It was a necessary choice."

"I know," I panted, my arms and legs churning forward.

"It will get easier."

I met that one with silence.

We were closing in when everything turned white. My screen blotted out completely and all of Greg's systems stuttered and then rebooted. When the light began to fade, we were still running, and a beam of energy was fading across the screen. Mac had fired, and the damage was horrifying. The blast had struck the midpoint of the support beam running over the hangar. Everything was still for a fraction of a second, and then the air ruptured and shook, the shockwave tearing across the field and blasting leaves from the trees. Everything swayed and shuddered and the sound of air being rent cut through the early morning silence.

Metal groaned and whined and then the struts gave. Rock fractured up the face of the mountain and then all at once the ceiling collapsed. Our view was obscured by the approaching wall and gate, but the noise was unmistakable. A thousand tons of rubble and steel colliding with a Free ship. It crunched and screamed, and then it exploded in a fireball that licked the side of the mountain and spat out a plume of black smoke.

"Fucking hell!" Mac yelled.

"Didn't you mean to do that?!" I yelled back, deafened by both blasts, even inside the cockpit.

"I didn't think it would be that effective— oh fuck, here come the cavalry! Fish, scramble," Mac ordered exasperatedly. I glanced left as the treeline lit up with a dozen sidewinders that all curled into the air and snaked toward the base, raining down on the wall and gate that troops were scrambling through. Ground vehicles spewed through the fence and fixed-wings wound into the air all around us.

Alice popped off two grenades and blew the eastern gates clean off their hinges. We swept inside, muzzles lit. I figured if I never let off the trigger, I wouldn't have to reconcile pulling it again.

The scene inside was carnage. One of the hangars had completely collapsed and a huge transport ship had been totally crushed. Its nose was sticking into the air, bent that way under the weight of the debris. Flames shot out of the cockpit windows and covered the hull, burning the fuel that had spilled from the ruptured tanks.

Hundreds of Free soldiers were mobilizing from all parts of the base, funneling out of the mountain or rushing from their positions on the runway. Fixed-wing and tilt-winged jets drop took off haphazardly and circled around, laying down fire on Mac and Fish as we closed in from the other side, pincering a chunk of their forces and mowing down the soldiers as they rushed away from us. Alice peeled right and I went left, firing wildly at everything that moved. The Free soldiers caught on immediately and split up, doubling back to take out the two crazy F-Series that had just blitzed through the eastern gate.

"We're going to be torn apart down here," I grunted, shielding my camera dome and body with my arm as a fixed-wing swept in overhead and peppered me with minigun fire. I chased it through the sky with my Samson, but it corkscrewed away and then rocketed into the clouds.

"Just keep firing and look for a way inside!" Alice called back through gritted teeth. I could hear the vibration in her voice from the Samson against her shoulder.

I stared at the huge hangar door — the one that hadn't collapsed

— but it was beyond the rubble, and there were soldiers pouring out of it. I turned my muzzle right and squinted through the flash. We were getting hit from both sides.

"Greg, where the hell are these guys coming from?"

"Preliminary sonic scans show that there is a troop entrance nearby that leads to an auxiliary armory. I believe that the Free rebels inside are seeking egress via that route."

"Show me."

The wall of the mountain lit up with white lines as Greg took a guess at the layout.

"And the Federation soldiers?"

"Deep within the base. I detect large spaces, but I am unable to effectively map them from here."

I cursed and turned to Alice. "We have to get inside, but the entrance is too small for our rigs. We have to go in on foot."

"You're not suggesting we go in through the door that all these rebels are coming out of?" she scoffed.

"You got a better idea?"

"There is another way," Greg cut in, spinning me around to leap out of the path of another barrage of fixed-wing fire.

"Start talking," I coughed against the harness cutting into my shoulders.

"There is a ventilation shaft that runs deeper into the base, though I cannot say where it leads."

"Show me!"

A flashing green reticle appeared overhead and I twisted until it flew on-screen, pinned to the face of the mountain about a hundred meters above us. A thin line of smoke was billowing out of it.

"You've got to be fucking kidding me!"

"I am not," Greg said flatly. "I estimate your chances of success very low in a ground engagement. This is your best option."

"And how the hell am I supposed to get up there?"

The words 'Ejection Sequence' appeared in front of me and flashed. "Oh no, you're crazy if you think you're ejecting me!"

"We will not be able to sustain this rate of engagement for much longer. Ammunition is at forty percent and depleting quickly, and our hull integrity is also falling. This is your only chance, or we must fall back." His voice was flat and without emotion, but I couldn't shake the graveness of it.

"Alice?"

"Yeah?"

"You get that?"

"We've got to try something."

I sighed. "Fuck it." My hand reached out and I jabbed the 'Initiate' button underneath it. 'Eject now?'

"Line me up, Greg." I sighed, my hands shaking, heart pounding. "Alice? Count us in."

"I recommend you install my AI link in your helmet. I may be of assistance," Greg said with something nearing sincerity.

I growled, but I knew he was right, and I'd need all the help I could get. I reached down and he opened a panel on the console next to the chair. A chip was sitting in a little cradle there with a label saying 'AI Mobile Uplink' next to it. I grabbed it up and clipped it onto the side of my helmet just as Alice began the countdown.

"Three."

Greg turned and made for her mech.

"Two."

He drew level and spun next to it, firing widely to clear out the nearest Free rebels.

"One."

I pushed my head back against the headrest and held on to the harness. I knew it was going to suck.

"Now."

Greg dipped at a weird angle and the hatch popped. My guts hit the seat and pinned themselves there as I shot upward. The chair rocketed into the air with a bang and then there was nothing but windrush. The altimeter inside my visor climbed and then levelled. I looked sideways and saw Alice, flying almost parallel. We crested at the same time and began to tumble together. Greg had angled me toward the mountain and I was right over the vent.

He and Alice's rig both turned and fired simultaneously at the rock, the bullets tearing through the grate that covered the shaft until it flipped over and tumbled to the ground.

Our chutes popped at the same time, suspending us over the cliff. Greg and Alice's rig were still firing below, but the Free rebels knew what was going on and had directed their fire upward, too.

Bullets ripped through the air around us like tiny fireflies zooming into the gloomy dawn-riddled clouds. My heart was a blur in my chest and my throat was a pinhole. I could barely move my hands. They were stiff, like talons. I fumbled at my belt, my breath fogging inside my helmet, and spidered my fingers down my leg toward the grip of my pistol.

In the distance I could hear Mac laying down as much fire as his HAM could produce, and the muffled screams of terror as Fish did what Fish did best, gutting unsuspecting rebels before they could get the fuck out of the way.

The vent loomed. Greg had put me right on top of it. Alice was next to me, both of us plunging toward it, our chutes speckled with bullet holes.

I fumbled for my buckle with my free hand and pulled the release, holding on to one side to keep myself in the chair.

I only had one shot at this. My brain was fog, and all I could see was the vent. Everything else was shimmering. Fear. Adrenaline. They fought inside me as the hole grew below us. Now. I let go and pushed out of the seat two seconds before it clattered into the mountain. I tumbled the last ten feet and curled into a ball, landing in the mouth of the shaft. My heel clipped the near edge and I tumbled.

I could hear yelling, but I didn't know if it was my voice or Alice's. I couldn't see anything, just flashes of light and darkness. I spread my arms and legs as wide as I could and felt them connect with the sides of the shaft. The friction burned but I kept them pinned, feeling myself slowing. There was a crash and pain ripped through my back. I heard a yelp — definitely me that time. Then a groan — Alice.

She'd collided with me, which was almost good. Meant that she hadn't been shot to pieces while she was coming in.

The friction burned my elbows and hands, my knees. We started to slow, but I couldn't see anything. I had my eyes screwed up, teeth gritted so hard I thought they'd crack. We kept sliding, tumbling, entwined together, until we landed in a heap. The shaft cut sideways at a right angle and we lay in a pile at the crook, panting, hot, and in pain.

I could feel her against me, her fists in the fabric of my jumpsuit, her chest rising and falling rapidly against my ribs.

"Are we dead?" she muttered.

I dragged in a slow breath, smoky with whatever was in the shaft. I coughed twice feeling a jolt of pain in my ribs. It felt like one was cracked. "I don't think so..." I coughed again. "Unfortunately."

We unfurled slowly, checking ourselves for breaks, but miraculously, it seemed like we were both okay — albeit a bit beaten up and bruised. Though, being in the Federation, that seemed to be a common occurrence.

I planted my hands in the soot on the bottom of the vent and looked around. There was only one path — forward. I'd lost my pistol in the fall, but it was lying just ahead. I crawled over and picked it up. It was greasy. I grimaced, thanking my helmet for the filtration system. I'd be choking on smoke otherwise. But where the hell was it coming from, and why was my pistol greasy?

"You smell that?" Alice asked, pulling up next to me.

"I'm trying not to breathe through my nose."

"Well, do. What is that? Food?"

I sniffed a couple times. "Smells like..."

"Cooking meat?"

I shook my head a little, smirking. "This vent comes out of a goddamn kitchen."

We made it along to the end quickly and found ourselves hanging above a set of stoves. Pots of broth were bubbling, but there was no one manning them. I wiped the sweat from my brow and kicked one down, waiting to see if anyone came to check out the noise. They didn't. With everything going on outside, it was all hands on deck, but we still had to be fast. If anyone saw two pilots heading down a damn vent, then they'd likely try to head us off.

I gripped the slick edge and swung down, landing square on the stove before hopping to the floor. I stayed low and pressed myself against a set of cabinets that made up the end of a long work island. The kitchen was a huge industrial affair with sinks and work surfaces running the full length of the room, nearly fifty meters.

Alice landed next to me like a cat and pressed herself against the island cover. She had her pistol drawn. I couldn't see her face through her helmet, but I knew her jaw was set determinedly. She nodded to me. "Ready?"

I took a deep breath. "Yeah, I'm ready." I touched my finger to the AI chip on my helmet. "Greg, sitrep?"

"We're still engaging, but have fallen back to draw their fire. Pilots MacAlister and Sesstis are still alive, but are under heavy fire. I would recommend hurrying."

"Okay," I sighed. "We're on it."

As I said it, the doors at the end of the room burst open and two Free rebels rushed in — both biggish guys, out of breath and carrying rifles. "They must have come through here," one said, panting.

"This is the only place that vent comes out," the other one added. "You circle left, I'll go right."

I swallowed hard and felt my heart kick up. I tapped the AI chip again. "Greg, I could really do with some help here."

"Of course. Active targeting engaged. I recommend turning to face the assailants. Chances of survival are greatly increased if you do so."

I wasn't sure if he was kidding. I sighed and twisted on my heel, ignoring the pain in my ribs, and flexed my fingers around the greasy grip of my pistol. Alice was tucked in against her counter. I could hear her breathing in my ear, softly. "On my mark. You tag the one on the right, I'll get the guy on the left. Ready?"

I tried to say no, but I didn't have chance before she said, "Now!"

She popped up from behind the counter and I followed on instinct. She wheeled left, took two steps and put a bullet in the first guy's chest. He reeled backward and she put another two above it.

One hit between the collarbones, and the other struck him just below the eye, sending him spinning to the ground. I watched, frozen. In my peripherals I could see the second guy rounding, rifle coming up. Everything slowed down. I saw Alice, the guy she'd shot falling, and my target, rising to pump her full of bullets. I saw it all happening—unless I did something.

My hand moved, my teeth clenched, and my finger pulled twice. I barely aimed, barely thought. The only thing that occurred to me was that if I didn't put him down, he was putting Alice down, and I realized then that killing wasn't hard. Killing for no reason was hard. But if there was something to shoot for — a reason to kill— then pulling the trigger was a lot less complicated.

The first round hit him mid chest on the right side. The second went straight through his temple. I stood like a statue, barrel smoking in my outstretched hand.

I heard Alice sigh in my head and then felt her hands on my shoulders. "Come on — there'll be more coming."

WE GOT into the hallway and started running. We stopped twice at stairwells to consult the fire escape plans bolted to the walls. It seemed like the only place big enough to keep thousands of soldiers locked up that was able to be secured was a huge vault two floors down — a self-contained room with blast-proof doors that would have been used for secure storage, development, or anything else that needed to be kept locked away and protected. It would stand up to everything except an orbital strike — which was what the Free were counting on.

We made for it quickly, my rib screaming at me as Alice hammered along. She pulled away at one point, as something between a stitch and a knife stabbed me in the flank. I doubled, my hands on my knees, panting hard. "You go," I wheezed, massaging my side. "I'll catch up."

She nodded to me. "Alright." Her eyes lingered on me for a

second before she turned and disappeared around the next corner. I had every intention of following her until I saw someone else.

We hadn't come across any other Free since the kitchen. We guessed that everyone else had made it outside to try and combat what they had to assume was a Federation counter attack. They'd need to neutralize it and get off planet as quickly as they could, or risk getting caught in the blast. No one was going to risk getting left behind either. No one, it seemed, except for the only Free rebel I'd ever met.

I dragged a couple of breaths into my lungs and glanced behind me, just to make sure I wasn't being snuck up on. But as I did, in the crosscut of the nearest intersection of hallways, the blonde rebel slid to a halt, breathing hard. She rested her hands on her knees, just like me, and sucked in lungfuls of air. She'd been running.

My eyes stayed with her for a few seconds. I wasn't sure if I was hallucinating or not. Maybe I'd taken a bullet in the kitchen or breathed in a few too many smoke-filled breaths in the vent. I blinked a few times, but she didn't disappear.

She turned away and looked down the opposite corridor, and then glanced in my direction and froze. She stared at me for a moment that seemed to stretch out forever, and then she bolted.

"Hey!" I yelled, taking off after her, pistol in hand. My side ached, but it didn't matter. For some reason, I couldn't help but chase her. I don't know what it was — something between bruised pride and an unrelenting curiosity built on a bedrock of empathy.

Her long legs carried her like a racehorse, and by the time I even caught another glimpse of her, she was disappearing through a steel door at the end of the hallway.

I made up the ground as quickly as I could and burst through, throwing my pistol up at the last second, realizing I could have been bumbling into an ambush. But, I wasn't, and there was no one else around.

I was in a room the size of an assembly hall. In the center, a Federation tilt-wing that would have rolled off the assembly line a century earlier sat, the Federation logo sprayed over. The rear doors were open but otherwise the room was quiet. Along one wall was a huge shutter, and through it I could hear the muffled sounds of gunfire and explosions. I racked my brain to get a sense of direction, and figured that this had to be an auxiliary hangar that led into the main hangar of the base, and that beyond that shutter, the fight would be raging and hundreds of Free rebels would be waiting with guns.

I swallowed hard, forcing down the knot of sickness in my gut, feeling the gun slick in my hands, and made for the rear doors of the tilt-wing.

# 25

"Freeze," I said.

She did. She lifted her hands slowly from the controls and held them over her head, but she didn't make any attempt to get up from the pilot's chair. The buttons and controls were lit in front of her, casting a dim green glow in the cabin, the ignition sequence half started.

I'd stalked up the ramp and through the cargo bay, made the climb to the upper deck and then crept into the cockpit, not announcing myself until I was close enough not to miss — but not close enough to get hit again.

"Get up," I growled, keeping the muzzle trained on the back of her head.

She turned a little so she could see me, and sighed. "Please," she muttered.

"Up."

"I have to unbuckle myself," she said quietly, reaching for the harness on her chest.

"Slowly!" I half yelled, trying to keep the gun steady.

She nodded. "Just— just don't shoot, okay?"

I didn't reply. I just waited for her to get up. Really, I didn't know what I was going to do. I'd half expected to find her in the cockpit, have her lunge at me, and then put a bullet in her. But now, with my gun pinned on her, defenseless once again, that doubt crept back in.

She raised herself from the chair and turned around it, ready to step out, and then she did it. It was idiotic — she was almost six feet away. There was no way she ever could have reached me, and looking back, I think she knew that, but it was the only play she had. If I wasn't going to shoot her, then I likely would have imprisoned her and then handed her over to the Federation. She'd already made it clear that she wasn't going to entertain that idea.

Her hands stretched out, muscles tensed, eyes full of fear. I skipped backward, angled down and fired. She yelped, and twisted in the air, and then sank to the floor, blood pouring from her thigh. I'd hit her about halfway up on the outer side. Didn't look like I'd struck bone, but it was enough through the muscle to put her down. I sighed and stepped back a little more. She clutched at the wound, half sobbing, half cursing herself.

"Just fucking do it!" she yelled without warning. "Just finish me." She stared balefully at me from under hooded eyes. "Just don't hand me over to the Federation." The words dripped from her mouth like venom.

"I'm not going to kill you," I said incredulously, as if I'd even entertain the idea of executing someone in cold blood. "But I wasn't going to let you kill me, either. You already got the drop on me once. I wasn't buying it a second time."

She stared at me in confusion, and then it dawned on her. She couldn't see my face, but she knew who I was in that second. "It's you." She shook her head. "The goddamn kid. So what are you going to do with me then?" She raised an eyebrow, her voice thin all of a sudden.

I hadn't thought that far ahead. I didn't really like the options. Either I was going to put a bullet in her, or I was going to hand her over to the Federation and let them do it. Both resulted in her death, and I was sure that if I told her it was the second, she was just going to let the pressure off her thigh and bleed herself out.

"Well?" she scoffed, thumbing at the spreading crimson stain on her trouser leg in an attempt to squeeze the blood back in, or tourniquet it with her fingers.

"I'm thinking" was all I could say.

"You know," she said quietly, shaking her head, "I was just trying to get away. When shit started hitting the fan — your doing, I'm guessing — I was in detention. You know they threw me in lock-up when I got back. Suspected desertion. Didn't quite buy the story that I managed to escape on my own while everyone else from the transport died." She laughed abjectly. "When I told them what happened with this dumb Federation kid-pilot, they told me that I was lying — badly. They said that no Federation pilot in the universe would be dumb enough to let a Free rebel sneak up on them and then disarm them. I told them I killed you with your own gun." She looked up at me, staring into the muzzle pointed at her head without a hint of fear. "They didn't ask, but I knew that was the question they were wondering. What I did with the pilot I disarmed. They liked that part — the only part that was a lie." She stared at her leg, soaked with blood. "I let you go. You know, I thought, here's a kid who's not been so fucked by their propagandized bullshit that he may still have a chance to get out and do something with his life. And not just throw it away like the rest of us." She took a slow breath and let her eyes wander to the ground at my feet.

Alice's voice crackled in my ear suddenly. "Hey, Red — I've got the prisoners, or I've found them at least. Where the hell are—" I tapped the side of my helmet, cutting her off mid-sentence.

I let the blonde go on, seeing myself in her with every passing second.

"But I was wrong," she said quietly. "I gave you that chance, and here you are — good deeds come back to bite us, don't they? You know the whole world is fucked when the people who do good get punished and those who take and kill and hurt people without remorse are the ones that are rewarded." She spread her arms. "Well, come on then. Claim your reward and climb the Federation ladder." Her voice was cracked like old veneer.

My throat was tight. "You said you were in detention," I squeezed out. "How'd you get out?"

She smirked a little, looking drawn in the halflight all of a sudden, a pool of red forming under her leg. "I was being questioned when things went wrong. The whole fucking base shook. We heard the blast — knew it was rail by the way the lights dipped. Felt it as the ceiling caved in the hangar. The guy interrogating me pushed back from the table and ran out of the room. After that, I was alone. When I figured that no one was watching me anymore, and the explosions kept on coming, I knew that it was too late. I had to get out. I had a chair, so I used it. Took me until now to smash the door handle off." She shook her head again. "You ever try to break a door handle with a chair? It's no fucking picnic."

I swallowed, trying to stay focused. "And now what, you're joining the fight?"

"I'm running. They didn't like my story — so if they survive, they'll come back and kill me for attempted desertion. The Federation and the Free differ in a lot of ways — but in a lot of ways they're just the same. So no, I wasn't joining the fight. I was running. I want off this planet, and out of this fucking fight for good. The Federation left me for dead and now the Free won't have me either. I was just going to find a nice peaceful planet somewhere very far away and not think about either of them ever again." She smiled at me, showing off straight white teeth. Her eyes were full, blue and bottomless, shining with tears. "Because honestly, what's the point in any of it? Huh? What are you even fighting for? Why don't you just kill me and take the ship yourself? Fly off into the sky and never look back. It's what I was going to do. It's what you *should* do. It's what anyone who can gain the clarity to see what the Federation and the Free really are *should* do."

My mouth wasn't my own as the words began to form in it. "What if we went together?"

Everything was still. She looked at me unwaveringly, her face a mixture of suspicion and fear, eyes twitching with trepidation, as I reached up and took my helmet off. I didn't know what the hell I was saying. In that moment, everything was peaceful. The thought of a peaceful life, away from all of this — away from the pistol in my hand and the Federation logo on my chest — seemed perfect.

But then it faded away, as quickly as it came. I stared down at the Free rebel that had jumped me, that I'd shot, and that I'd just offered to run away with, and realized that I didn't even know her name. That I didn't care about her. That I didn't know her.

I looked over my shoulder at the door and thought of Alice. Thought of what we'd come through already. Thought of what would happen to her if I left. Where she'd go and what she'd do. I thought about her going into the next battle, with guys like Jonas at her side — people she couldn't rely on. I swallowed hard, and let her face float in my mind. I sighed and closed my eyes, turning away.

I stepped toward the door and laid my hand on the frame, not looking back. "I'm sorry I... I'm sorry about your leg." I took another step. "I hope you find your peaceful planet, and that it's everything you want it to be."

"Wait," she said quietly. "Where are you going? We can—"

"My fight's not over yet. Not until I don't have anything left to fight for, at least." I hit the door panel with my clenched fist and heard it slide shut behind me.

In a blur, my feet were back on the smooth concrete of the hangar floor.

The doors to the tilt-wing rose behind me and sealed, and then the roller shutter started clanking upward, exposing the hangar beyond. It was quieter now. No one was running or yelling and the sound of fire had dwindled to a distant rumble. Either the fighting was over, or Mac and Fish had retreated. Either way, in that moment, I didn't care. In the distance I could see the burning wreckage of the read end of the pinned transport, crushed under the collapsed roof.

I watched the flames lick the smoky air as the tilt-wing trundled slowly forward and then pulled right, heading for an open door at the far side.

It picked up speed and left a trail of blue jet wash in its wake as it zoomed into the morning sunlight and then banked into the sky and out of sight.

My heart beat slowly in my chest and the pistol felt heavy in my fingers.

"Red?" came a familiar voice.

I turned, watching Alice come through the door. I could hear voices beyond —shouts and commands. The prisoners. She'd gotten them out. I smiled. "Hey."

"Are you okay?" She sounded concerned and jogged over, helmet under her arm.

I nodded. "Yeah."

"You killed your comms? What happened?"

"I, uh..." I stalled for a second. "I got into a scuffle. They cracked me with the butt of a rifle, blew out my comms — I had to ditch it."

She narrowed her eyes at me. It didn't look like she was buying it, but she didn't pry. "What happened then?"

I followed her eyes to the fresh tiremarks leading into the hangar and toward the door. "They got away."

She nodded slowly, accepting that much. "Mac came in while you were off comms. They had to retreat — low on ammo, but they said that the Free rebels started to split, anyway."

I smiled slowly. "That's good. And you got the prisoners out."

She smirked a little. "Yeah, there was no one guarding them. Guess the Free never figured on us attacking or making any sort of rescue attempt. They had them locked up in a storage vault downstairs — was a cinch to crack." She shrugged, but I could see the sadness in her eyes. The Free had just locked them up and left them to die — obliterated by their own forces as the base went up, or just to starve to death if it didn't. I tried not to think about it.

I looked back into the hangar, watching as the liberated Federation soldiers started to appear, heading for the door as they poured out of the base. "That's good."

She licked her lip slowly, and then bit it. "For a second, I thought you'd gone."

I furrowed my brow. "Gone? Gone where?"

She shrugged in my peripherals. "I don't know. Just *gone.* I came back up, looking for you, heard that tilt-wing spooling up, and I just thought..."

I grinned, to myself more than anyone else. "Don't worry, you can't get rid of me that easily."

She seemed to hear the sadness in my voice and nodded. "You did well. I'm— I'm glad you were here."

I turned to her now, the sadness gone, replaced with a sort of hollow numbness. I couldn't say what lay ahead, or whether I'd made the right call, but as I stood there, framed in the doorway of the base, staring at her, the words just seemed to come to me. "You know what, for what it's worth — me too."

Made in the USA
Middletown, DE
27 December 2018